# TriQuarterly

T0164109

*TriQuarterly* is

an international

journal of

writing, art and

cultural inquiry

published at

Northwestern

University

# TriQuarterly

**issue 113** *summer 2002*

**Editor**
Susan Firestone Hahn

**Associate Editor**
Ian Morris

**Operations Coordinator**
Kirstie Felland

**Production Manager**
Bruce Frausto

**Production Editor**
Laura Ploszaj

**Cover Design**
Gini Kondziolka

**Assistant Editor**
Eric LeMay

**Editorial Assistant**
Cara Moultrup

**Triquarterly Fellow**
Ryan Friedman

**Business Projects Manager**
Michael Workman

**Contributing Editors**
John Barth
Rita Dove
Stuart Dybek
Richard Ford
Sandra M. Gilbert
Robert Hass
Edward Hirsch
Li-Young Lee
Lorrie Moore
Alicia Ostriker
Carl Phillips
Robert Pinsky
Susan Stewart
Mark Strand
Alan Williamson

# CONTENTS

*Donna Seaman*

# Many Shades of Green, or Ecofiction is in the Eye of the Reader

The living flowing land
is all there is, forever

We are it
it sings through us—

—Gary Snyder

I write to make a difference . . . I write to give pleasure
and promote aesthetic bliss. To honor life and to praise
the divine beauty of the natural world. I write for the joy
and exultation of writing itself. To tell my story.

—Edward Abbey

To read outside, to sit with a good book in the backyard, on a beach, or in a park, and glide between the page, the realm of imagination and ideas, and the sensuous world of sunlight and dappled shadows, leaf-lifting breeze and spangled water, birdsong and the tangy smells of grass or sea, is to satisfy every aspect of being. It's blissful to absorb both what we call wildness or nature (all of life that isn't human) and language

9

and story (intrinsically human creations). To do so is to be aware that we dwell on a threshold between the wild and the civilized, and to recognize just how steeped our language is in the earth's lexicon.

Metaphor, our most intuitive tool for making connections, for finding meaning and order in the tumble and dazzle of life, has, from the earliest days of storytelling and spoken poetry, been based on observations of the natural world. Spring, the poets tell us, signifies renewal and hope; winter is death. Mountains are forever; rivers embody change, and a garden symbolizes the ideal union of the wild and the human. The tropes are endless and universal and all but instinctual, and writers have been occupied with the question of our relationship to the rest of nature ever since the first alphabet was scratched in clay.

Not only is it bliss to read outdoors, reading about the outdoors is also a profound pleasure, beginning in youth, when one's sense of place, of home, is so intimate and vivid. The Mid-Hudson Valley, where I grew up, is curvaceous, lush, and secretive. The rolling land, rising and falling beneath my feet and bicycle wheels worked its sinuous and enchanting way so deeply into my consciousness I learned to think in curves and convolutions, following twisting and shadowed pathways of thought that open out into sudden vistas filled with light only to plunge once again into tunnels of striated rock and filigreed forest. Living in a place of hills and valleys teaches you that everything can be seen from different perspectives, and coming of age in a place where maples and pines stand side by side teaches you about dramatic change and consistency. Place, as every writer knows, is tightly woven into the fabric of one's character and sensibility.

I was all eyes for the distant mountains, the pelts of green, then gold, then white that blanketed the rocky terrain, the great tidal river with its serpentine currents, sparkling in sunshine and brooding under clouds, and the stirring trees. The landscape spoke to me, its beauty penetrated my being, often making my breath catch hard in my chest. I sensed the earth's power and nature's indifference to human desire, and I preferred it to the aggression and pettiness of human society, which was making itself felt so unpleasantly in school. I was the sort of moody child who was scolded for staring longingly out the classroom windows. Like so many sensitive misfits, unhappy with myself and bored with uninspired instruction, I turned to books for help, searching for clues to the nature of the larger world, the contours of a meaningful life.

I respectfully read Thoreau and was stunned by the beauty and alarm of Rachel Carson's books about our careless abuse of the living world. I was profoundly disturbed to learn about the atom bomb and air and water pollution. I felt cheated. I found childhood annoying enough—how tiresome it is to be bossed around by adults who insisted that they knew more than I did, but to discover that these authority figures had gone and poisoned the earth was a rude and alienating realization. How smart is that? And how dare they! The beautiful Hudson River was full of something awful called PCBs, and the older I got, the more toxins at loose in the world were identified and decried. The more I read about the wild, the more my frustration and dismay over our cavalier attitude toward life on earth, this astonishing planet, increased.

My ardor for reading led me to work in libraries and delivered me to the American Library Association, the publisher of *Booklist,* a book review magazine for librarians that has been offering succinct advance reviews, the haiku of book reviewing, for close to a century. Here was a reader's paradise, it seemed, and there I continue to feed my appetite for nature writing. I've read all the rediscovered and republished works of such pioneers as John Muir, John Burroughs, and Aldo Leopold. I've been electrified by contemporary writers who extend the reach and turn up the volume of the genre, courageous writers who pay close and reverent attention to the world around us and to our impact on nature and its impact on us. Writers such as sage and eloquent Barry Lopez, passionate and daring Terry Tempest Williams, meticulous John McPhee, Gretel Ehrlich, Edward Hoagland, and Evan Eisenberg, whose brilliant book, *The Ecology of Eden,* a gutsy and path-carving synthesis of history, religion, ecology, and the poetics of jazz, has been woefully overlooked and underappreciated. And Diane Ackerman, who marshals her wit, lively intelligence, and lyricism to convey the essential truth that we are nature as much as a dolphin or a rose. These writers have greatly expanded readers' understanding of the fine and intricate web of life, while at the same time, they stoke our distress over the damage done by our marauding and greedy species.

Many nature writers protest environmental degradation, defining the complicated problems we now face in scientific, political, and economic terms. My preference is for nature writing that addresses the quandary of our species' ability to annihilate ourselves and all other life forms from psychological, philosophical, ethical, aesthetic, and spiritual perspectives because the loss of wilderness, the loss of the splendor of biodiversity, is a crisis for the body and the soul. Acutely descriptive, nature writing moves from the intense study of a particular aspect of the wild—the lives of wolves or hummingbirds, the cycle of the seasons as witnessed along the shore of one pond—to insights into the human condition, and back again, tracing over and over again the net within which we exist. Here's a startling passage from Annie Dillard's much treasured *Pilgrim at Tinker Creek*:

> Another time I saw another wonder: sharks off the Atlantic coast of Florida. There is a way a wave rises above the ocean horizon, a triangular wedge against the sky. If you stand where the ocean breaks on a shallow beach, you see the raised water in a wave is translucent, shot with lights. One late afternoon at low tide a hundred big sharks passed the beach near the mouth of a tidal river in a feeding frenzy. As each green wave rose from the churning water, it illuminated within itself the six- or eight-foot-long bodies of twisting sharks. The sharks disappeared as each wave rolled toward me; then a new wave would swell above the horizon, containing in it, like scorpions in amber, sharks that roiled and heaved. The sight held awesome wonders: power and beauty, grace tangled in a rapture with violence.
>
> We don't know what's going on here. If these tremendous events are random combinations of matter run amok, the yield of millions of monkeys at millions of typewriters, then what is it in us, hammered out of those same typewriters, that they ignite? We don't know. Our life is a faint tracing on the surface of mystery, like the idle, curved tunnels of leaf miners on the face of a leaf. We must somehow take a wider view, look at the whole landscape, really see it, and describe what's going on here. Then we can at least wail the right question into the swaddling band of darkness, or, if it comes to that, choir the proper praise.[1]

Dillard is drawing connections between the wild all around us, which ambushes us with its magnificence and terror, and the wildness of our own minds, no less wondrous and frightening a realm. Her entire book is arresting testimony to that interplay, and to the value of observation, the revelation of language, and the poignancy and mystery of our eternal quest for understanding. In *This Incomparable Land: A Guide to American Nature Writing*, Thomas J. Lyon states, "The crucial point about nature writing is the awakening of perception to an ecological way of seeing. 'Ecological' here is meant to characterize the capacity to notice pattern in nature, and community, and to recognize that patterns radiate outward to include the human observer. There is nothing exclusivist about nature writing. The perception of pattern has been the moving spirit of American nature writing almost from the beginning; this is why, for example, it is concerned with ethical questions."[2]

There is no "us" and "them," no divide between humanity and the rest of nature, but this is not what we are taught. This is not a vision supported by Western civilization or consumer society. Most Americans growing up in the nuclear age are profoundly alienated from the wild, and tend to commodify, trivialize, or romanticize nature. Many people choose not to think about how dependent we are on every other living being, from the microbes and worms that make soil fertile to pollinators such as bats, predators such as the much maligned coyote that keep the populations of other animals in check, and all the trees and plants that sustain us with precious oxygen and food. Those of us who have not been taught to think ecologically fail to recognize that contempt for and exploitation of wilderness, crimes against nature, are equal and inextricably connected to crimes against humanity such as virulent prejudice and the attempted genocide of Native Americans.

Many readers steadfastly avoid picking up the sort of metaphysical nature writing Annie Dillard excels at, just as many flatly refuse to read anything about environmental issues. They feel that it's too depressing a topic, or too polemical, or that "green" writers are just too holier-than-thou. This disinterest and denial is a serious obstacle to the dissemination of the sort of deep ecological thought necessary for coping with the numerous decisions society faces regarding such fundamentals as land use, the protection of biodiversity, sustainable energy sources, and the maintenance of clean air and water. If what wilderness remains is going to be preserved, if we're going to change our habits of consumption and attempt to halt pollution and reckless development, if we are to evolve as a species and therefore survive, people need to change the way they think about our relationship to nature. And reading is essential to instigating and sustaining this change.

Fiction, a far more popular form than nature writing, may be the ideal conduit for introducing ecological thinking to the common reader. In my own reading, I've noticed intriguing correlations between what nonfiction writers report from the field and how nature is depicted in contemporary novels and short stories. Many works of fiction either deliberately or intuitively explore our conflicted feelings about the wild in an age in which the profound consequences of our burgeoning population and insatiable appetites are becoming visible to even the most reluctant eyes. As I began to keep track of writers who launched imaginative inquiries into our perception of nature I noticed a curious equation: these writers were aligning the loss of wildlife and wilderness with emotional and spiritual crises. They were working their way through the souls of their characters toward an understanding of why we truly do need forests and wolves, coral reefs and whales. They were articulating the recognition that while we stand to lose the beauty, mystery, and bounty of our fellow creatures, plants, and unspoiled places, we will also lose a sense of our own wildness, our animal selves, our bred-in-the-bone wisdom that is not dependent on culture or technology. We need wildness because we are wildness.

Fiction is more open and supple than nonfiction, which explains why nature writers such as Rick Bass and Barry Lopez turn to writing stories and novels to express the more emotional, less issue-oriented facets of their insights into the natural world. Nature writing is often so exquisite and so knowledgeable it makes some readers feel excluded, small, ignorant. Fiction, on the other hand, is all about flaws, errors, weakness, and confusion. Stories and novels make room for everyone, and while fiction exposes our faults and failings it also expresses compassion and finds nobility in our struggles and strengths. Stories can be funny and irreverent. Fiction is more tolerant of ambiguity and contradiction. It asks questions without forcing answers. Fiction is about feelings not statistics. Love not politics. Beauty not resources. Stories are our most instinctive way of understanding ourselves and our world. As William Kittredge writes, "We ride stories like rafts, or lay them out on the table like maps."

Writers have been pondering our skewed perception of our place in the natural world from the dawn of literature, attempting to understand the paradox of our sense of separateness from the rest of life in spite of the fact that we know, however subliminally, that we are thoroughly enmeshed within it. We are inextricably and eternally a part of nature no matter how much we try to civilize ourselves, no matter how many barricades against the wild we create for our bodies and minds. Every myth about a lost earthly paradise, including the story of the Garden of Eden, the bedrock of Western civilization, seeks to illuminate this puzzle, and each stage in our technological development, which seems to outstrip our ethical and intellectual growth, ups the ante, arouses more fear, and inspires more stories.

There's a movement in academic circles called ecocriticism. This sounds deadly but in fact it's a vital outlook shared by many nature-loving readers without our being aware that it has a name. Ecocriticism is a form of reading that pays particular attention to a narrative's ecological attunement, or emphasis of environmental interests and concerns, however subtly or overtly expressed. Ecocriticism of a work of nature writing is a fairly straightforward proposition, but to read fiction ecocritically is a more interpretative act. In its most simplistic mode, this can mean searching for environmental advocacy within a story. A more open-ended and hence more appropriate approach to imaginative works involves the reader's sensitivity to the work's illumination of the basic tenet of ecology—the pattern of relationships among organisms, including human beings, and their relationship to the environment as a whole. An ecocritic may pay close attention, for instance, to a novelist's insights into how place shapes the psyches of his or her characters, or to how characters relate to plants and animals.

I'd heard the term but didn't realize that I was practicing ecocriticism when I first began collecting short stories with a "green" aura. An avid admirer of the form for its all-at-once comprehensibleness—like a painting, film, song, or poem, a short story resonates in the mind whole and complete—I began to set aside stories that I felt illuminated some psychological aspect of our relationship with nature, and soon I conceived of the idea of a "green" fiction anthology, the first ever compiled. I fully intended to include stories by nature writers who also write fiction, and both Barry Lopez and Rick Bass are present in what became *In Our Nature: Stories of Wildness*. But I was especially interested in short stories by writers who have no overt environmental orientation but who nonetheless write about wildness in a time of its diminishment, and I found many that qualified.

As I read dozens and dozens of short stories published over the last two decades searching for "green" perceptions, I was amazed and gratified by the connections writers make between the wild and the domestic. I ended up selecting stories by Bass, E. L. Doctorow, and Percival Everett in which childhood is depicted as an interlude of profound intimacy with nature, deep knowledge that comes into sharp conflict with the demands of civilization. Characters' livelihoods are sources of environmental conundrums in Francine Prose's story about a wildlife biologist, Lopez's take on the visions of a paleontologist, tales of the farming life by Kent Meyers and Rick DeMarinis, Pauline Melville's dramatization of corporate greed, and Tess Gallagher's story about loggers. Lorrie Moore explores our need for animals in her tale of a woman's love for her cat, and Margaret Atwood writes from the point of view of a bat. Chris Offutt examines the consequences of displacement from one's home turf, and both Simon J. Ortiz and Linda Hogan subtly explore the sharp divide between Native American and Anglo perceptions of nature. Each of the fourteen stories in In Our Nature touches on the irony and paradox intrinsic to our headlong species, the dire and confounding fact that we destroy what we love.

I didn't abandon an ecocritical approach to reading fiction when In Our Nature was published. In fact, I found myself even more attuned to "green" themes in imaginative works, including those written in the past. Writers such as Herman Melville (Barry Lopez told National Public Radio's Susan Stamberg that Moby Dick is his favorite novel) and Jack London readily lend themselves to ecoreading. Others, such as Joseph Conrad, can yield surprising results. In the midst of Conrad's powerful tale of life-transforming moral dilemmas, Lord Jim, published in the watershed year of 1900, he introduces a character named Stein. A wealthy merchant and passionate entomologist, Stein is a vehicle for Conrad's pondering of our perverse species' persistent feeling of being separate from nature. When Conrad's narrator, the indefatigable Marlowe, visits Stein, he finds him deep in contemplation of a butterfly specimen:

> ". . . I respected the intense, almost passionate absorption with which he looked at a butterfly, as though on the bronze sheen of these frail wings, in the white tracings, in the gorgeous markings, he could see other things, an image of something as perishable and defying destruction as these delicate and lifeless tissues displaying a splendour unmarred by death."
>
> "Marvelous!" he repeated, looking up at me.
>
> "Look! The beauty—but that is nothing—look at the accuracy, the harmony. And so fragile! And so strong! And so exact! This is Nature—the balance of colossal forces. Every star is so— and every blade of grass stands so—and the mighty Kosmos in perfect equilibrium produces—this. This wonder; this masterpiece of Nature—the great artist."
>
> "Never heard an entomologist go on like this," I observed, cheerfully. "Masterpiece! And what of man?"
>
> "Man is amazing, but he is not a masterpiece," he said, keeping his eye fixed on the glass case. "Perhaps the artist was a little mad. Eh? What do you think? Sometimes it seems to me that man is come where he is not wanted, where there is no place for him; for if not, why should he want all the place? Why should he run about here and there making a great noise about himself, talking

about the stars, disturbing the blades of grass? . . ."

"Catching butterflies," I chimed in.[3]

This passing moment in a sweeping tale of cultural dissonance and life-or-death conflicts speaks worlds about the state of science and humankind's self-image at the dawn of the twentieth century. Religion's incessant adversary, science was still in its hunter-gatherer stage, when the quest for knowledge of the natural world precipitated a frenzy of collecting, naming, and ranking in an all-out effort to catalog and therefore control the wild. Courageous and zealous wilderness explorers amassed entire museums' worth of captured and killed fauna and plucked flora that were dutifully tagged and displayed as discrete objects. Even zoos were in essence museums, the animals cataloged and boxed according to zoological conceits in stark confinement that denied the true nature of nature with its profound meshing of species and rampant mutualism. An ecocritical reading of Conrad reveals traces of this rigid viewpoint which would soon be challenged by Einstein's radical vision of relativity, and the shock of our sudden ability to manipulate atoms and bring on the apocalypse.

Thrown out of paradise where we were one with the rest of life, our species has been wreaking havoc ever since, and writers have struggled to understand our folly and perversity. Now, at the dawn of a new century, the stakes are infinitely higher. We've left nothing untouched; we've devoured entire species, emptied the seas, and decimated the forests. We live under the pall of nuclear weapons and the promise and threat of bioengineering. And yet we love animals, are moved to tears by sunsets, garden ardently, flock to national parks, and hang photographs of unspoiled forests and mountains on our walls like icons worthy of worship.

One hundred years after Conrad's philosophical entomologist praised nature's artistry, an American biologist turned novelist, Barbara Kingsolver, brings her deep knowledge and respect for nature to fiction. She has made humanity's troubled relationship with the rest of life on earth her signature theme, culminating in *Prodigal Summer,* which any ecocritic would tag as a work of ecofiction. A term coined in the latter third of the last century once the full extent of our impact on the environment became clear, ecofiction refers to short stories and novels that foreground nature and our self-serving and stubbornly destructive responses to it.

Set in Appalachia, Kingsolver's econovel combines ethics with romance in the braided stories of three sexy women versed in the ways of the wild and vehement in their resistance to all that threatens it, from insecticides to men intent on killing predators essential to the health of an ecosystem. Deanna Wolfe is a reclusive yet passionate wildlife biologist working for the Forest Service in the mountains above her southern Appalachia hometown. An early scene involving Deanna offers a variation on Conrad in its depiction of the capture and scrutiny of a winged creature:

> Luna moths were common enough up here but still never failed to move her because of their size and those pale-green, ethereal wings tipped with long, graceful tails. As if they were already ghosts, mourning their future extinction. This one was out of its element, awake in broad daylight. A busy chipmunk might have rousted it from a lower resting place. Or it was possible she was witnessing the fatal, final disorientation that overcomes a creature as it reaches the end of its life. Once, as a child, waiting with her dad in a gas station, she'd found a luna moth in that condition: confused and dying on the pavement of front of their truck. For the time it took him to pump the gas she'd held it in her hand and watched it struggle against its end. Up close it was a frightening beast, writhing and beating against her hand until wisps of pale-green fur slipped off its body and stuck to her fingers. Her horror had made her want to throw it down, and it was only her preconceived affection for the luna that made her hold on. When these creatures dance above their yard at night, she and her dad called them ballerinas. But this was no ballerina. Its body was a fat, furry cone flattened on one end into a ferocious face like a tiny, angry owl's. It glared at Deanna, seeming to know too much for an insect, and, worse, seeming disdainful. She hadn't given up her love for luna after that, but she'd never forgotten, either, how a mystery caught in the hand could lose its grace.[4]

Deanna's determination to protect a coyote family puts her in conflict with her new and unexpected lover, a hunter and sworn enemy of the animal she reveres. Meanwhile down in the valley Lusa Maluf Landowski, a scientist of Polish Jewish and Palestinian descent, has married into a clannish farming family skeptical of her city ways and obsession with studying insects. When her young husband dies, Lusa is forced to become more involved in running the farm, and she eventually figures out how to integrate her scientific insights into the work of everyday life, something septuagenarian Nannie Land Rawley learned long ago. An organic apple grower and jane-of-all-trades, she feuds with her crotchety, uptight neighbor, Garnett Walker, who, unbeknownst to her, dreams of creating a new strain of blight-resistant chestnut.

As these brief descriptions and the obviously "green" names of her characters indicate, Kingsolver uses the predicaments of her Appalachian earth goddesses as opportunities for dispensing ecological wisdom, praising the old ways of living in harmony with nature, and glorying in nature's beauty. Her fervor to impart her invaluable message frequently overwhelms her story, rendering it didactic, a bit pat, and very sweet in the a-little-sugar-helps-the-medicine-go-down mode. Clearly, she hopes to reach as broad a readership as possible, and that's all to the good because, in fact, her prose is fecund and spellbinding, her humor sly, and her story genuinely compelling, intelligent, and cathartic.

Kingsolver's tightrope act reminds the critic that novelists driven to write by strong moral convictions have to walk a thin line between proselytizing and telling a convincing story, between burdening characters with ideas and allowing them to emerge as complex, fully-dimensional personalities the reader will care about. An ecocritic, in particular, has to be careful not to let their environmental and political beliefs cloud their literary judgment. No matter how painstakingly realistic fiction can be, no matter how masterfully contrived, it is still a work of the imagination, and as a work of art it must leave room for ambiguity, mystery, and all the craziness and unpredictability inherent in life.

John Steinbeck wrote *The Grapes of Wrath*, his 1939 masterpiece, with tremendous empathy and anger, but he did not oversimplify the social and environmental forces that gave rise to the terrible Dust Bowl of the 1930s, or the subsequent migration of so-called Okies to the so-called promised land of California, or the fear and loathing with which they were treated, nor did he create caricatural characters. Like all great writers, Steinbeck infused his characters and landscapes with his compassion and moral perspective, making his values as intrinsic to his writing as blood is to the body, water to the earth. It's clear that he knew that there is no difference between human and environmental rights, between social injustice and the abuse of land and mistreatment of animals. In fact, his profound ecological awareness is immediately palpable in the grand and sonorous overture to *The Grapes of Wrath*, in which he describes the relentless drought that has desiccated the land, transforming once green fields to restless dust. As his hero, Tom Joad, just released from prison, makes his way to his family's farm, a land turtle also embarks on a journey:

The sun lay on the grass and warmed it, and in the shade under the grass the insects moved, ants and ant lions to set traps for them, grasshoppers to jump into the air and flick their yellow wings for a second, sow bugs like armadillos, plodding restlessly on many tender feet. And over the grass at the roadside a land turtle crawled, turning aside for nothing, dragging his high-domed shell over the grass: His hard legs and yellow-nailed feet threshed slowly through the grass, not really walking, but boosting and dragging his shell along. The barley beards slid off his shell, and the clover burrs fell on him and rolled to the ground. His horny beak was partly open, and his fierce, humorous eyes, under brows like fingernails, stared straight ahead.[5]

Steinbeck describes exactly how this powerful and determined turtle heaves itself up a highway embankment, scales a four-inch high concrete curb, balances on the ledge, then tips itself over to the pavement. As the turtle begins to walk slowly across the blistering hot highway, a woman in a sedan swerves to miss him, then a man in a light truck "swerved to hit it," and does. The turtle lands on his back, but manages to right itself and plod on into the dust on the other side of the highway where Tom Joad picks him up, and wraps him in his coat. Tom's intention isn't murderous, he wants to present the turtle to his kid brother—he has no other gift and it's been four years since he's seen his family. Once he discovers that the farm has been abandoned, he lets the turtle go. Soon the Joads will also be on the move, carrying their home with them, as the turtle does, and, like the turtle, they will be vulnerable to the mayhem and brutality of man and machine.

Zoom forward to 1975 and the release of America's most radical econovel, Edward Abbey's notorious and celebrated *The Monkey Wrench Gang*. No discussion of nature writing can overlook Abbey, an irascible, brilliant, and protean champion of liberty and wilderness. Born in Appalachian Pennsylvania, Abbey came to love and revere the red rock canyon country of the Southwest, writing a peppery and passionate work of nature writing, *Desert Solitaire* (1968), an account of his experiences as a park ranger in Arches National Monument in southeastern Utah, as well as bold, kinetic, and provocative fiction. Many of his writings are uncompromising yet funny calls-to-the-barricade, including "A Writer's Credo," which begins:

It is my belief that the writer, the free-lance author, should be and must be a critic of the society in which he lives. It is easy enough, and always profitable, to rail away at national enemies beyond the sea, at foreign powers beyond our borders, and at those within our borders who question the prevailing order . . . But the moral duty of the free writer is to begin his work at home: to be a critic of his own community, his own country, his own government, his own culture. The more freedom the writer possesses the greater the moral obligation to play the role of critic . . . That's all I ask of the author. To be a hero, appoint himself a moral leader, wanted or not. I believe that words count, that writing matters, that poems, essays, and novels—in the long run—make a difference.[6]

Himself an ecowarrior—rumor has it that Abbey torched highway billboards—he based his fictional band of anarchistic nature-lovers, the Monkey Wrench Gang, on close friends and comrades in wilderness adventures, animating his ornery characters with his own anger over the pell-mell development of the mystically beautiful Southwest. George Washington Hayduke, Seldom Seen Smith, Bonnie Abbzug, and Doc Sarvis fight back by becoming saboteurs, throwing monkey wrenches into the ill-conceived plans of government and big business. So convincing was Abbey's depiction of such ecotage methods as tree-spiking and disabling bulldozers, they were used as a blueprint by the radical environmental group Earth First! Smart, outrageous, funny, and thorny as cacti, *The Monkey Wrench Gang* ends like a good old-fashioned cliffhanger, the fate of its hero, Hayduke, uncertain, as is the future of the spectacular wilderness he loves.

Abbey died in 1989 at age 62, just months before his last book, *Hayduke Lives!*, the long-awaited sequel to *The Monkey Wrench Gang*, was published. Here he renews his assault on the complacency and greed that made possible one of the greatest crimes against nature ever perpetuated, the building of the Glen Canyon Dam, which flooded a stretch of the Colorado River so unique and magical in its beauty, its loss is still sharply felt by those who knew that holy place, and those who wish they could. Abbey's wit and storytelling skills are even more finely honed than before, his ire even more molten. But as radical and fresh as his viewpoint and approach are, he is keenly aware of and grateful for his predecessors, a debt he pays in the opening scene in *Hayduke Lives!*:

Old man turtle ambles along the deerpath, seeking breakfast. A strand of wild ricegrass dangles from his pincer-like beak. His small wise droll redrimmed eyes look from side to side, bright and wary and shrewd. He walks on long leathery legs, fully extended from the walnut-colored hump of shell, the ventral skid-plate clear of the sand. His shell is as big as a cowboy's skillet, a gardener's spade, a Tommy's helmet. He is 145 years old—middle-aged. He has fathered many children and will beget more. Maybe.[7]

Abbey pauses to describe the turtle's bred-in-the-bone attachment to his beautiful canyon home, a meditation that is abruptly interrupted when said turtle smells "something rank, vile, poisonous, of a thing hot and burning, an entity not alive but nevertheless in motion." He doesn't know this alien smell. He feels the ground vibrate. He hears an unidentifiable sound. And then:

> Something huge and yellow, blunt-nosed glass-eyed grill-faced, with a mandible of shining steel, belching black jolts of smoke from a single nostril of seared metal, looms suddenly gigantically behind the old desert turtle.[8]

Clearly, this is an unabashed homage to Steinbeck, a writer Abbey greatly admired. Abbey's turtle is walking the earth fifty years after Steinbeck's turtle crossed that dangerous highway, and this venerable creature is facing far more dangerous adversaries than his Oklahoman cousin. Abbey's turtle is soon buried alive, and Abbey peers balefully inside the terrible killing machine:

> A dim anthropomorph, helmeted, masked and goggled, fixed in place under a canopy of steel, attached by gloved forelimbs to a pair of levers, moves jerkily half-blindly inside the fog of dust, one small component of a great machine.

This is another variation on a scene from *The Grapes of Wrath*. Steinbeck also recognized the malevolence of bulldozers in his empathetic portrayal of poor farmers losing their land to banks and big business, faceless entities who send in their machines to eradicate all evidence of the former occupants:

> Snubnosed monsters, raising the dust and sticking their snouts into it, straight down the country, across the country, through fences, through dooryards, in and out of gullies in straight lines . . .
>
> The man sitting in the iron seat did not look like a man; gloved, goggled, rubber dust mask over nose and mouth, he was a part of the monster, a robot in the seat. The thunder of the cylinders

sounded through the country, became one with the air and the earth, so that earth and air muttered in sympathetic vibration. The driver could not control it—

The destruction of wilderness and the corporate takeover of private lands and displacement of families are inhumane acts, Steinbeck and Abbey imply, carried out not by individuals but of robotmen brainwashed by the powers-that-be and made machinelike in their enslavement, stripped of identity, conscience, and soul. The confounding blend of boon and curse inherent in the Industrial Revolution, the harsh reality that machines both improve and degrade life, is examined in many nineteenth- and early twentieth-century novels, a theme ratcheted up tenfold after the advent of nuclear energy and computer technology. Steinbeck detected the first hints of what was to come and alluded to it in his keen depiction of the then-new interstate highways and the high-speed parade of gleaming air-conditioned automobiles whizzing arrogantly past the heavily loaded and lumbering trucks of the homeless farmers. Abbey picks up the thread and robustly satirizes these same highways, which have become even more offensive, as well as the burgeoning and absurd bureaucracies of business and government, the crass megapresence of commercial media, and the ever-accelerating pace of everyday life.

Now, a dozen years after *Hayduke Lives!*, no fiction aimed at capturing the texture of contemporary American life can fail to take into account the effects both obvious and nuanced of the precipitous Electronic Revolution. There's the ubiquitous presence of computers and their spawn—VCRs, Gameboys, Walkmen, laptops, and cell phones—machines that further separate us from the living world, dazzling us with images and messages of our own devising. The rapid spread of these inherently narcissistic and cocooning devices is occurring in inverse proportion to the decimation of wilderness. There's irony, too, in the absurd popularity of gargantuan, gas-guzzling SUVs. Built for terrain few people should traverse, they jam up the streets of cities and suburbs instead, some equipped with monitors so that passengers can watch the screen rather than stare at the heavy traffic and hideous line-up of franchised stores and junk food dispensers that has replaced forests and prairies.

Edward Abbey declares, "Growth for the sake of growth is the ideology of the cancer cell," yet bulldozers and earthmovers have triumphed nearly everywhere while we watch TV, play computer games, and worry about our weight. As we use technology to alter the environment, it is also affecting our bodies and minds. Technology is designed to extend our reach and our senses, so that while our bodies remain parked at desks, our brains process the views from space telescopes and electronic microscopes, sounds that orbit the globe instantaneously, and the ceaseless stream of digital information. In an observant and imaginative novelist's hands, consideration of these extreme changes to the ambiance of life and their effect on our psyches results in new shades of ecofiction. The environment, after all, does not consist only of ocean, desert, or forest but also of commuter trains, offices, city streets, and suburban shopping malls. Everything we do is part of nature because we are nature, and a true ecological viewpoint encompasses everything from cockroaches to condors to mold to people and their cars, computers, and cell phones.

Alan Lightman, a physicist and a novelist, bravely explores this cluttered and cacophonous new world in *The Diagnosis*, an unforgettable drama of the tyranny of the status quo and the malignancy of human life lived out of touch with nature. As the novel begins, his hero, Bill Chalmers, a workaholic corporate drone who has calculated his suburb-to-city morning commute to the minute, hurries within a stampeding herd of stressed-out fellow travelers to catch the rush-hour train into Boston. People are cramming muffins into their mouths and clasping newspapers, briefcases, and laptops as they hurry blindly along. Chalmers is jostled and nudged, but he slows down to give a homeless woman his change. He reaches the platform, surely a circle of hell:

> He glanced at his watch, 8:23, and forged a path to the kiosk. Above his head, the digital sign flickered and hummed and something clattered repeatedly against the high concrete ceiling and the air sagged with the burnt smell of hot brake fluid. Several radios blared, jumbling their throbbing bass notes in competing rhythms. Huddled against the kiosk as if battling a strong wind, a woman in a smart linen suit was delivering instructions into a cellular telephone. Chalmers couldn't help noticing that her phone was a new model, considerably smaller and sleeker than his. He took out his own phone from his briefcase. As he began dialing, he found that he was still shaken by the poor woman on the stairs. Her misery had cast a gloom over him, which he tried to forget by pushing the tiny buttons as fast as he could. First he

called Jenkins, to make sure that the proper documents would be ready for his 9:15 meeting. All was in order. He hung up and stood on his toes, peering down the dark tunnel of Track Two. Over the track, hundreds of glowing red neon tubes dangled down from the ceiling, one of them broken and blinking like a Christmas tree light. His telephone rang. Two men reached inside their briefcases, thinking it theirs . . . Chalmers looked at his watch and dialed his voicemail. As the connection was being relayed through space or wherever—who knew exactly where cellular transmissions were at any one instant?—he twisted his neck and gazed up at the digital sign: "8:24 . . . Introducing a new feature of Providential Services: Providential Online . . . Get stock quotations on your pagers, minute by minute . . . Think of Providential Online as 'Work wherever, whenever'(TM) . . ."[9]

This is the first of many sharply etched scenes in which Lightman captures the frenzy of our loud, discordant, crowded, toxic, digitized, and information-addled world. He does it again in descriptions of gridlocked traffic, and when he has Chalmers, who tells his psychiatrist that he's angry at everybody, say, "No one sees anything. . . . I was driving to work this morning, and I saw a mother duck on the side of the road, with six or seven babies waddling behind her. I slowed down to look and everybody started honking at me." The same aggression, impatience, and indifference rules in scathingly parodic scenes of frantic office life—Chalmers works for a cutthroat company that promises to "process the maximum information in the minimum time"—and in the bureaucratic, machine-dominated, surreal realm of contemporary medicine, where doctors barely look at or touch patients.

Lightman's suspenseful, darkly comic, and disquieting novel ignites when Chalmers has an inexplicable and devastating breakdown on the train, followed by a harrowing emergency room stay and a reckless, late-night journey through a demonic cityscape where every stranger is obsessed with obtaining cash at any cost. Chalmers manages to find his way home, where his wife has been having a cyber love affair (tenderly taking her laptop to bed) and his teenage son prefers email to conversation. He resumes his normal life, but not for long: he has contracted a mysterious, slowly progressing malady that soon forces him out of the whirlwind of work and into a strange limbo. His symptoms escalate from numbness to paralysis, and in his stillness, he finds himself paying attention to the most commonplace and yet most wondrous phenomenon, such as the play of light and shadow on his bedroom floor as the earth turns, or the delicacy of a leaf. And he is inexpressibly grateful for these revelations.

Nature's beauty nourishes the senses and the soul. It is the baseline for existence, the wellspring for consciousness. The cosmos itself, scientists have determined, is a web; life is a web; all is connection, flow, and mutuality. Our fascination with and aggrandizement of our own species and the helter-skelter, money-driven technocracy that enables us to live hermetically-sealed lives, distances us from the greater living world, the realm our ancestors called sacred.

In the overtures to Steinbeck and Abbey's novels, man's machines and man's greed first threatened, then buried alive a land turtle, one of the earth's most ancient creatures. Lightman's novel begins with a man who is under assault by a virtual bulldozer as he is buried beneath an avalanche of noise, image, and information. What will happen if we turn our gaze away from the wild so long there is no wild left to see? We are, indisputably, a hardy and adaptable species. It's very possible that we'll thrive in a less splendid future in which we and a few other weedy and invasive organisms dominate, in which the biodiversity that has created countless and astonishing variations on the theme of life—thousands of different butterflies, trees, fish, mammals, flowers, each a work of art—has given way to a more pragmatic and static homogeneity. Cultural diversity, a reflection of biodiversity, is fading, too, as corporate images invade and eradicate local culture just as industry destroys wilderness.

Once upon a time, each village, each town, each landscape had its own unique look, texture, sound, and scent. Now name-brand franchises, the zebra mussels of architecture, degrade the countryside. Television and advertising, the invincible seeds of business, travel far and wide and put down strong roots everywhere they land, strangling indigenous languages, art, and customs like kudzu chokes out other plants. And yet no matter how sterile our habitats and popular culture become, we seem to adapt physically, psychologically, even spiritually. Some individuals, like Lightman's hero, may break down, but most of us conform, seeking safety and comfort, even finding beauty in the most compromised and contrived environments, driven by the same needs, fears, and desires that drove our ancestors, however different our surroundings.

To despair or hope? This is the question that goads and inspires today's ecominded writers, and there are many. Just as Edward Abbey paid tribute to John Steinbeck in *Hayduke Lives!*, T. C. Boyle offers a rollicking yet empathic homage to Abbey in his econovel *A Friend of the Earth*, which features an ecowarrior named Tyrone O'Shaughnessy Tierwater, and explores the trials and traumas of serious environmental activism: the soul-crushing sense of the futility of small efforts, however heroic, in the face of an immense maelstrom of destruction. Other novelists, such as John Hockenberry, are writing ecothrillers and literary quasi-science fiction, such as Kathryn Davis' haunting tale, *The Walking Tour*. Native American writers, including Leslie Marmon Silko, Louise Erdrich, Linda Hogan, and Eden Robinson, have written novels that link the spiritual loss attendant on the attempted ethnocide of indigenous North Americans, people who live in harmony with nature, with the concomitant obliteration of wilderness through clear-cutting, strip-mining, and dam-building.

It's the work of writers, of all artists, to observe change and determine what remains the same. To gauge what is lost and what is learned. To help us see where we've been, who we've been, and to foresee what we are making of the world, and who we will be. To keep reverence—the awareness that there is a force far greater than our own, the awe we feel in the presence of the wild—alive and valued. Will people still read the poetry we treasure now in the spirit in which it was written centuries, even decades ago? Will late twenty-first century readers know what it means to watch a windhover? To walk through a meadow of wildflowers and buzzing bees? To hear the courting songs of frogs? To see a sky bright with stars on a clear and quiet night? Or will all the tropes of the wild become mere symbols, contrivances no longer connected to living entities and sensuous experience? How will language evolve to reflect the diminishment of life's gorgeous improvisations and our species' mental migration into the cyberworld, or whatever artificial realm lies ahead?

Change is inevitable and usually painful, but it needn't be dire. Writers of ecologically-attuned fiction help us see life's modulations from fresh and imaginative perspectives. They inspire us to think about difficult questions we'd rather ignore, and be open to unexpected revelations. They remind us to be aware of life's complexity, to, simply but resoundingly, pay attention. Jane Weddell, the misunderstood paleontologist in Barry Lopez's evocative short story, "The Empty Lot," has it right: "She saw no greater purpose in life than to reveal and behold." To look not to abstract or otherworldly forces, as poet Edward Hirsch writes in "Earthly Light," but to life itself:

*Because this world, too, needs our unmixed*
*attention, because it is not heaven*

*but earth that needs us, because*
*it is only earth—limited, sensuous*
*earth that is so fleeting, so real.*[10]

Earth is our home, our mother and father, our tabernacle, the one true testament, the ur-book, living scripture. Reading and writing can be acts of reverence, the prologue to the preservation of all that nourishes us body and soul.

## Endnotes

1   Dillard, Annie. *Pilgrim at Tinker Creek*. Harper & Row: New York. 1974. pp. 8–9.

2   Lyon, Thomas J. *This Incomparable Land: A Guide to American Nature Writing*. Milkweed Editions: Minneapolis, Minnesota. 2001. p. x.

3   Conrad, Joseph. *Lord Jim*. Modern Library: New York. pp. 207–208.

4   Kingsolver, Barbara. *Prodigal Summer*. HarperCollins: New York. 2000. pp. 65–66.

5   Steinbeck, John. *The Grapes of Wrath*. Penguin. pp. 14–15, pp. 36–37.

6   Abbey, Edward. *Hayduke Lives!* Little, Brown: Boston. 1990. pp. 3, 4, 5, 6.

7   Ibid.

8   Ibid.

9   Lightman, Alan. *The Diagnosis*. Pantheon: New York. 2000. pp. 4–6, 239.

10   Hirsch, Edward. "Earthly Light" from *Earthly Measures*. Knopf: New York. 1997. p . 89.

Linda Gregerson

# Maculate

I remember going door to door, it must
               have been nineteen-
           thirty-six and half the town was out of work,

we always had the Red Cross drive in March
               (*consider*
           *the lilies how they grow*). The snowmelt

frozen hard again, and cinders on the shoveled
               walks.
           I was wearing your grandmother's boots.

(*Consider the ravens, they have neither storehouse*
               *nor barn.*)
           The grocer gave a nickel, I can see him yet,

some people had nothing at all.
               And I came
           to Mrs. Exner's house (*no thief*

*approacheth, neither moth*). The woman
               was so bent
           with arthritis, nearly hooped

when she walked up the street with her bucket and mop
               (*not Solomon*
           *in all his glory*). The people

29

she cleaned for wouldn't keep a bucket in the house
(*nor*
*moth*). She gave me three new dollar

bills, I'll never forget it, I wanted the earth
to swallow me up.


2

Oilcloth on the kitchen table, linoleum

under his chair, and both of them an ugly hiero-
glyphic
of yellow scorchmarks ringed with black.

My father must be tired, to let the ash
between
his fingers and the still-lit butt-ends of his

days befoul the world around him so. Bone-
tired
and all but hammered to his knees

with drink. (*Burnt offering I have not required.*)
The morning after
the night he died (the undertaker's taillights

on the snow-packed drive), my mother sat just
there
(*burnt offering I will not have*) and said

(*but only love*), I'm going to get a new kitchen floor.

3

    The raven is not
an unmixed consolation. What is manna

to the raven leaves a crust of blood
        above
    its beak *(a treasure which no moth*

*corrupts)*. The freckled lily festers. The unspotted
        lily drops
    its trembling stamen in a smear of gold

*(laid up for thee)*. And still it is no little
        thing
    to think we shall be eaten clean.

# A History Play

Months later—I'd been cleaning
      my desk—
    these bits of gold foil spilled to the ground

a second time, five-petalled blossoms of public
      gaud
    unloosed from the folded playbill as in

August from the heavens at the Swan, Act
      Five,
    to mark the child Elizabeth's birth.

The old queen has been put aside *(I am not
      such a truant as not
    to know)*, the new one's doomed *(the language*

*I have lived in*), the girlchild is herself
                    a sign of grace
              withheld. But look at these sumptuous

velvets with their branchwork and encrusted
                    pearl,
              you'd think the hand of death would be afraid

to strike. That's wrong. You'd think
                    that death
              had held the needle and dispensed the worm-

wrought thread. The players will be wanting their late
                    supper soon, while
              we—we two and our two girls—

set out across the footbridge on our way back
                    home.
              The waterfowl will be asleep—they're sleeping

already—their willow-strewn and fecal
                    island silent
              in the summer night. The past that for a moment

turned, backlit, thick
                    with presence, as though
              leading to us somehow, in its very

inadvertence giving way to this
                    slight stench
              beneath a moon-washed bridge, the past

that has a place for us will know us by
                    our scattered
              wake. (A *strange tongue makes*) And morning

meanwhile yet to come (*my cause*
                    *more strange*):
              the girls will have hot chocolate with their toast

and eggs. The play? (which we will talk about) Tenacious
in its
praise and fierce in its elisions. So

father, mother (older than the cast-off queen), two
girls: an open book.
And spilling from the binding, gold.

*Carol Frost*

# Nature Has

Nature has a sexual sense of humor. A bee swigs nectar, the tail
of a neighborhood cat lifts, a shawl of white blossoms wafts from
the apple tree onto the dirt, until a breeze tweaks an exposed place,
a bottom—storms of pollen and flitting laughter—What birds
are these? They are singing. *Sex in the wind, love in the trees, sex
in the grasses, eggs in the nest.* But yourself, surely more complex,
with your imaginary lives and your off-keyed moon,
do you blush toward the meeting in the bower, a lark fluent in the leaves,
soft fires underneath and the trilling
ruthless? The fallen angels love you and what they do to you—
your senses and little white lies and rampant heart.

# Kayaking in the Gulf after Dusk

All the way back to the harbor
gray phosphorous and saffron as the night
comes on I keep turning to look for the island
in its lee in head winds

and look for furls beneath the water
of dolphin and scarcer shark as the west
blazes then shuts over the gulf

I paddle to the few lights after sunset
counter balanced the hours
caught like baits till I and the water
and the sky are mixed as if the moment

I rinsed my mouth and spat
and the ocean was a jar for me to do this
I was a part of the tide and rocking

the dark comes over the water
and looking outward in that dark
is the same as looking inward

only the harbor stay apart and divisible
seeds on the black sill

the unforgetting seeds look
the harbor burns

*Alice B. Fogel*

# The Owl

If it can be called staring when no eyes are visible . . .
I thought I could wait staring back till I could see

some glassy feedback or glare of light in the socket
indicating reception, recognition, retina.

No wonder, for some, the owl encountered
presages a death: its eyes look

as if from the dead—all soul, or none at all,
it's hard to tell. It was a trap, a trick, the way

I had to crane my neck up, while it faced me down
from its perch with its empty eyes, its round

dark holes for eyes, till I glanced past it to see
if forest blackness was what came through its skull

from behind. It slid its own neck slowly
all the way away from me, its head with its cannily

judging eyes swiveling like mockery,
and then, deliberate, the face swinging back.

Caught at the brink of woods as if guilty, and it
a thing of weight and judgment, a beauty, a boast.

Cold blew through me at the thought of its swoop,
even more at the memory of its sound

like sudden coyotes howling, or like the sound
midnight might make falling

before twilight.  And at the question
of what it saw in *me*, craving up at it, as at the last

desire of the damned. Of course
*it* was the first to let go, before I found any answering

light reflected in the place of its eyes, deep there
in the feathers of its cowl. And as it turned upward

and flew, with my new trove of religion in tow,
the fear and awe I never felt for God

nor ever knew the sense of until then, skewed
all laws of perspective in the heavenly

way it grew larger in expanse of wing
and wing, still lifting

my eyes along like an undercurrent
below it, the ground for once gave out

from underneath so that I was like the condemned
standing for one impossible instant above the collapse

beneath his shoes, the noose still limp and loose,
the neck expectant of its clasp.

*Ray Gonzalez*

# Hymn for the Tongue

There is nothing more to say.
Chile pods in the nose and on the tongue.

When the fire strikes, raise your hand.
You will be recognized as a new element in the universe

long after everyone has disappeared.
The angels can't be mentioned here,

only the waving girl on the street who warned you
about yourself, how often you had to eat and translate

desire into a flowery thing, how last summer you killed
fourteen scorpions at your mother's house in one week,

the awful things appearing day and night, their springing
from the walls making you fear your appetite,

the hooked tails you gathered in a sandwich bag
causing a commotion across the stars,

galaxies imploding to get out of your way when
you touched the largest stinger with your fingertip,

sent the cosmos flying to find other ways to feed itself,
other means of being able to talk to you.

# The Sign in the Lava Bed

Its creator was here seven hundred years ago,
Its shape embedded in the fields of tomorrow.
When I stood over it, the worn figures were constant
and I missed the key to the silence that looked at me.
When I tried to copy what I saw on paper,
its boundaries realigned themselves in the black rocks.
When I studied it again, the sign was a word I once knew
but could not recall in the 106 degree heat of the desert.

When I stepped back, the Gila monster crawled out
of the crevice a few feet to my left, its pink
and black bands pausing on top of the bubbled surface.
The huge thing flicked its tongue,
its heavy head turning toward me.
It carefully moved one swollen paw after another,
sliding through the black holes, until it rested
between what I had discovered and
what I thought I could steal.

# The Cities Are Wounded
# by Another Year

The stillness in the mimosa, the cry
of the killdeer vanishing in the wind.
Of the window, only the picture frame,
the bed where the grandmother died,
miles of abandoned railroad tracks,
the desert tortoise I found as a boy,
its wrinkled head retracting when

I picked up its heavy shell, set it under
the largest tumbleweed as I followed
the city into a storm of years
the way men lean into their silence
after the arrows find their mark,
the old plaza rebuilt in concrete.

Even the mud in the alley dries
into a new country, streets filled
with maps for the end of the world.
Broken treaty, red drops, blue stains,
one emerging canvas bursting with
the shadow in the cottonwood
that is always there, my approach
not making it disappear,
the tree growing without me,
how I left by breaking its
branches so I could see.

*David Roderick*

# Grass

GRASS BECOMES MY FATHER. SHOOTS GREEN FROM HIS KNUCKLES. Sproutlets push from his chin. Father burns his days with grass, primping and trimming, manicuring the surface with snips. He sleepwalks angry engines over his grass at dawn, making wakers of the neighbors.

Father sears himself with chemicals. His skin is soaked with knowledge, with compounds that syndicates hock in kegs. Shelf-life alkalines that rag his warcoat. Fluorescent dressings that stain his skin green, steep there, flare from his pores and follicles.

All this because of Plato, says Father. All this for a lawn that is perfectly beautiful, he says while yanking the tussocks, while shaking soil from their roots.

But at night, polecats burrow their snouts into his grass. They lace stink through the yard, delve out pocks of soil that peek through, holes in Father's green blankie. Someone needs to repair those holes, and that someone is Father, the him that is half-me. Someone needs to quell Hed at night, that mutt who howls at skunks.

Hed, that dung-piler, that purveyor of pustules and pests, that barkridden slothmouth, he loves me. He swabs my ears with his tongue. His tongue is a grit tongue. His tongue is a sandpaper tongue that burns my cheeks with laplicks.

String becomes my Mother. Snip snip. String through her tresses. Goldstring and whitestring. Strings defiantly bright, iridescent in the bluegloom house. She stitches lampshades of string, the couches, the banisters. She darns steps of string, an amazing staircase that spirals up to her lair.

We live at Ten Unity Circle, Mother and Father and Hed and me. Ours is a house of string, string that ties up Mother with tasks like shelling the peapods, like burning the bunts. Hers are fingers that ravel, that sterilize the silver. She darns things with those strings, tighter and tighter around us. Our house is a strange cocoon.

Sometimes I think that darning makes lonely my Mother. She sits in the bluegloom house, knitting and weaving, waiting for birds to sing from their nests.

Grass becomes my Father when it burns in the summer waveheat. He limps over it, smokes from his nose, cups a blunt in his hand. He rolls his eyes and spreads each Hed pile with lime. Hed, he says, don't mess you lousy mutt this grass. Hed, he says, dragging the dog to his stringpen, these dung-piles must cease. Plato would not approve of a lawn that is not perfectly beautiful, of a lawn messed with dung-piles.

I ride on Father when he mows the grass. I press my face into his beard and the scent of grass lodges in my hair. Sometimes I find clovers in that beard, whiskered through it. Sometimes I find a damselfly or moth. Father's cuticles are vaults of grease. His palms reek of gas. When he rides across the grass I link to his neck. His Apple-Adam throbs, a huge lugnut, a knot of string that lunges from his throat when he swallows.

My Father, this half-me, grass becomes him. He yearns for grass in the swallows of his dreams. I spy him, hammock-slung in his toolshed: that dented quonset, corrugated, rusting. I spy him bathing in a badbirth, his beard in the panes of that shed. His fingers pry into his beard, picking out the dandelions and timothy, the weeds that are starting to sprout there.

Lawn-edges whacked. Weeds choked. Alkalines spread on the grass. Father sweats more and more quickly than the lemonade I serve him in tumblers. A quencher pressed from real lemons, honey from the bees stirred in, bees that hover over the grass to pollinate and cross-pollinate. Bees that communicate, that land with lust in the flowers. When Father shoos them away, they sometimes stab his wrists. I read the strange marks stung to him, like braille, a pink language of buzzes. This is how they battle, those bees, their needles piercing his skin.

It's like a war out here, says Father, while holding his poison-prong and kneeling over a dandelion. If one goes down they all go down, he says, as he uproots it with his glittering tool. Father follows that job by lacing the lawn with toxins. Then he cups a blunt and watches the sky, scours the cloud formations, waits for rain to soak the subsoil.

I like to scour the cloud formations too and ask which cloud would suit Plato. Plato does not like clouds because they lack perfect form and beauty, says Father.

That is why Father coils his grass with snakes that spout water. Our tricky weather makes it a must. But the coils are tricky too, unpredictable. One time they snarled me while I was a secret in the yard, holding out a banana peel for the polecats. Before I could feed those toe-snuffers, the coils snarled me, and Father with his penlight scolded and spanked me to bed.

I didn't give Father any buttons that week, I was so sore from the spanking.

Green is the secret urging toward the sun, that star that wants to yellow it. But the grass doesn't know better. It needs less sun, more water than Father can quench. He carries his coils out to grass and waters, splattering it with life. This is how grass survives the waveheat at Ten Unity Circle.

Our house is a strange cocoon. Mother darns it, stitches its foundation into the ground. She darns the walls, the tiles, the kitchen engines. She understands only fabrics and weaves of string. She understands nothing about the polecats and the Dominoes that torment my Father.

I must prevent the Domino Effect, says Father, stalwart in his warcoat. I can't let a blade fall to the weeds. It's a war out here, he says, while shoveling compost, his eyes blazing with compounds.

While Father stumps his declarations against the polecats, I sit on the grass and listen to him, my back on Hed's sun-stomach. I look for Plato in the clouds and I hide a button under my tongue.

Sometimes Mother spreads string over the grass, but Father doesn't mind because he says that Plato was a birdfiend. A bird is perfectly beautiful, says Father. It has a knowable form. So Mother darns the hickories and fences and the suet bells. She strings Hed's wigwag and Father's beard. Purplestring and redstring braided with green. String webbed between her fingers and toes, tight around my whitewrists, looped around Father's neck. She gears up birdsongs by stringing around the badbirths.

Here is how Father fills the badbirths. First he trickles seeds around each base. Then he coils the spouts until water teems at each lip. One badbirth is built of brick and the other is nailed wood. The birds like the wood badbirth better because it reminds them of hickory, says Father. Sometimes he sinks little twiglets in there to make them feel at home. Sometimes Hed woofs them off and angers that half-me that is Father. Sometimes the birds aren't nice and scat on Father's lawn, even in the badbirths, even in the wood one. But Father says they are good for the grass, and that Plato would think so too.

The birds weave nests with Mother's string. Mother the lonely one, to whom the birds sing songs about the common orb of day. They plunge into their afflictions, mechanically. They have wind-up pins under their throats. Their songs are strings of mirth, unspooling over sprockets. Their flights are sometimes dumbdeaths in the mirrored toolshed panes.

Mother whines about buttons swiped from her sewchest. She whines to Father about the stolen nubs, but I am the great button-filcher at Ten Unity Circle. The buttons clasp us tightly to this address.

There are many good places to slip a button. Sometimes I slip a button into Father's sleeve. Then I watch as he says whoops, what do we have here. A shiny new button. A pink one. I must submit this fine button to your Mother. Then he vanishes inside the house of string for an hour. Those are the times when I climb a hickory and plot secret visits to my polecat pets. I grin when I hear Mother cry out with happiness for her button.

Or sometimes while Mother cries out with happiness I lie on Father's grass and look at the clouds that Plato scorns. They make strange, riveting shapes, those clouds. Sometimes they look like a polecat or a banana peel or Hed. Sometimes they look like a wind-up bird or a boot. But the clouds never shape into buttons. I don't know why the clouds don't wish to be buttons.

Or sometimes while Mother cries out with happiness I sneak into the toolshed and sit in Father's little quonset room, his hammock and Hed-eared books, his greasy lantern that holds a flame. The machines tinkered down to mere parts. Sprockets and wheels. All the dull blades nailed to the walls. And webs, pinned into sills and panes. The hammock, where Father sleeps like a sort of spider himself, waiting to hear movements out in the yard. I bet that Father would like the polecats to be flies, and for his hammock web to spread out in the yard, trapping them.

The polecats have striped-whites down their backs. I like to feed them banana peels from the compost pile, but Father doesn't know. Father doesn't know much about how things work here at Ten Unity Circle. Sometimes I slip him a button and he never finds it in his sleeve. Sometimes I bite a hole in his trousers so that Mother will visit him in the yard.

Hed is trapped in a pen that Mother wove from string. On certain occasions, Father frees Hed into the prison of the yard to scare off the polecats, but Hed woofs and woofs and harries the wound-up birds. Or Hed leaves dung-piles in the grass, irritating Father. Once Hed snarfed at a polecat and earned himself a tomato bath. Stupid Hed, said Father, soaking him in a zincbin.

So many weeds infest the yard, so many polecats hole, so much grass becomes my Father. As the summer drears on, his hair thickens, sodded from the lawn. Father weaves forth and back across the yard, for noons and noons, forth and back on his mower. I ride him when he mows with a blunt in his hand, his Apple-Adam throbbing under his neckskin. He mows again at dawn, when the birds gear up and the waken neighbors complain.

Buttons become me. I steal them from Mother's sewchest and slip them into Father's pockets, into compost, into the corners of the toolshed. Father knows that I steal the buttons but he pretends that it is Mother, romanticizing him. He pretends that the buttons are the gift from her heart. He finds the buttons and returns them to Mother, saying, look what I have here. Look what I discovered under a badbirth, hidden in the grass.

Mother tricks each button from Father. She employs her strings for reconnaissance. She pleasures over each of them, the plastic ones and wooden ones, the buttons carved from bone. After each session with Father, she returns the buttons to her sewchest. After she locks up her buttons, she sings a song through the rooms.

This is the flow of commerce at Ten Unity Circle.

Weeds kill my Father because Plato would have scorned them. They wind Father into angry storms. He battles back with all his chemicals, his glittering trowels. He leads with his toxins, sprays each fiddlehead, sometimes draws a draught for himself. The shed glows at night, rife with green spectres, but Father sleeps there in bluntsmoke, dreaming a slaughter of weeds and slugs, of polecats that pock his grass.

The polecats snuff at my toes. They nibble banana peels from my palms.

Father catches a slug tracking through the grass. See, he says, this is a nasty, but the slug looks cute to me, with its antennae blurging over his finger. It's magic, he says, sprinkling some dust, making the slug vanish from his palm.

The sewchest has a lock, but I pick it with one of Father's glittering tools. Then I slip buttons into the toolshed shadows. I hide them in the cups of tulips, in hickories, in the ducts of angry machines. I pat them into anthills, in Father's beard, in the pockets of his warcoat. When Mother notices they are missing from her sewchest, she plays her strings into whines. Then Father visits her and the buttons pleasure her. What a happy family we are at Ten Unity Circle.

Funny how the warcoat is the same color as grass, green fatigue. Which is good because a war takes place on this lawn, a place where Father can blend. He worries that Dominoes are taking Effect here, that the blades are withering one by one, falling to polecats, juicing in the bellies of slugs. Father broods in his tangled hammock. He smokes over the sprockets and screws, the loose axles. With grunts he greases each squeak.

My hair was the color of Father's. That is why I am a half-him.

But from carrying the poisons, Father's hair is tainted with chlorophyll. When I link around his neck I can smell toxins in his breath, even through his bluntsmoke. The butterflies collect in his beard no longer. The slugs die at his touch.

Father shucks his warcoat and boots. Too hot for summer, he says. I take them from their hooks and wear them when I climb up into hickories, where birds sing mechanical songs. If I wear Father's warcoat, I think I might see the Dominoes taking Effect. I want to see what they look like, those Dominoes in the grass.

When Father's angry engines fail to rev, he crawls under them, his feet sticking out. This is another good time to hide a button in his pocket. While he tinkers with his tools, a hankie covers his mouth. He wears goggles and is absorbed with his engine. I slip my hand in his pocket and march across the lawn in his warcoat. I salute the wind-up birds in the badbirths, chirping from their nests of string. I salute Hed, my imaginary general, lolling in his hotsleep.

Once Hed was a bread oven. Mother was pounding some dough but Hed wolfed it and slept heavily on Father's grass. Then the dough began to rise in Hed's sun-stomach. Imagine that, Hed's sun-stomach like an oven, with bread expanding inside. Hed's sun-stomach baking a loaf of rye.

Usually I bring lunch to Father, yet another opportunity to slip him a button. I hide one between his ryeslabs, and sometimes they break his teeth, or vice-versa. This is a game that Father and I play. Button button where hides the button he sings as his fingers spider over my body, giggling me. I giggle softly though, so as not to wake the neighbors, so as not to distract Mother who is sewing our house with string.

So many weeds infiltrate the lawn. And so many Dominoes, but I still can't see them. Father sees them though, pointing here and here and here. The Dominoes are taking Effect, he frets, his brows knit with concern. If one goes down they all go down.

I admire the way that Father uses wrenches and screwdrivers and other glittering tools. He always has one in his hand, even when his hand is smoking. Once he let me hold a tool while he was tinkering, and I was surprised by its weight. It felt greasy, like grass juice, the kind that the crickets spit into my palms when I clamp them.

One of the buttons looks like a bird and one of the buttons is yellow. Many of the buttons are made of plastic: pink and red and blue. Some wood, some painted, some are old like trinkets. Some are white buttons of sharkbone or amber ones with bubbles trapped inside. Sometimes I keep a button on my tongue, rolling it there, metallic. Once I swallowed a button by mistake, a shiny button from Father's warcoat.

I march the warcoat out onto the grass and cut that out, says Father. He won't talk about the warcoat or the war that won it. I roll up its sleeves and salute him. Father spanks me to bed, even though it's dawn and the clouds make riveting forms.

Mother darns Father's clothes while they hang on his body. This is the only other time she visits the yard, to stitch his clothes together while he stands there, leering over his grass. Looking for polecat traces. Scheming against them. Muttering. This is what makes Father and Mother happy, I realize, that they both know their roles. This is why we are one happy family at Ten Unity Circle.

The polecats have striped-whites down their backs. They like to burrow slugs from the grass at night. I don't think that they know the difference between good slugs and bad ones. I don't think they see their role in the Domino Effect. They will eat any slug that blurges under their claws. I wonder how the polecats hear them beneath the grass, those slugs with juice in their stomachs.

Hed, that barkridden mongrel, that crotch-nosing wigwag, he loves me. And I him, but not when he chases the polecats. The polecats walk funnily, burrow little holes in the grass. They nibble banana peels from my palms at midnight, and they snuff between my toes.

I think that I love them.

And the polecats are winning the war over grass. Father has only poisons for the weeds. When I ask which is worse, the skunks or the weeds, he tells me that Plato would feel disgraced with the stinking polecats and the bad weeds equally. He was a sucker for perfect beauty, says Father, of that Thinker named Plato.

When Father bathes in a badbirth, I see that the grass is somehow part of him now, grass sprouting from his skin, from his pits, growing like nothing other than grass.

Father is losing, and Plato too. The wind-up birds are doing their part and the water its part and the compost its part and I my part and the poison its part and Hed his part and the angry machine its part but still there are patches of weeds. The Dominoes are taking Effect, says Father. One blade lapsed and now others are lapsing, falling to weeds and pests, to slugs that lure the polecats.

I try to find Plato in the clouds, but Father says no, Plato comes from books. Then he shows me one greasy and Hed-eared, one with missing pages, yellow, one with a library stamp on its cover. Tsk tsk, I say to Father, stomping around in his boots. While Father reads aloud, I salute the hickories and Hed, the clouds that make riveting forms.

More and more often, Father spanks me into the house when I share my love of polecats or march around in his warcoat, saluting the clouds. So Father gets fewer buttons than before. And Mother whines lonely through the bluerooms.

Patches of grass are turning brown, deadishly, and Father starts pulling them out of his hair. This isn't from polecats, he says. He goes to his little grass book and tries to identify a blade to find out if it is grass or a weed.

I am beginning to suspect that grass is a kind of weed. Some of the blades are mysteriously red. Mysterious red they are. Some, if I open them with my thumb, have fibrous strings inside.

String does not become me. Grass does not become me.

Father believes that there is a whole world beneath the grass. He says that a cross-section would show us all of the nameless worms that live there. Some of them are bad and some good. Some feed the grass and some eat it. This is Father's problem. He cannot peer beneath the grass so as to protect it, to weed out the bad from the good. Sometimes he wishes that he could peel back the grass and eradicate all of the nasties, the bad eggs and maggots, the blurging slugs that feed the polecats at night.

Father builds a trap with an angry tool that spits out sparks. Father says that Plato would appreciate such a trap, that he would see a beauty in its functioning, that he would understand the quest for the perfect lawn. Father intends to snuff out the polecats by trapping them, by dragging them off far from here. Father spanks me to bed when I protest, when I salute him in his warcoat. He will get no more buttons from me.

When I wake up at dawn and go down to the lawn, I see Father peering through the bars of his silly trap, the hatch slid down. Inside isn't a polecat at all, but a pussycat. Relief becomes me.

See I got one of the little nasties, says Father. I got her with a right tin of fish. But Father, I say, that's not a polecat at all. That's a pussycat. Nonsense, says Father. I know a stinking polecat from a pussy. And that ain't no pussy.

Then Father drags the trap deep out into the woods and blasts it with his pistol. He doesn't even release the pussycat. Blasts the trap to remnants. That Father. Chemicals green his skin. Grass becomes him.

But the polecats keep returning, just as I told him, back for grubs, back for the secret peels in my palms. There isn't a point to the silly trap and the killing, I say to Father, before he can build another trap. I think that Plato the Thinker would agree, I tell him. The trap is smithereens.

Father is gloomy from the Domino Effect and my love for polecats and the lack of buttons in his lunch. He decides to web his hammock out in the yard, a long veil dragged behind his feet. He drags it there to humble himself in the night. To listen for the polecats himself. He drags that hammock there and here, but none of the hickories lend their trunk to the cause. Poor Father. He can't find two hickories to hold up the webbing, and he looks like a dejected spider. He can't find two columns to hold him up at midnight, so he knots his web to the badbirths.

Placements of light pin Father in his hammock, where he sleeps, where he turns more green. Even buttons are no use, after I forgive him for the war. I hide buttons in his beard, in the folds of his ears, but they spill out onto the grass. And Father's tools glitter over the lawn. When I pick them up to store them in the toolshed, they leave strange yellow shapes in the grass. Tool-like shapes, forms that fail to fade. Father sleeps or reads his Plato while the sun seeps into his greenskin.

And Mother doesn't darn his clothes anymore. She is waiting for her buttons, she says, while she darns within those bluerooms.

They make my life so difficult here at Ten Unity Circle.

Then, after days of greening in the sun, Father untangles from his hammock and crawls to the edge of his grass. He pries up a corner with his fingers. He looks beneath it, searching for grubs and nasties.

This will be the new method of battle, he explains. To roll the grass. To crawl under it as if it's a blankie. The answer lies beneath the blankie, says Father, and I must find it. I must go down into that other world. I must stop the Domino Effect, lie down within the secret, he says, of grass. I must find out why the patches die, which of the nasties lures the polecats.

He peels up edges, looking for the best place to start. He blends with the grass at times, his hair a tract of turf, his ears filled with sod. Father is absorbed with his grass and it with him. Perhaps this is the Domino Effect, I think, high in a hickory, near the clouds. If one goes down they all go down, I whisper to myself in the branches.

And then, one dawn, I go out into the yard and Father is gone. His web is back in the toolshed with the axles and kegs, but no Father smoking there, no Father sleeping. I check the bulkhead and hickories. I check in the hedges and Hed's stringpen. Yoo hoo Father, I sing, Button button where hides the button.

But all I can find is a lump under the lawn, slumping there, sniffed by Hed. I poke it with a tool, but nothing says ouch. Father is down there in that other world, I think, looking for Plato. I begin digging with his glittering tools, with a button under my tongue. Mother continues to darn. Hed laplicks my face. The banana peels rot on the compost pile. I dig and dig for Father, under the hickory trees and clouds, and all the while the wind-up birds are singing.

David H. Lynn

# Mistaken Identity

THE SLEEPY SACK OF A MAN WAS WAGGLING A STRIP OF CARDBOARD with her name on it as passengers wearily surged through the arrivals gate at Gandhi International Airport. Only now did Vera Kahn first suspect that perhaps, after all, she'd made a mistake by accepting this invitation. Next to the driver, a U.S.I.S. bureaucrat—he could be nothing else—was craning his neck and failing entirely to see her as she approached. Ludicrously, he was still trying to spy something, someone else, over her shoulder even as she dropped a heavy bag nearly on his toes.

"I'm Vera Kahn," she said with hardly any smile at all.

His pale eyes registered the problem in a series of stages he did his best to mask despite the very late hour. "I'm sorry?" he managed first, belatedly.

"Kahn. Vera Kahn. I'm your poet."

The poor man, straw haired and tie limp—Vera was glad he made sympathy so difficult—struggled not to say the obvious: that there must be some mistake. There *had* been a mistake. She was very well aware of it. She wasn't about to let him off the hook.

"Are we waiting for someone else," she asked, "or can we go? I'm pretty well shot."

"Right—okay. But can I see some ID first? You know, security's sake. It's standard procedure over here." Although he looked miserable and confused, struggling to maintain his official good cheer, not to mention his authority, Vera was impressed that he'd managed to improvise the lie at this hour. She handed him her passport.

He studied her photo. "Right. Okay!" he shouted more cheerfully to conceal his greater dismay. "Shankar, let's get a move on." With a nod, the driver shooed away a scatter of boys eager to help and, reaching for the bag himself, let her name drop to the floor where it joined a ragged swirl of scraps even now being swept away as travelers and greeters, officials and porters and pickpockets dispersed into the Delhi night.

The air felt less tropical, less exotic than she'd expected as they emerged from the airport. It was plenty warm—laden with a muggy haze and wood smoke and the less acrid stink of burning cow dung. Vera felt a stab of disappointment. The irritability and disaffection she'd hoped would somehow magically lift on arrival in the East was instead merely chafing into a raw, weary restlessness.

"I'm Walter Tyson," said the American official more genially as he directed her toward a small red car parked in a reserved space. "I've read your work." Then he stopped lamely once more, doubting his own truthfulness.

"That's so thoughtful of you," said Vera Kahn and left it at that as she climbed into the back of the Maruti. She knew he hadn't read her poetry, either the one book from a good press or the couple of smaller chapbooks she'd all but paid for herself. Not that the lie was intentional this time. No doubt he'd read, more or less out of a sense of duty—whose idea had it been to extend this invitation? she'd probably find out in the next day or so—some selection from the poetry of Veera Kahn, a black woman of almost precisely her own age who taught, not at the small Catholic college in southern California and not with the glorious view overlooking the ocean (this one of the few satisfactions of the common misunderstanding), but a few miles inland at the much larger school by the same name, but with a U. C. in front. It used to be that Vera would imagine the two of them getting together and giggling over drinks about their ongoing entanglements. But Veera had made it clear on the occasions when they did meet, usually by accident or confusion or someone else's sense of jolly fun, that she wasn't interested in playing pals. Never did she let on how *she* came saddled with such a name, Kahn. Being confused with a now middle-aged white woman of little fame could have done Veera's own career no particular good.

For twelve years, on the other hand, Vera had felt shadowed by the other woman's celebrity. Every professional charm coming her way—

engagements to read, solicitations for new work, even the occasional call for a date by some friend of a friend—increasingly seemed tainted by this confusion of identity. She knew it wasn't true. Not entirely. But she'd grown used to spying similar symptoms of mistrust, disappointment, resignation that had flitted across Walter Tyson's brow. It hadn't grown easier. It had grown harder, especially of late.

So what should arrive on her desk in mid August but an invitation from the United States Information Service to spend two weeks on a reading tour in India? Only eight weeks warning. Someone even more prominent than Vera's near namesake must have canceled on them, not quite at the last minute. U.S.I.S. Delhi scrambled. Hence, no doubt, the sloppy research, the mistake. She'd had to scramble too, bargaining with colleagues to cover her classes, with students to water her plants and feed her cats.

That look had been in the Dean's eyes too when she requested permission—he'd grown used to such confusions between Vera and Veera. Not that he'd complain or admonish her: he was perfectly thrilled for the sake of the college reputation. Still, that knowing smile on his face. She ignored it, she loathed it, any doubt about the wisdom of taking the United States Information Service up on its offer, honest mistake or not, eased itself from her thoughts.


Five hours sleep was all she could manage that first night, and Vera rose, woozy and disoriented. She was sniffling too. Apparently, a cold had stowed away for the journey. Most of the hotel's other guests had already breakfasted by the time she appeared in the dining room. Its tightly sealed windows overlooked the bright bustle of Connaught Circus—and shielded her from it. She'd been so eager, yet now she lacked the courage to venture immediately into the mayhem. Cranky, annoyed with herself, she sipped at a second cup of tepid coffee. Perhaps she'd been expecting too much of India, or of herself. She didn't want to be disappointed.

Oh, bullshit, she thought, pushing the cup away and staring out at a street of swarming scooter taxis, of buses spewing swathes of dark smoke, of pedestrians and peddlers and darting children with shoeshine kits, all wrestling for advantage. Only a faint but constant bray of horns seeped through the windows.

A little past one in the afternoon Walter Tyson appeared, freshly shaven and shirted, his face lacking any trace of the suspicion and discouragement it had betrayed a few hours earlier. No doubt he and the U.S.I.S. staff had already made some calls. They'd discovered their own mistake. Like it or not, intended or not, it was Vera Kahn they'd invited, not Veera. And Vera had taken them up on it. Here she was, and at least she was a poet too. Perhaps some careful political calibration about race or fame, or both, had been vexed. No solving it now. A later program could be altered. Crossing the lobby, he smiled at her with an enthusiasm that went with the job. His face was pinkly tanned and round, faintly boyish. Vera smiled back.

But it wasn't so easy as that, of course. Tyson drove her to the American Center to meet the staff and check out the room where she'd be giving a first reading that same evening. With each of the senior officers, even with the librarian who'd already hidden away the copies of Veera's books specially ordered for the occasion and who, without question, had spent the morning trying to discover whether a single copy of Vera's book existed on the subcontinent, she spied or imagined spying in their eyes the smoke of disappointment that she was only she. They probably also suspected her complicity in the matter. Her anger flared. One young cultural liaison, lips glossy with color, hair in a careful bun, nearly got herself slapped.

What right, Vera forced herself to acknowledge, sagging a bit, had she to claim any innocence at all?

"Can I sneak away from here for a while?" she whispered to Tyson, tugging at his sleeve in a hallway.

"No problem," he said, apparently relieved to be asked so little.

She hadn't really intended that he escort her, but on the other hand she had no clue where to go or how to get there. He seemed well accustomed to the task. "Let's swing you through some of the national monuments," he offered as they climbed into the Maruti, "mostly built by the Brits. Then we can try the Old City—you'll like that."

She wanted to be filled with wonder and exhilaration. Yet the broad avenues and Edwardian monuments of New Delhi only soured Vera's mood still further. India Gate, the Parliament buildings, cracking pavement and peeling paint, waves of stench and billowing heat, a welt of mosquito bites just behind her knee, Tyson's enthusiasm, all nagged and niggled her into a raging petulance she hadn't felt since adolescence. She was aware of it and ashamed and unable to govern her own mood. Gritting her teeth, she nodded at each banality the man offered with a wave of his hand.

Slowly the car began tacking toward the north. They passed a railway station, teeming with solitary men wearing only strips of cotton wrapped around their waists, families besieged by bundles, and young Americans weighed down by enormous backpacks. The streets narrowed, traffic slowed, boys tapped on the car's fenders as they slid past. Vera's nerves were taut with exasperation. She struggled not to shriek at Tyson, demanding that he return her to the hotel, where at least it would be cooler and she could take a shower.

Around another corner they finally made out the cause of this particular tie-up—a dozen tree trunks had slipped their chains and tumbled from a long flatbed truck. How could such a huge truck be allowed in this part of the city, on streets as narrow as these? Scooter taxis and cars were inching up one by one onto the ragged sidewalk and crawling around the blockade. And suddenly Vera realized what she was seeing, as if until this moment she'd been unable to recognize or make sense of it: an elephant heaving one of the logs off the ground and back onto the lorry. A scrawny boy perched just behind its ears tapped the animal's attention towards another piece of lumber straddling the road. It wrapped its trunk around the near end of the log, hoisting it at an angle and leaning it against the bed of the truck. Then, using the edge of the truck as fulcrum, the elephant deftly grasped the bottom end of the log and swung it up and over with a last, delicate thump. Dust and exertion were smudging the elaborate pink flowers chalked across the elephant's flanks.

"Probably on its way to a wedding," Tyson said. "The mahout figures he can pick up a few rupees from the truck driver."

Vera nodded. That's what blind-sided her—the apparent ordinariness of such a sight. Her heart thumped hard in her chest. Her throat swelled. Joy—there was no better word for what swept over her, so glad was she to be right here, right now, watching this elephant at its task. How long had it been since she'd experienced such joy? Tears welling in her eyes, she felt amazement as much at her own reaction as at the scene before her. Such violent swings were entirely unlike her. In an instant she'd been wrenched from raw misery to this wonder, this elation. Joy, yes, but harsh too. She sniffed and blew into a tissue, hoping to disguise her emotions. Again Tyson glanced at her. She wouldn't face him.

By the time they reached Old Delhi's web of narrow streets, she'd regained her composure. They parked the car and made their way by foot through thick crowds. As they penetrated deeper, buildings were leaning towards each other above their heads like trees in an ancient forest. Yet this strange world all seemed distant, as if she were still peering through a window. It was the wooly congestion in her head and a haze of fatigue and jet-lag—everything seemed pushed beyond arm's reach.

Old men in pajamas and skull caps gathered in stalls and tea shops. Women, mostly wearing scarves over their heads or with full chadors hiding their faces and limbs, scurried by with infants in tow or picked at plastic shoes or soap trays or children's T-shirts hanging from a wire frame. Young men hovered about Vera and Walter Tyson, shoving packs of handkerchiefs and small chess sets at their faces. Jeeringly persistent, the pack of boys flitted along through the winding lanes, darting forward, trying again and again. Tyson flicked his hand, shooing them, and pressed forward. "This is the best walk to the Red Fort," he cried over his shoulder.

The boys circled and swooped, calling out to her in a sing-song chant. "Buy this, sweet lady. It's good for you! I make it nothing for you, no money at all. A gift from my heart. Buy, sweet lady." She couldn't quite make out all the words. The boys were pressing closer. The sing-song danced about her head, mocking, crude, taunting, obscene. The boys were laughing, leering.

Suddenly a hand groped hard at her buttock and she jerked in pain. From another direction fingers jabbed one of her breasts, pinching for its nipple. Other hands snatched at her shoulder bag.

"Stop," she shouted. Was there any sound? Did anyone hear? The grabbing, pawing, clutching spun her around.

"Help!" she shrieked, flailing out, her hands balled in tight, child-like fists.

The boys scattered in a single gleeful instant as Tyson waded towards her, and he was hurrying her back the other way, back towards the car, and he was saying something or asking something, but she couldn't really hear in the clotted silence all about them now. Tyson was apologetic and courteous, yet he couldn't quite mask his impatience too, as if she were making a lot out of nothing. She was furious with him, furious at those boys. Yet, curiously, the anger seemed distant too, almost beyond reach, and she wasn't weeping in the car: she was sniffling and blowing into her tissue, that was all.

"It's a terrific turnout," whispered the woman with her hair in a bun, Bridgit, the one Vera had wanted to smack earlier. She seemed sincerely pleased that the room was better than two-thirds full as the two of them peeked through the doors. Both were aware that they owed the crowd of middle-class Indians, expatriate Americans, and local academics to a grave misunderstanding, but neither was going to mention it.

This moment was worse even than confronting Tyson at the airport—only now did Vera feel truly a fraud. Nervous, irritable, she strode to the podium. The small auditorium might have been on any college campus in America, the kind of place she'd given dozens of readings in her career. She had nothing to be ashamed of. She was sweating despite the air conditioning.

"Good evening," she said brightly. "I'm honored by the invitation to read to you, and I'm delighted you've turned up to hear." A few people applauded politely, unaware of anything amiss. Vera smiled bravely past confused looks and harsh whispers from others.

Once she plunged into the first poem, however, the audience settled and so did her nerves. Now she was on home territory at last. She relaxed and read well. Once or twice, glancing up, she spotted a face here, eyes there, a pensive smile, listeners who were with her. Such delicate connections were all she sought from any public reading.

Earlier in the day she'd tabbed the selections she'd read from her book and a new manuscript. Yet the pages were in fact mere prompts— as always she was reciting from memory. And she had the odd sensation that she was observing her own work from something like the distance she'd been seeing Delhi since her arrival. The poems were hers, yet separate too. They pleased her. Their workmanship, their sensibility and insight, the knowledge they demonstrated of the craft, all of this pleased her. What more did she have to say than she was sharing this evening?

That question startled her for a moment, and she stumbled, reciting a line twice. Was this enough? she wondered. Did this mean she'd finally matured as a poet—or that she was finished as one? The prospect suddenly seemed unclear, unnerving, the footing of her career treacherous.

For forty minutes she held the audience and then ceased, smiling, sipping at a glass of water. A long, pleasant moment passed as both she and they took stock. No better evidence of success than such silence. Could anyone from U.S.I.S. complain now? The applause when it broke was warm, dissolving only slowly into a fluster of people rising, chattering, making their way up the aisles. Among those who ventured forward to thank her, a woman in a gold and crimson sari waited her turn. "It was delightful—a wonderful treat," she said, proffering Veera's book for an autograph, despite the back cover photo of a noticeably different woman than the one who'd been reading on this podium.

No American official was stationed in Jaipur to welcome Vera as she descended from the train into a blast of desert heat and scalding sun. Instead, an Indian in gray trousers, blue shirt, and a short black tie hurried up to her on the platform. Someone at the American Center in Delhi must have tipped him off about whom not to expect.

"You are Miss Vera Kahn? The poet?" he said. He seemed uncertain about whether to shake her hand. "I am Dr. Kanthan, head of the English literature department. We are so very delighted you have made this arduous journey to grace us with a reading. It is the event of the year for our students. They are so very, very excited."

"I am too," she said, and allowed him to lead her toward a car. She welcomed the dry heat and cleaner air of Rajasthan—though the congestion in her head and chest stubbornly refused to clear away. The train's first-class compartment had been sealed tight for the entire journey, its air conditioning oppressive and only partially effective. She much preferred this, even though sweat was already prickling along her arms and legs.

No one had mentioned any plan or particular schedule, but she was rather surprised that Dr. Kanthan drove directly to a small bungalow which, she soon gathered, was a guest house. Without switching off the car, he stepped out and pulled her bag from the back seat. "The remainder of today is for you to rest and perhaps to visit something of our most beautiful city," he said. "Tomorrow morning, 9 a.m. bright and early I will fetch you here to the university. It will be a grand treat no doubt." With a little wave of his hand, he was back in the driver's seat and pulling away.

For three days Vera had yearned for some freedom, for some time alone, unshepherded by Tyson or anyone else. But now that Kanthan had so unceremoniously abandoned her on the hot asphalt, she wasn't so eager to be on her own.

Her room was spartan but adequate, with a heavy A. C. unit in the wall. Black scorch marks around its plug made her nervous. She'd sleep later without it running. In the meanwhile, she had no intention of remaining cooped up here. Strolling once more out onto the road, she spotted several bicycle-rickshaws huddling in a patch of shade a hundred yards away. A dark-skinned old man with a turban and no shirt was cleaning his teeth with a twig. He spat and looked up at her as she approached. "City?" she said. He nodded.

The rickshaw gathered speed enough to bathe Vera's face in a dry breeze. The old man pumped slowly from one leg to another, standing, his legs young and thin and powerful in their rhythm. As they passed through an ornate wooden gate into the city he glanced over his shoulder at her. "Go," she said with a smile and waved him on.

Through the streets and sprawling market they wove, sometimes quickly, often slowed to a walk. A bright pastel pink wash covered almost all of Jaipur's buildings as if defying the surrounding blankness of desert and grey dust. Likewise, the Rajasthanis themselves dressed with a far greater exuberance than people in Delhi—scarves of orange and flaming red, scarlet cotton shifts and leggings.

Spying one woman, no youngster but with beautiful dark eyes, a persimmon duppatta over shoulders and head, walking two children by the hand, Vera careened with a fresh surge of joy. She'd never been anywhere so beautiful, so full of life that was strange to her and yet palpably real—ordinary even in its strangeness. She was also keenly aware that she could only hover outside, riding a rickshaw like any tourist, and watch.

Along one avenue stretched the stalls of spice merchants with their careful heaps of cardamom, stalks of ginger, bright orange mountains of other spices and seeds. Swaying around a corner, she found herself sweeping among the silversmiths. Trays of bangles and earrings, rows of goblets and cups. In the back of larger shops Vera could make out young men working the metal, tapping with mallets, etching with an instrument that looked like a razor.

"That's what Andrew would love." The thought startled her. It had been months and months since she'd thought of her former husband. But it came to her now that *he* was the one who'd always hankered to visit India—a desire that seemed extravagant and childish to her when they were young. Northern Italy, perhaps, if he insisted on traveling. Jamaica if it had to be exotic. Wasn't it enough they managed to steal a few days together in bed in New York, a city where the publishers had him chained? India—they could have their pick of East Sixth Street take-away, hauling the cartons and little cups of chutney right into their tangled nest of sheets. Or if he stole out to California every few months, why shouldn't that count?

She wondered, possibly for the first time, whether she should have taken his name after all. He'd shrugged, said it didn't matter. Had it mattered? Over time, a continent apart, they'd forgotten each other or failed to keep up with the stiffer, more mysterious adults they were becoming. Vera looked about her. Andrew would love Jaipur.

Every few minutes the rickshaw-wallah glanced back for directions. He seemed increasingly suspicious—his trade was to ferry riders from one place to a specific destination. Such casual touring as this made him uncomfortable. Finally, in the middle of a square, he climbed off the bike. Without quite looking at her, he held out a hand. "You pay now. I eat." He scooped his fingers at his mouth to help her understand.

For a moment she considered exploring the city by foot. But she still felt a bit light-headed from the deep-rooted cold in her chest. "No," she said, shaking her head. "Take me back, please—I will pay you." The old man shrugged as if he'd merely been seeking this reassurance and mounted his cycle once more.

More quickly now they whizzed through the streets, up an alley and out a different gate into Jaipur's more modern precincts. Disorientation soon dizzied Vera. Vaguely uncomfortable, she had no sense of their direction. Had the old man understood her?

Several ancient buses were jammed haphazardly into a lot. Some stood empty, waiting for future assignment, one or two abandoned entirely. Others, arriving or departing, overflowed with passengers squatting on the roof with bags and parcels or clinging to doors and window bars.

Hardly slowing, the rickshaw-wallah swung wide around a corner and peddled along a narrow lane, past a row of low derelict buildings. Scabby trees covered in dust threw a paltry shade here. It wasn't cool, but the sudden escape from the sun seemed to silence a harsh and terrible sound that had been ringing in her ears.

In the sand along this lane dark bundles lay scattered. She couldn't quite make them out. Large and small, they'd been dropped casually in odd contortions. Off to the side, a stick collapsed in the dust. Vera turned her head toward it. And still it took a moment as she was being driven past to realize it was a leg that had fallen. Above the haunch lolled the uncovered head of a young woman, jaw slack, eyes naked and blank and unfocused. Now Vera could translate: men, women, children, sprawling motionless, sparsely covered in scraps and rags. Their entire absence of movement was horrible, testimony to an equal absence of hope or purpose. What had brought them here? What were they waiting for? Were they waiting for anything?

Rage at the deception flooded through her—the beggars in Delhi had been toying with her after all. Those young mothers holding infants and banging on car windows near Connaught Circus wore bangles on their arms. Those babes had flesh on their bones.

Not the sordid shapes lying here in the sand. She spied a shoulder—a small boy's shoulder—no more than socket and bone. These shadows made no appeal. Indifferent in their lethargy, they didn't notice this stranger rolling past. Had they called out she might have flung her bag, her ring, the clothes she wore. Instead, she sat frozen and horrified.

The rickshaw-wallah took no more notice than he had with earlier marvels on this improvised tour. Shade and convenience were his only purpose in fetching his passenger along this particular route.

But the vision of such casual detritus pummeled her. The exhilaration she'd been feeling only moments before disappeared like smoke in a sudden gale. Tourist, she'd already been borne safely past, the only trace a sickness in her belly, a spot on her soul.

Bright and early as promised, Dr. Kanthan fetched her from the guesthouse. She'd taken a simple dinner in her room and then spent the hot night tossing with dreams she couldn't recall.

Rajasthan University stretched across a large swathe of desert, its concrete subsiding in reddish sand and ragged patches of wild grass. Kanthan led her first to his own office where the eight other members of the English department were already gathered. The one woman among them rose and stepped towards her. "Dr. Shukla," said Kanthan.

"We are so happy you have come to visit us," she said. Her hair was pulled taut. A streak of henna marked its severe part. Vera had seen looks before like the one Dr. Shukla offered her. Senior women in American universities shared it. They'd broken the bastions first; they'd made a place for themselves, suffered what had to be endured, compromised too deeply in order to survive, and would brook no latecomers, wanted no sisters or sympathy. Their claim was too precious. "Please, you will take a cup of tea with us before your talk?" she asked. And handed her a cup, a saucer of sugar biscuits. Vera didn't dare refuse.

She'd been asked by U.S.I.S. to prepare a lecture for occasions such as this, and so a few minutes later she entered a large bare room packed with at least three hundred students. Perhaps thirty-five chairs were reserved for faculty and administrators, all but swallowed by the crowd. Most students sat on the floor. At the front of the room a bare wooden desk and chair perched with cold authority on a platform. But Vera couldn't bring herself to sit in that chair. Giggles exploded and were shushed as she propped herself on the edge of the desk. "I'm more comfortable this way," she said with a smile, hoping to win them over. She coughed, wishing she could clear her lungs even for a moment.

Certainly the students were smiling and eager, willing to accept anything this visitor might offer. "My talk today," she said slowly and clearly, "is called The Best of Times, The Worst of Times: the contemporary literary scene in America." She glanced up from her paper and saw them eagerly nodding, these hundreds of young people. They were gazing so intently. Without warning, a surge of dread swept through her, leaving ash in her mouth. Bone deep she knew, only now when it was too late for anything but to soldier on, that this was the wrong talk for the wrong audience. She'd intended it as a light introduction to American themes and authors, with diplomatic bows to Rushdie, Desai, Roy—Indian writers who'd been fashionable of late. But the students before her had no clue what she was talking about, not enough context to imagine a context. And she could tell from their eyes, gazing at her with fascination as though she were an exotic creature babbling some strange gibberish, that they could hardly understand the sounds she was making. It wasn't that they didn't speak English: their English wasn't hers but a language whose sounds were trained to a different clef altogether. Sitting amidst department colleagues jotting diligent notes, Dr. Shukla stared up with a grim triumph at her helplessness.

When Vera finished—she ceased speaking somewhere in the middle of the talk, middle of a thought, middle of a phrase—a ripple of polite applause passed quickly. But then, to her amazement, the students surged towards her. "Miss Vera," a brash boy cried out, "please sign for me." He thrust a pen at her. Laughing at the joke, she autographed a scrap of paper. "Miss Vera," crowed two or three girls side by side and giggling with excitement. They too pushed pens at her.

"Miss Vera, Miss Vera," swirled calls from all sides. A throng of dozens seethed towards her. "Miss Vera!" shouted another boy. "Sign this book—*please*—you must!" She found herself backing away, herded towards a wall. No one came to her aid. No sign of the faculty. It seemed Kanthan had abandoned her once more. Arms flailed about the celebrity, all waving pens and markers and pencils. Someone's pad struck her accidentally, dislodging her glasses. She clutched at them.

She was shaking her head, waving her hands, chagrined at the adoration of this mob. Besieged on all sides, still she could recognize the scene as ludicrous. "You don't want this from me," she kept saying over and over. "I'm just a teacher, a poet."

It was clear that at some level they all knew this, but it didn't matter. She was American. She'd been brought to see them and for them to see. When had they ever been visited by someone from beyond Rajasthan—when would they ever again? She was signing note pads and the frayed covers of textbooks, shirts and even bare arms and hands, all thrust demandingly into the path of a pen. The students kept pushing forward with desire but without intent. They'd pinned her against the wall and still they pressed tighter. It was hard to breathe. Just a little panic giggled in her throat.

"Miss Vera, Miss Veera, Veera." The sounds grew confused in her ears. Whose name were they calling? Even here the mocking pursued her. "Veera!"

"How you holding up?" asked Walter Tyson, reaching to give her a hand off the train at the Delhi station.

She shrugged because the answer wasn't easy. How could she explain the buffeting her own ambitions had subjected her to? His glance quickly took in the dark shadows around her eyes, the loss of flesh along her jaw and throat—his sudden concern a more reliable gauge than the mirror in her bag.

"We can slow all this down if you need. The symposium in Simla can manage without you—and you're supposed to be having some fun too. How about I arrange someone to run you to Agra."

"No. Thanks." She shook her head and didn't cough. "I kind of like the working just now. I'll go back to being pure tourist at the end." She didn't want to confess that lingering in Delhi seemed impossible— she needed to keep moving. She also didn't want to let on quite how pleased she was to see him. Oh, she was confident she could manage on her own, but a lift to the hotel was certainly easier this way.

"Okay," he said. "Better get some sleep then. It's an early start tomorrow. Train's at 4:30."

"Can I get a taxi at that hour?"

"No need. I'll pick you up on the way. Didn't I mention the symposium's my baby?—months and months getting the arrangements settled. So this leg of your tour we'll be traveling together."

It was only after they'd sleepily switched trains at Kalka that the sky lightened enough for the world to gradually grow visible. They'd begun to climb now, and the air was fresh and cooler. In the lingering darkness of the mountain train's old-fashioned compartment, thick stands of pines seemed to cluster close to the rails like a ragged blanket. But the trees fell away along with the darkness of night, and as they moved from hills into the first smaller mountains of Himachal Pradesh she was surprised by long vistas of naked reddish and yellow rock. No telling whether the train had already crept above the tree line, or whether men had long ago scraped these slopes bare of stumps and brush and soil.

The rails stretched where the mountains allowed, not blasting their way through but clinging to each bend, sometimes dipping, sometimes climbing sharply, always searching for the next pass, dragging the train higher. Long ago during an undergraduate history course Vera had happened to read about the summer capital of the Raj—a quiet retreat in the distant skirts of the Himalayas where the British sought relief from the furnace of May and June. Her distant studies hadn't prepared her for this: a jagged landscape of high peaks and blasted ridges. How desperate for relief the British must have been to carve this railway all the way toward Simla, 7000 feet high and misleadingly called a hill station.

Walter Tyson's small pair of binoculars perched on a shelf by the window. Looking up from the book in his lap as the train jolted sharply around a bend or soared for an instant at another crest, he'd gallantly offer them to her first. Twice, and then again, she couldn't bring herself to say no, delighted by the rock and sky. She studied the landscape and she found herself, rather as a surprise, studying her companion.

"Any must-sees in Simla?" she asked for the sake of hearing his voice again—she hadn't really bothered to listen to it before.

"Not much beyond the mountains themselves, as far as I know," he answered with a smile over the rims of his reading glasses. "There's the old Viceroy's palace, or course, and a famous monkey temple too—supposed to be worth the walk."

Vera nodded. Whatever adventures she might have conjured for herself in the frantic weeks between the mistaken invitation arriving and her own departure, some wild sexual fling hadn't figured among them. Oh, well, perhaps at the margins, as a never entirely not-present hope or possibility of possibility. Middle age had brought her some relief from the humiliating urges of youth, a relief ratified daily by the young men, the *boys*, in her writing and literature classes who gazed at her or through her as if she weren't entirely visible. Nor did the harried, pallid men in her department cause her pulse to race with any dangerous temptation.

Relief from urges. She shook her head now and immediately glanced up to see whether Tyson had noticed—she didn't want him thinking her any crazier than he might already suspect. Relief came at a price: a withering, a numbness on the tongue that wine and poems in small magazines and nights out with her sister never entirely chased away. If she hadn't come to India looking for a fling, no doubt somewhere in the impulsive deception lurked a desire to fly free from that lingering taste of mortality for a few weeks at least.

Walter Tyson. She smiled at the thought, deciding him a kind man, with his granny glasses perched at the end of his nose, with his slight paunch, and the prissy way he rolled his cuffs back with such care, once, twice. Ever since his initial shock at the airport, denying she might be who she claimed, he'd been quite thoughtful. Could there be any more to it than professional responsibility? She wasn't sure. She doubted it. It didn't matter.

Maybe if she could ever shake this heavy cold in her lungs and the light-headedness dogging her, maybe then it could matter.


Simla clung to a long, sweeping ridge in terraces of markets and brightly colored houses and shacks. Like a haphazard book shelf, these terraces were articulated along three or four narrow streets, one stacked above another. As Walter Tyson and Vera Kahn emerged from the station, she was surprised by a cloud of diesel exhaust and soot hanging low about their heads. Traffic was snarled worse than Delhi, trucks too big for the streets wedged snarling one against the other.

"Are you up for a short hike?" shouted Tyson in her ear. "A porter can fetch our bags, and the hotel should be walkable."

"Absolutely," she cried back.

The station sat at the bottom of the town. They set off at an easy stroll. Yet even before they'd begun to climb towards the next street she was feeling the altitude, panting heavily. She tugged at his shirt.

Distracted or daydreaming, he was startled at her touch and immediately abashed. "Sorry—sorry. Do you need to stop for a minute? Should I grab a taxi after all?"

She shook her head. "No. I'll be fine." The acrid smoke hovering in the air stung her eyes and throat and congested lungs.

Tugging out his binoculars as if he'd just noticed something, Tyson pretended to study the rather limited view west and south, the landscape through which the train had passed, giving her another moment or two. When they set off again it was at a more leisurely pace, and she could manage it, just.

The hotel was new and pleasant, not very fancy. That suited her fine. The scholars and teachers who'd been invited from across northern India to a symposium for which one Vera or another's visit was the instigating opportunity hadn't yet arrived. Dinner was scheduled as the first official function. And lunch wouldn't be served for another two hours. Despite the cough she tried to sneak away into a handkerchief— the altitude no doubt—she was restless. She wanted to see something of the town, the mountains. "Care to explore a little bit?" she asked Walter in the lobby after the porter delivered bags to their rooms.

"Oh damn, I can't right now—after lunch, for sure?" he said, looking disappointed. "I'm meeting the hotel manager about preparations for the next two days."

His straw-colored hair, thinning to be sure, still fell with a hint of boyish wildness. She was quite pleased at his reaction and smiled at him in a way she hadn't yet—hadn't in years—and headed off with a little wave in any case. She didn't want to waste what was left of the morning.

After a couple of easy switchbacks, Vera found herself on a road gradually rising. At one twist in the pavement, just below the mall, a sign marked the spot beyond which Indians weren't allowed to trespass during the days of the Raj. All about her, of course, Indians were strolling, pushing, hawking souvenirs. The only creatures not allowed beyond this marker any longer were cars and other motor vehicles. Their absence made Simla's mall, a spine of macadam along the top of the ridge, quite pleasant. The stinging cloud of soot and smoke remained trapped in the terraces below. Up here the air was fresh and even chilly, with a quick snap of wind.

Other colonial vestiges remained intact. A small stone theater where, according to the plaque, amateur performances of Shakespeare had once been staged, now offered Hindi films and touring concerts. Banks and other looming gray-stone edifices mimicked the architecture of other distant precincts in a vanished empire. Yet at a peak in the road, next to mounted telescopes where for ten rupees one could get a clear shot to the north, a large bust of Indira Gandhi commanded the city.

But what a disappointment: the Himalayas themselves were shrouded in haze. Looking out across long valleys and lesser peaks, Vera could make out nothing beyond. The haze didn't appear terribly thick—the day's light simply seemed to fall short before it could reach the great mountains. Even plunking coins into a telescope yielded nothing.

Frustrated, she strolled farther along the mall. Narrowing gradually and climbing again, it soon turned into a lane running past private residences with high gates and bungalows guarded by lounging men in khaki and berets. At one bend in the road a fresh fit of coughing brought Vera to a halt. When it finally passed she was left with a blossoming headache. She nearly turned back in despair. But just above her head and nearly hidden by the branch of a tree—only by chance, only right here should she notice—a faded monkey urged her with all six arms to keep climbing. Intrigued by the sign, as though the message were hers alone, and unwilling to skulk back to the hotel so early, headache or not, she remembered Walter mentioning a temple.

She expected to discover it over the next rise, but nothing lay waiting for her but another sloping bend in the path—pavement had disappeared a hundred yards back. A first smudge of dirty snow appeared at the base of a pine. Other travelers were picking their way up from the town as well, she now noticed. Mostly young Indian couples attired in silken shawls and well-polished black shoes, they wore the shy, eager grins of newlyweds. Apparently a visit to Hanuman's shrine offered an auspicious beginning. So be it—she welcomed the company, the occasional conspiratorial smiles thrown to her by young brides. And, guiltily, she also wished she'd waited for Walter Tyson's company.

She was panting again, straining for thin air. At home, treadmills and twice-a-week aerobics kept her in decent enough shape. She brushed away a glaze of sweat from her lip. If these young couples could manage the climb in saris and stiff shoes and suit coats, she could too, middle-aged westerner or not.

Any pretense of a casual stroll had long since disappeared. The slope had grown steeper, more treacherous. Rough hewn steps had been hacked into the rock, but these were slick with old ice. Beside them a gully of packed mud and scattered stones offered better footholds.

Gradually a prickly sensation of being watched put Vera on edge. Sharply she snapped her head to the side, then again up into the trees, trying to catch a glimpse of the spy. Out of the corner of her eye she noticed the dull brown rock twitch alive—a monkey swung by one arm from a tree branch and dropped to the ground. Once recognized, dozens appeared out of the thin soil, young ones darting and tumbling over each other, older, much larger monkeys staring at the human visitors, appraising them with hostile indifference. As patches of snow along the route became more frequent so did the monkeys.

Forewarned, many of the newlyweds had packed along popcorn balls as offerings. Once these were tugged free, the monkeys approached more boldly, screeching and demanding their due. One young bride fumbled with a paper bag of loose popcorn. She giggled nervously. Her husband, embarrassed by such behavior, stood stiffly beside her and pretended not to notice. A great gray male ambled toward the girl with its hand outstretched, impatient and querulous. She struggled not to drop the bag, clutching it against her chest, trying to extract a handful. A few grains splattered to the ground. Too proud to scrabble for stray kernels, the angry monkey hopped forward and with a scolding shriek snatched the bag from her hand. The girl shrieked too. Popcorn peppered about her feet. Her husband strode silently, furiously away.

As the peak in this ridge finally drew close, Vera panting hard as each step skittered treacherously across loose gravel and ice, a pack of teenage boys seemed to emerge from the rock as well. They hovered about a large clearing. "You need a guide, Miss," one boy announced with a shout to Vera. Thirteen or fourteen, he was cocky and very handsome, with long lashes and delicate dark skin and a clove cigarette dangling from his mouth. Dramatically, he tossed it into a mound of snow. She couldn't hear the hiss. She shook her head.

"I'm okay," she said.

"Miss, you need a guide for the temple."

Again she shook her head and trudged forward, yearning only to reach the damn temple so she could tag it accomplished, catch her breath, and begin the hike down to the hotel. Could she make it back in time for lunch? The question occurred to her, and suddenly she was ravenous.

A blow slammed her head and shoulders from behind. Vera staggered forward, startled, terrified, trying not to fall. An attack? One of the boys? A heavy weight was riding on her back. Lurching, hunched over, she struggled to keep her balance. Something rubbed past her ear. A small hand was reaching from behind her head. It clasped angrily at her eyes, closing on her glasses and snatching them away. Eerie and disorienting, the moment froze her. The monkey leapt from her shoulders and scurried away.

Monkeys were screeching, boys were shouting. The one who'd offered his services—for bodily protection, she now understood, rather than for particular guidance into Hanuman's mysteries—raced after the animal. Vera was already picturing her appearance at the seminar, how foolish she would look staring out vaguely at the Indian scholars, attempting to recite from memory her talk on the worst of times.

Fuzzy shapes were scrambling higher off the path. The boy halted for an instant at the top of a boulder to hurl a chunk of ice at the monkey, then leapt in pursuit once more. Vera couldn't make out just when it happened, but the animal must have surrendered at last, flinging its trophy away. Because abruptly the boy was back, shoving the glasses into her hands.

"Here, good lady. I save them for you," he declared proudly.

"This deserves a big reward," suggested another voice helpfully at her elbow.

The lenses were smeared, the frame wrenched awry at one corner as she tried to reestablish the glasses on her head, hands trembling.

"You must do something for him," offered still another advisor.

Vera was aware of tourist couples watching. Gratitude, relief, embarrassment flooded her with warmth. She shoved a hand into her pocket and tugged out something more than a hundred rupees. Hardly equal to her relief, yet far beyond what the rescue warranted, she knew. Wouldn't the others despise her being such easy prey? The boy didn't hesitate, didn't wait for her to consider, but sealed her generosity by pulling the bills from her hand with a cry of "thank you, dear lady," and a whoop of glee. In another instant Vera was abandoned, boys and monkeys and tourists vanishing with the conclusion of this particular show. What cut had the monkey earned? she wondered.

Ahead and through a thick stand of trees she glimpsed the gray bulk of Hanuman's temple perched on a rounded knob. Shaken by the attack and its abrupt reversal, she felt no yearning to delve any further. Her mouth was dry. She coughed and coughed again, harsh and deep, a fit that doubled her over and wouldn't let her snatch a breath. At last it eased. Hesitant, teary, afraid of triggering another attack, she limped to the far side of the clearing's bare rock and snow. She needed to gather herself before braving the descent into town. And casually looked up.

Startled, Vera fell back a step as if she'd been struck again. Distant and impossibly close and impossibly massive, the Himalayas loomed high above the world. No trace of haze protected her any longer. Glasses damaged or not, she made out sun striking rock, shadow caressing snow with a clarity that snatched the last air from her lungs. Earlier, on the mall in Simla, haze erasing all sight, she'd tried to imagine just where on the horizon these mountains might scratch the sky. Here and now, her vision restored, the Himalayas towered above any such human measure.

Yet this view wasn't exotic. It wasn't alien. It simply was, with a certainty of overwhelming fact. Had she been chasing illumination on this journey? No illumination here, beyond the sun striking the mountains themselves. Each stage of her journey so far, each powerful jolt that jerked her between joy and despair, might have been in preparation for this moment, softening her up so she could see. She saw, yes, and she had no idea what to make of it. Poetry failed to soar from her soul as it might have done when she was younger. Barren, spent, her spirit cowered before the ordinariness of the rock before her eyes and beneath her feet. She felt able to see and she felt small and alone and afraid.

She was aware that Walter Tyson had summoned a doctor. She was grateful to him, wished she could tell him so, accepted the fact she couldn't.

"It is altitude sickness. No doubt about it," the young doctor was saying. She felt the distant stab of an injection. "With any luck this will do the trick for her, quite quickly no doubt."

She felt very bad that the seminar would be disrupted and Walter put to more trouble. Well, surely they could carry on without her. She wasn't whom they'd been expecting anyway.

"It is a puzzle to me. No, if it doesn't work already, another dose will be without effect and as well may be dangerous."

The side of the bed sagged and Vera opened her eyes. Walter Tyson was leaning on an arm, studying her closely. Startled to find her gazing up at him, he drew back. She tried to smile. He lay his hand on her arm—she could feel it.

"Should I get a med-evac helicopter up from Delhi?"

She wasn't sure which of them he was asking.

"I think it is a bug I don't know," the young doctor was saying. "It may be one she brought with her."

As she approached the edge of waking, she sensed a light in the room and a larger darkness beyond it. A jumble of quiet voices. Were they close by? Where was she? she wondered, without opening her eyes. She wasn't sure yet, wasn't quite awake. Those voices—were they her parents?

For a terrifying moment she wasn't sure quite where she was, quite who she was. She was sick—that much she knew. Her face felt hot, her throat parched. But still she wouldn't open her eyes. It seemed far too great a challenge. She wasn't ready. The only certain fact was her own awareness. She took that in. She was a she and the rest of the universe, small or large, was not she, lay outside, beyond her closed eyes. Terrified and determined—with all her soul and all her might she'd cling. Teeth clenched, she wrestled to hold her own.

The electric light in the room had been switched off but, coming to herself, Vera saw a grayish light leaking in from beyond the windows. Dawn or dusk, she couldn't tell. Walter Tyson was sitting, arms on knees, in a chair by the window. Realizing she'd awakened, he rose and drew close. His face was dark with shadow and with concern.

"The copter's already landed, but the ridge wouldn't let them get very close. We're waiting for an ambulance to come ferry us up to the mall."

She wanted to smile at him again, at Walter Tyson, but she was weak—when had she ever felt so weak, her body and her head and even the muscles of her jaw so heavy. And yet she also felt light, terribly light, as if the faintest puff of breeze might sweep her away entirely.

"I'm sorry about all this," she whispered, surprising them both.

"Don't be," he said and touched her arm again. She wished he'd keep his hand on her arm. Just a little while. "It was our mistake, not yours. I should have done my homework better before sending an invitation."

A giggle—did she have the strength for a giggle? "Not that, silly man. You'd have liked my talk." Exhausted, she couldn't say any more.

Tyson snorted, laughing for them both. "One damn talk? You can recite it for me later. Once we get you to the East-West Hospital in Delhi. It's their copter." Prattling on, he was sounding worried again.

Vera guessed the journey back down, even by helicopter, would be all she could manage. Thirsty, she glanced to a side table and, understanding, Walter Tyson brought a cup of water to her lips.

*Willis Johnson*

# Vienna, City of My Dreams

MRS. PISZKOS TURNED OVER IN BED AND FOR THE LAST TIME PULLED from off her husband Mr. Piszkos their winter quilt whose floral pattern in deep peach so perfectly matched the ruffled curtains on the casement windows. It was a cold night in the cellar where they slept, the thermostat having been lowered to fifty-eight degrees because their son Joey preferred to sleep in a cool house and he said it got too hot in his room upstairs with the furnace running all night. His covers gone, Mr. Piszkos, who had very little fat on him, felt the cold and woke up. He tugged at the end of the quilt but Mrs. Piszkos, who had on her an abundance of fat, had rolled over onto it and it was stuck.

The parts of Mr. Piszkos that froze first were those with the least flesh, his bony hands and his two long feet. They were soon followed by the freezing of his thin arms and pointy shoulders and hairless white legs. When he rose from the bed he was just shaking. He felt his way into the bathroom where he sat in order to urinate quietly because boy could Mrs. Piszkos get mad if you woke her. For the same reason he did not flush when he was finished. Creeping back to their bed, he tugged lightly once more at the quilt but Mrs. Piszkos didn't budge. Mr. Piszkos sat on the edge and rubbed his arms and legs and rubbed one foot against the other and waited in vain for his wife to roll the other way. Finally he got out his flashlight from the drawer and climbed the cellar stairs. Even under his slight weight they groaned from bottom to top. In the linen closet he found two winter blankets which he hoped would be all right to use. Rather than risk the noisy stairs again, he headed for the attic where they stored their old divan. Though in the living room stood a perfectly comfortable sofa, sleeping or even sitting on it was forbidden. One previous winter night when his wife also had pulled off the covers, Mr. Piszkos had very rashly bedded down on this sofa. Mrs. Piszkos' revenge was to stop cooking dinner for two days. She even refused to heat up the left-over soup in the refrigerator. Mr. Piszkos and Joey had to eat out at the diner, which made Joey really sore at him too.

Joey's room was next to the attic door. The instant Mr. Piszkos slid back the bolt, he woke.

"Who's that?"

"It's me," his father whispered. "Shh. Don't wake Mommy."

"What the hell are you doing?" Joey demanded. "What time is it?"

"It's early yet. Go back to sleep. I'm just going up the attic."

"You woke me up," Joey said aggrievedly. "Thanks a lot."

"I'm sorry, sonny," Mr. Piszkos said. "Shh, now. Close your eyes. That's a good little fellow."

"Little fellow, my ass," Joey said. Mr. Piszkos was holding his hand over the head of the flashlight to keep it from shining into the bedroom. In the light that slipped through his fingers he saw his son sit up in bed and try to read the hands of his watch. When Joey saw the time, he got even madder.

"Mom!" he cried out.

"Joey, son," pleaded Mr. Piszkos. "Let your poor mother sleep."

Joey yelled again, but his mother didn't answer. "Never mind," he warned. "You'll get it in the morning."

But in the morning after he had creaked down the cellar stairs to put on their coffee and to watch to flush the toilet before she should have to use it, Mr. Piszkos found his wife not asleep inside her flowery quilt, but dead.


Martha Piszkos' funeral was held at the Hungarian Reformed Church in Bridgeport after a delay of nearly three weeks, which was the time needed by her sister Anna to secure a visa and fly out from Budapest. Anna was a poor widow who lived with her son's family in the Zugló District where, with the introduction of a free-market economy, they now had a telephone in the house. It was about the only good thing anyone in Zugló could say about Capitalism, no more twenty-year wait for a phone. With Joey's help, Mr. Piszkos was able to obtain the number and ring with the news of Martha's death. Joey was unable, however, in spite of his urgent hand signals, to prevent his father from offering to pay for Anna's plane fare so that she could attend the funeral.

The day she arrived they drove straight from the airport to the funeral parlor. Anna, who had not laid eyes on her sister for forty years, found herself gazing into the coffin at a stranger. "That's my sister," she kept having to remind herself. "We went together to the harvest dances in Tengelic and that one time in Paks. She was the pretty one. She was the spoiled one. She was the smart one who knew enough to get across the border when she could."

But Anna could not cry for her. No, when she wept it was for her own vanished life. Her tears at the cemetery the next day were likewise not for Martha but for what she saw in the faces of Joseph and young Joey. The one looked so imperiled, the other so utterly doomed.

After the burial everyone returned to the church hall where the Ladies Guild had prepared a big pot of stuffed cabbage. On each table stood a variety of soft drinks and a paper platter with the good rye bread from Ziesler's Bakery. If you wanted wine or beer or something stronger, you had to bring your own.

Whenever anyone spoke of Martha, the heart-broken widower cried. Joey on the other hand seemed to have recovered tremendously. He sat at the head table with his long-time girlfriend, Arlene Bako. They were drinking vodka. Arlene's nose was already pretty red. As dessert was being served, Joey squeezed her hand and said, "I'm going to do it." He stood and clinked his spoon against his glass. Arlene tried to pull him back into his chair but it was too late, people had turned to listen. Just now, maybe three minutes ago, Joey said in a voice like a broadcaster, he had asked Arlene to marry him and she had said yes. "So no more tears, okay? Hey, Pop, you listening?" he said down the table to his father. "All of you—it's time to be happy. Happy for us. I know Mom would be." With that, he gave Arlene a passionate kiss in front of everybody. The mourners applauded even though it seemed a funny thing to do, getting engaged and kissing in such a way at the funeral of your mother. While Arlene tottered among the tables receiving congratulations, Joey had himself a big shot of vodka. Arlene kissed Mr. Piszkos on his bald head. "We want to do it next week, Dad. We figure what's the sense in waiting," she said. "There'll need to be some rearranging, of course. I mean, with our guest here and all."

What they had in mind was outlined for Mr. Piszkos that evening over tea. She and Joey had talked it all out. They knew just how difficult these coming days and weeks would be on him. So instead of looking for a place of their own, they had decided to set up housekeeping there in the cellar "to be here for you." Anna, who was staying the month, would move upstairs into Joey's room where the bed was sure to be more comfortable than the recliner on which she was sleeping. Mr. Piszkos would have to go into the attic: there simply was no other place for him. For it was Joey's wish, above all, to maintain in memory of his Mom the sanctity of the rooms above.

Arlene inhaled a last mouthful of smoke from her cigarette. "Later on," she said, scrunching the butt into her saucer, "we'll see."

Mr. Piszkos was again in tears, that's how fragile he was. More than by their devotion to him, he was moved by their reverence for Martha, who had made those rooms upstairs her life's work. My God how that woman could sweep and scrub, polish and dust, not to mention align and fluff! Visitors escorted along the hallway (where a clear plastic runner protected the carpet) could only gape at so much tidiness and taste. The speckless shelves of knickknacks and attractive Avon bottles. The shiny displays of cookware whose bottoms had never known heat. The burst of velour flowers at the sunny south window. The fringed feather pillows. The crocheted covers for the bathroom scale, toilet seat, and extra toilet paper roll. The splendid color coordination between soap and washcloth, dishtowel and napkin, waxed fruit and window drape. And of course all that wonderfully untouched-unsat-unlaid-upon furniture— save for the living room sofa whose ivory plush had been marred on one arm where Mr. Piszkos had rested his oily head after his pillow on that one winter night had tumbled onto the floor. Martha had also kept the cellar very tidy. It had scatter rugs and curtains and comfortable furniture. But it was not invested with such perfection that you could not sit in its chairs or cook on the stove or rest your heels on the hassock when you watched TV. It was also where everyone, family and guests alike, went in and out of the house, through the cellar door that opened onto the driveway. The only room in habitation overhead was Joey's, whose door (except at night when he needed to have circulating air so his nose wouldn't stuff up) had always stood closed. "Joey's room," his mother would say to the escortees, giving them to understand by a quick elevation of her eyes that it probably had posters on the walls and maybe clothes in piles, which is often the condition of the bedrooms of boys, although Joey was no longer a boy, he was thirty-seven for heaven's sake.

It can be very upsetting for a son to watch his father weep, even when it is in gratefulness for the son, and for a moment something tender stirred in Joey. It was a memory from long ago, in their mutual time of innocence and love: his Daddy kissing his forehead, assuring him as he lay in his solitary bed that night was only the day drifted to sleep, the way he too now must sleep and not cry and in the morning they would go to the park and feed the ducks, would he like that? And Joey had to drop his eyes and sip his tea, holding the cup steady with both hands, he could not watch his father longer.

But eventually these tears dried too and when they had finished their tea and swallowed the last of the left-over pastries from church, Arlene kissed her fiancé and drove home. Joey headed upstairs to watch on the TV in his room the latest Star Wars movie from the video store where he worked. As he passed he gave his father's shoulder a pat not devoid of affection. Anna lowered the recliner and spread out her sheet and blankets. As he had the previous night, Mr. Piszkos said, "Anna dear, take the bed, I can sleep there," but she wouldn't hear of it. It had been a long, draining day. Yet tired as he was, Mr. Piszkos could not sleep. As Anna snored across the room, he switched on the bed lamp, took out his notebook from the nightstand, and began to write a song, his first since Martha's death. Yes, Mr. Piszkos was a songwriter, well-known among his neighbors, a composer unique in the music field in that he fitted all of his lyrics to a single tune, that of his all-time favorite waltz, *Vienna, City of My Dreams*, which he first had heard on an album of Austrian zither hits. It went *Tum tum tee tum-tum-tum, tum tum tee tum-tum tee tum-tum-tum* and you could make of it a lullaby or a love song or a sad or a happy song, it was adaptable to just an endless variety of themes. Now into his notebook he set in his scrawly hand the words that had come to him as he lay awake.

> *Gone, gone, you're gone away*
> *Into the sky where the angels play*
> *On harps they pluck with the tips of their wings—*
> *Oh, wings are handy for all sorts of things.*

That was the first verse. The second went:

> *Up on your cloud you'll be sprouting them too,*
> *Soft white wings fitted specially for you.*
> *Feathers fashioned for heavenly chores*
> *Like dusting God's shelves and sweeping His floors.*

Mr. Piszkos read it over grinning with rank delight. His songs, even the saddest of them, always lifted his spirit, for with them he sang what he seldom could speak, the content of his heart. Instead of putting away his notebook, he laid it open on the pillow beside him—Martha's pillow—and turned off the light. He tried to envision his wife with her new wings, tidying up, making a place ready for when he would join her. It was better to see her that way, high on a cloud, scented by her favorite cleaning liquid, than to picture her in her current earthly condition under the heap of dirt and stones at Mountain Grove Cemetery. It was true she had treated him at times pretty unangelically about removing his shoes at the door and not spitting in the sink and about changing his underwear and socks each day even if they weren't soiled and not scratching his scalp at the table where they ate. Yet to him her harshness was understandable. How could any woman saddled as a bride with the name of Mrs. Piszkos—in English, "Mrs. Dirty"—help but resent the responsible party? Mr. Piszkos remembered the many times little Joey had fled in tears from the playground where a gang of fresh kids constantly teased him as "Junior Dirty" or as "Dirty Joe from Muddy Creek"—the name of Mr. Piszkos' hometown—Sárospatak—in Hungary. So she was not alone in her suffering and shame. They might well have been right, those who speculated it was this at the beginning that drove her to keep her house so clean, so that the joke on the family, on her and her son, whom she always took care to dress in the best of clothes, would just fall flat, and that anyone with eyes to see would know she was ten times cleaner and neater than the cleanest and neatest of them. And indeed some in the neighborhood soon began to refer to her not as *Piszkos Martha* but as *Tiszta Martha*—"Clean Martha"— who, as time went on, became more and more obsessed with shiny faucets, crumbless countertops, twinkling toilet bowls, untrodden floors. That her poor brain eventually went pop was a guilt he must live with. His song gave him a measure of relief. As did the thought, as he lay in bed waiting for the sky to lighten, that if it were so that cleanliness stood as close to godliness as the fingers on your hand, then his dear departed Martha was sure to be in line soon for promotion from angel to saint.

After her marriage Arlene made some effort, with Anna's help, to carry on Mrs. Piszkos' great work. But she wasn't so fussy, Anna noticed, if a pot soaked in the sink overnight or, for that matter, a good deal of the supper dishes. Finger smudges on a window, the odd dust ball under the bed, grease spurts from the frying pan were for Arlene part of the patina of life. Nor did she much enjoy living in a cellar, she confided to Anna, "like Mr. and Mrs. Mole." Yet she recognized an ascent to the surface would have to wait. The upstairs was still too hallowed. That was made plain to her by Mr. Piszkos' song.

"I mean, my God, come on already," she said to Anna. "What's next, a statue on the lawn?" Even as she spoke, Mr. Piszkos was up in his attic quarters, which she and Joey had taken pains to make extremely comfortable for him, working on a new piece. "And talk about dumb! First prize goes to that song. I don't know how you kept a straight face."

Though she hadn't understood the lyrics, which were in English, Anna had thought the song was actually pretty nice. She thought the same of the new song, which her brother-in-law performed the next night at the supper table.

"Ready?" he asked. He stood before his chair, all proud.

Joey, just home from work and really hungry, said, "Fuck, how about giving us a break? I mean, we're eating."

"You don't have to stop," said Mr. Piszkos, blinking at his son's language. Where had he learned to talk like that? He put on his reading glasses and cleared his throat. "It's very short," he said. "Anyhow, it's dedicated to you."

*Dear son Joey and charming Arlene*
*You're the kindest couple I ever have seen.*
*A table, a lamp, a kerosene stove,*
*From the attic, to be sure, I never will rove.*

*Up under the eaves the love I'm feeling*
*I share with the mouse who lives in the ceiling.*
*Alone like me, he's glad for the chat,*
*Having lost his wife to the neighbor's mean cat.*

"Well, that's beautiful, Pop," Joey said. "Really fucking beautiful."

"Pretty melody," said Anna. "Dee dee dah duh-duh-duh. Somehow it seems familiar."

Arlene was nearly choking.

"I don't think it's anything to laugh at," Joey lectured her. "He's just being sarcastic."

"Joey!" cried his father.

"Oh, how silly," said Arlene.

"You don't know him yet," Joey said. "But I do. Our reward for thinking of him."

"But that's exactly what it's about," Mr. Piszkos said in appeal. "How good you've both been. I've said it to Aunt Anna many times. Haven't I, Anna?"

In fact, he had. She had listened, not saying a word, to how the considerate couple had laid in for him several small frozen potpies, chicken, beef, and veggie, so that he could just pop one in the microwave for himself whenever the swordfish or Porterhouse—Joey's personal favorites—wasn't quite enough to go around. And that money for the kerosene heater—they had yet to ask him for a dime of it. Now they were even talking about an electric fan for the summer! Their insistence he do his own laundry rather than mix his dirty stuff in with their nice clothes was their way of helping him to become more self-reliant. And who knew what jeopardy his savings might be in had Joey not assumed ownership of the bank account?

"For instance, suppose I got into a car accident? Or had to go to a nursing home?" Mr. Piszkos had felt the need to explain when Anna, still holding her tongue, just stared at him. "Why, between the doctors and the lawyers, the money'd be gobbled up in no time. Not that it's so much. No one gets rich on Social Security, I can tell you. Not with the price of things today. Do you know what they're asking for swordfish at the supermarket now? The whole check, it's gone—poof!—just like that."

The same could be said of the wages of a part-time video store employee. Which was one more reason for Joey to have taken over his father's account. He wasn't sitting on that money, either; no sir, he was investing it.

On one weekend business trip to Atlantic City he realized a profit of more than four hundred dollars speculating, if Anna understood it correctly, in a company named Craps. To celebrate, he and Arlene decided to extend their stay. Joey telephoned to ask his father to call in sick the next morning for him and for Arlene, who worked in the appliance department at Sears.

"He's a smart one, that boy," Mr. Piszkos boasted after telling Anna of Joey's good fortune.

Again she said nothing, only "Good, let's eat."

She had made for their supper that evening a batch of *palacsinta*. Half the crepes she filled with either prune or apricot butter and half with cottage cheese blended with sour cream and raisins. They were the first *palacsinta* Mr. Piszkos had eaten since Martha's death. Pretty soon he was having to stop and take out his handkerchief.

"I'm sorry," he apologized. "I just can't help thinking . . . and Joey . . . he loved his Mom's *palacsinta* too, poor kid."

Anna looked at him with sadness. "Jozsi . . ." she began, then stopped and said, "You've got something in your eyebrow. No, the other one. Here," she said as he felt around for it, "let me."

Her fingers were peasant fingers, big and rough, but she just gently plucked out the bit of curd that had got into his eyebrow instead of into his mouth. As she wiped the spot with her napkin she said, "You must forgive me, Jozsi, but it's really not true, you know. The goodness you keep talking about. I've yet to see it."

She folded the napkin and laid it back onto her lap. Mr. Piszkos shrugged his thin shoulders. "Maybe it's not always so obvious—"

"Obvious?" she said, suddenly angry with him. "I'll tell you what's obvious. The cleverness, the slyness, that's what's obvious. What, they can't even put your wash in the machine with theirs? After you and Martha spent how many years washing his diapers?"

"Diapers?—oh, my, yes," Mr. Piszkos answered with nostalgic digression. "And later, poor little fellow, his pajamas and sheets. Martha, God rest her, her skin was much too sensitive. A little pee, the tiniest smear of the other, she'd rash right up. Not to mention how the odor would turn her stomach. But I never minded. He was just so cute so . . . 'Our perfect angel', that's what I called him. 'Our own white star' . . ."

Anna frowned. "And when did he stop?"

"With his 'accidents'? Well, that went on for quite a little while. But in other ways he was a real quick learner."

Anna studied him. Was he really such an innocent?

"I meant the cute part. The 'white star, perfect angel' part. I see how they treat you. And I hear how he talks. Even when it's in English and I don't understand, I can hear it."

Mr. Piszkos slowly shook his head. "That's only the way he learned—"

"To be fresh to his father," Anna said.

Slowly he went on wagging his head amid his sighs.

"I don't know how it happened," he said. He sat forward with his hands clasped between his knees, his shoulders hunched into knobby peaks. "In all his life, he said quietly, "I swear I never gave him even one spank. If he needed disciplining, Martha did it. Made him sleep up in that room, for example, even though he was terrified to be alone at night. I mostly played with him. Tickled him, did little piggies with his toes. That's when I began composing songs, when he was little. They were for him. So he wouldn't be afraid. I had one that went, 'Baby Joey you are so sweet, with your pink cheeks and your chubby feet.' And when I sang 'cheeks' I'd give each of his a tiny pinch and when I sang 'feet' that's when he got tickled. How he squealed! But as he grew older he began to change. I mean, toward me. And I couldn't understand because I'd never done anything but love him."

"I don't want to hurt your feelings, Jozsi," Anna said sympathetically, "but you can see for yourself all that love that was just love has made of your Joey a real stinker. Your tickling only made him laugh. It did nothing to make him respect you."

"I didn't only tickle him," Mr. Piszkos made haste to say. "I tried to teach him good things. Not to lie, not to steal or to speak badly of people or to be envious of what they had. And not to be afraid. Yes, to try to have courage . . ."

"And meanwhile, you allowed my sister to terrorize you. What kind of a master is it who bows to such rules? A master belongs in the master bed, not in a cellar or on an old couch in an attic. Where was your own courage?"

As he lay in bed that night, Mr. Piszkos thought about what Anna had said. It seemed impossible. How could love engender anything but love? If love made someone dislike or even hate you, then what did kindness do, or truth? Was bad the spawn of good? Could laughter make you mean? Was that the problem with cranky people? They had got overly-tickled in childhood? It was hard for him to accept. He had always done what the Bible said: honored his wife, loved his neighbor—Mrs. Virag in the back, Beres the barber across the street, Mr. Szigeti next to him. He would have loved his enemy, too, he felt, had he ever had one.

Behind the whole idea of love, it seemed to him, lay peace, not an easy thing to come by if you looked at the history of the world or even just of Hungary. It puzzled him, was love so difficult a thing to learn, and then to show? Suppose, for instance, the Hungarian nobles and king had let Suleiman the Magnificent know that contrary to appearances they could really grow to like him—would the Ottomans have butchered the Magyars until almost none was left? Didn't anyone even think to suggest this at court?

Mr. Piszkos turned with a sigh and gazed out the attic window at the stars. He once had imagined God to be as big as the universe. That was why we could not see Him or fathom His shape. We dwelt inside Him, like Jonah in the whale. Perhaps the sun was His brain, all aglow with wisdom. His heart might be Mars or some other red planet throbbing behind it. The stars could be His million little corpuscles, the earth His fertilized seed. Love and peace. Not only the Bible but a lot of your Christmas card companies equated them. For him to have lain in the master bed, as Anna had proposed—it would have been akin to an act of war. Martha the Turk. How she had battled to make of her domain a perfection, to bring life's unruliness into line. She looked at the world and saw nothing of its loveliness, only toilet rings and tilted picture frames. Her baby burped and puked. Unsightly hairs sprouted from her husband's nostrils. Even her own body violated her sense of order with its various discharges and odors. Why, she once had pondered to her husband, had God in His creation of human beings not found a means of eliminating a hole or two, at least in the ladies?

Mr. Piszkos turned back and closed his eyes. Soon Martha stood before him. He touched a finger to her scowl. Up with one corner, then the other. And now she was smiling. As stern as her suzerainty had been, he was sure she loved him. Had she not lain beside him through all the nights of their long marriage? But now she was gone and of his son's affection he had not been sure for years. The boy could just fly off the handle and screech at him. And the names he called him, for the whole neighborhood to hear! It was as if the vessels exiting Joey's heart had so constricted that only the bile and none of the blood's sweetness got through. Anna was right. Love alone had not worked. Yet how to change him—this prince with his bride who acted as if the realm belonged now to them?


Anna returned to Hungary at the end of April with more than three hundred dollars in twenties sewn into her bra. This was money she had earned cleaning the houses of some of Bridgeport's better-off Hungarians. A dollar bought a lot of *forint* back in Zugló and she did not want to risk being frisked by Hungarian customs or mugged by the American Mafia on the ride to the airport. Because Joey and Arlene were occupied that evening, Mr. Piszkos got his neighbor Mr. Szigeti to drive Anna and him into Kennedy.

At the airport Anna held her hand tenderly to Mr. Piszkos' cheek. "You're a nice man, Jozsi," she told him. They had arrived at the gate where they check you for bombs you might be hiding on your person.

"You only have to learn to stand up for yourself," she said. "Do it by standing up to them." She glanced toward Mr. Szigeti who was waiting nearby and acting as if he weren't listening. "You know who I mean," she said.

Mr. Piszkos nodded. They were both wiping their eyes. They knew they would not meet again. It was hard enough for him to get out, "I will," never mind asking for any ideas on how to stand up to whom. The Malev flight to Budapest had already been called and now they called it again. Anna reached into her blouse and checked her cups. "Jesus and Mary," she said, "I hope I don't set off any kind of alarm."

It took a long time, some four months, for Mr. Piszkos to actually do it, stand up for himself, sort of, for the very first time. It was well into summer. Arlene was pregnant. Tests showing the child was a boy had set Mr. Piszkos to work on his most ambitious composition to date, the Joey the Third Concerto. He planned a verse for each month of Arlene's pregnancy with a big crescendo at the end, a triumphant ninth cannon-blast proclaiming the baby's birth. Night after night he labored away in the attic where he had continued to be quartered after Anna's departure. As Arlene had said, "What's the sense of moving down if he'll only have to move up again?" Joey's old room was to be redone in blue for their son: new paint, new paper, teddy bear curtains, crib from Sears.

One Sunday Mr. Piszkos came down to breakfast. Joey and Arlene were still in their pajamas. Arlene had not been out of hers for a few days.

"And how's my young fellow this morning?" Mr. Piszkos asked, bending to address Arlene's belly as she sat at the table with a banana she seemed to have trouble swallowing. "I've got something for you," he said tunefully.

Arlene looked at the sheet of paper in her father-in-law's hand. Above it stretched a familiar grin.

"Please," she said. "Not now. I'm not feeling up to it."

She did look awfully pale. Yet what better antidote than the one he held? It was the completed overture, the entrance to his concerto.

No sooner had he placed on his eyeglasses than Arlene dropped her banana, most of which was still in its skin, and hurried into the toilet.

Joey had been slicing his own banana onto some Cocoa Crunchies. The sound of his wife throwing up forced him to lay down his knife. Arlene coughed and spat. You could hear her through the door. Joey looked into his cereal like a prisoner into his swill. He nudged away the bowl.

Mr. Piszkos suddenly was not feeling so very well himself. He tucked the overture into his shirt pocket and went out the door and around the house to see how his tomatoes were doing.

Mrs. Virag was sweeping the flagstones around the barbecue in her back yard. Mr. Piszkos entered his garden and pinched off the suckers from a couple of plants.

"Good morning, Margit!" he called over the hedge as soon as she had laid aside her broom. "Guess what? I've got it ready."

Mrs. Virag was one of his biggest fans. Whenever he sang her one of his songs and asked how she liked it she always said she did.

"Care to listen?" he asked, unfolding the paper from his pocket. "You'll be the first."

The bathroom in the cellar had a window that opened on the back yard. From it came the sound of gagging.

"What's that?" asked Mrs. Virag.

"Arlene," he answered. "I think she got a bad banana."

With a wave of his hand and tap of his toe he gave himself the beat.

*The sweetest sound I ever heard*
*Comes not from the branch where twitters the bird.*
*It's the heart that beats with never a word*
*In the tummy home of Joey the Third.*

*In nine months he'll emerge cute as a dimple*
*A lad who began no bigger than a pimple.*
*God's great miracle, plain and simple,*
*Behold him, oh priest, oh nun in wimple.*

*From pimple to dimple he'll grow like a champ*
*To love Mommy and Daddy and love and respect his Gramp.*
*And one day for certain, I'll bet a buck,*
*There'll be a Joey the Fourth to try out his luck*
*To perpetuate the proud name we never will duck,*
*Long live the Piszkoses from Sárospatak!*

For a few anxious moments Mr. Piszkos looked at Mrs. Virag whose face bore a pained expression as if the retching from the bathroom was affecting her stomach as well. With good reason did he worry: This was a woman who knew her music. You should see her play the piano. She hardly ever had to look at her hands.

"It's just the opening," Mr. Piszkos said. "I'm working on the rest. I'm not certain how many verses the average concerto has. I'm shooting for nine."

The toilet flushed. It almost sounded like somebody was weeping in there.

"It's nice," said Mrs. Virag. "That pimple part is the only—"

"I know. That's what gave me the most trouble," Mr. Piszkos said. "Did you know there's only three words in the whole English language that rhyme with 'dimple'? Otherwise you liked it, though?"

"Yes, I did," said Mrs. Virag.

"I hoped you might," Mr. Piszkos said exaltedly. "Say, are you planning a cookout today? How about a couple of nice tomatoes?"

When at last she came out from the bathroom, Arlene looked just awful.

"I can't stand it any longer," she said, collapsing into her chair. "I really can't."

"I thought the throwing up was only supposed to be in the beginning," her husband said.

"I'm talking about him," Arlene said. "Him and his stupid songs. And all his pestering. Who knows what kind of body chemicals it's producing inside me?"

First the vomiting, now the bawling. Joey's appetite for his Cocoa Crunchies was completely ruined.

"It's part of the whole pregnant thing, I betcha," he said analytically. "You get overwrought."

"I'm not overwrought! Stop saying I'm overwrought!" Arlene's eyes abruptly filled with tears that turned them muddy. "I'm getting sick and tired, that's all. Tired of this cellar, and sick of him. Do you want me to tell you where he belongs? He belongs in an institution."

"Come on, Arlene. Just because—"

"Just? Do you call it *just* when he has a conversation with my stomach? Then goes out singing to the neighbors?" Beneath the mud you could see the red in her eyes. "I tell you, it's everything. Everything. You saw what he did last night to his food. Whoever heard of putting sour cream and paprika on Moo Goo Gai Pan?"

"Listen, I was the one who had to go all the way downtown for it. I should have got him the Chow Mein."

"He'd sour cream that, too, don't worry."

"Well, yeah. But at least the Chow Mein's only five and a quarter. Compared to seven twenty-five. I mean, if he's going to spoil it."

Arlene was prevented from detailing other of her father-in-law's offenses by his return from the garden. Against his narrow chest he cradled several tomatoes. He unloaded them onto the table.

"These are going to be a lot healthier for you than what you've been eating this morning," he said. "There's rats, I hear, running all over those banana boats."

Arlene glared at him.

Mr. Piszkos, still soaring from his overture's successful debut, seemed hardly to notice. He got a serrated knife and began to slice the ripest of the tomatoes. "Our little guy will like these, too," he said. "See, Joey, what Grampy's got for you?"

Arlene turned away.

"And do you know what else?" he said. It just killed her, he was so delighted with himself. "Grampy," he went on addressing her lower half, "is going to make sure you're never ever frightened like your Daddy was. Poor Daddy! How many nights he tried to crawl into our bed! 'Martha, let him,' I used to plead. 'Look, he can lie here next to me.' But Grammy wouldn't hear of it. 'I'm not having our good mattress soaked as well,' she said. She was right, of course. You have to be firm with children if you want their respect. Still, I'll bet that's what made Daddy do wee-wee in his bed. It can be awfully scary at night to be all alone. Unless you've got someone very close by."

Arlene was trying to remain calm. "No thank you," she said curtly, her lips tightly pinched, when Mr. Piszkos slid the plate with the tomato slices toward her.

"You don't want any? They're straight from the garden."

Arlene shifted her glare to Joey, who had raised his eyes to a corner of the ceiling.

"Pop, she doesn't want any," he said.

"Well, all right, but they're good for you," Mr. Piszkos said. "Time to time we get a rat out back, but that's nothing compared to the hundreds on those banana—"

"Are you deaf?" said Joey. Now he was getting really mad, too. "What did I say?"

Mr. Piszkos sprinkled salt onto one of the slices and ate it himself. "Would you like to hear the new song now? It's only the first—"

"Damn it, Pop!"

"Wait a minute," said Arlene. Her look was suddenly suspicious. "Back up a bit. I want to hear the rest of that. What you were saying before. About Joey."

"You mean his wetting the bed? It's true, poor little tyke. We had him all potty-trained and everything. And then he was made to march upstairs. Night to certain children, I think, must seem like death itself, that dark, that terrifying. Right through grade school, as I recall, we were using rubber sheets. . . ."

"That's not so!" cried Joey. "God, how he exaggerates! Okay, maybe a few times when I was really young—"

"Forget the bed-wetting," Arlene said. "I want to know what you mean, 'someone close by.'"

Mr. Piszkos began slowly to salt a second slice.

"Just so he . . ."

"What?"

"So he won't be afraid," he murmured. "I've given it a lot—"

"Meaning?"

Just as slowly as he had salted, he sliced the slice into quarters. "Anna thought so, too," he said, avoiding their eyes. For now they both were staring at him.

"We're waiting," Arlene said.

"She thought . . . well, that maybe I ought to, in her opinion at least, move into the master bedroom."

Joey laughed. "That'll be the day!"

"You're staying put," Arlene said.

"Yes, but I've already sort of decided," Mr. Piszkos said. "Just to be close. You know, in case—"

"Well, decide again," they said, almost in unison.

Arlene's pregnancy got no easier. The morning sickness stayed with her through the second and into the third trimester. At one period she had to be fed intravenously. The extra weight she carried caused her varicose veins to swell. After work she came home exhausted, only to endure her father-in-law waiting to sing his latest idiotic verse. In the seventh month she discovered she was bleeding. She had been experiencing some severe cramping, and now came this spotting which frightened her. The doctor ordered her to bed. Three days later they put her in the hospital and sewed closed her cervix.

Why was this happening to her? Why was everything going wrong? She wept this to her husband.

"My little worrywart," he called her.

"Hey, it happens, that's all," he said after aiming at her cheek a peck that missed somewhat when she moved her head aside. "Especially, I guess, if you're like, you know, a little older. You heard the doctor. All the tests are fine. All you gotta do is hang in there." Not that she had a choice, other than to hang. So in she hung until finally on a raw January morning with the wind off the Sound she gave birth to her child.

The baby had turned. The doctor struggled to get it out. He held it up, gave it a whack, and announced over its wail, "We've got ourselves a handsome little—"

He looked again. Just what *was* that tiny dangle there? He carried the infant to a table away from the mother. Holding apart its writhing legs, he said to the nurse, "What would you call that?"

The nurse peered. "Holy cow," she said.

They both looked closer. The baby squalled. "I don't know, but I don't think that's a penis," the nurse said.

But if it were a clitoris, where was the vagina? Yet of testes there also was no sign.

"It's got to be one or the other," she said.

The doctor tested around the protuberance with his fingers, measured it against his thumbnail. His face mask expanded with his breath.

"Well, you'd think so," he said.

Joey, who had his mother's sensitive stomach, had waited out the delivery in the waiting room. He had been camped there the whole night. The doctor found him slumped in his chair with his mouth open, a magazine fallen onto the floor between his legs.

"Good morning to our newest dad," he said cheerfully after waking him. "It was a bit of an ordeal. But all's fine. Just fine. Mother and baby both. Resting comfortably now. The two of them, just fine."

Joey sat up painfully. The bones cracked in the back of his neck.

"Looks like you could do with some proper rest yourself," the doctor said. "My advice is go home and get some breakfast. Clean up, take a nap. Come back this afternoon. Your wife should be alert enough then. We'll need to have a chat. It won't take long. One of my colleagues will be there. Some issues to discuss. When you're good and rested. Shall we say three o'clock?"

It seemed to Joey the doctor was having to work to maintain his smile, thin as it was.

"You said everything was fine."

"And so it is. You've got a fine, healthy child. A real little kicker. Stop by the nursery. You'll be very proud, I assure you."

The baby was sleeping. A nurse brought it out for him to see. Joey touched his forefinger to its cheek. He wiggled its tiny red hand. "Hi," he said to it, then peeked in on Arlene. She was snoring.

"Maybe it's just what they do," he thought as he rode the elevator to the ground floor. "With new parents. A kind of orientation."

On his way home Joey stopped at the diner. The waitress brought him coffee without his asking for it, he looked that bad. He ordered the Number 3 Breakfast Special: three eggs, three sausages, three pancakes with fake maple syrup. The waitress told him when he asked for the bill that it was on the house.

"Your Dad gave us the big news," she said. "Said he waited to hear from you, then rang the hospital this morning. We were his first stop. 'You watch what I'll make of that boy.' That's what he was telling everybody. 'I,' mind you! Really, he was so cute. Refill on that coffee?"

His father was still making the rounds, apparently, when Joey arrived home. He took a shower and lay on the bed but was too tired to sleep. At noon he shaved and drove into town. He dropped by the video store, where his manager clapped him on the back: his father had been there, too. For a while Joey wandered around the shopping center. He bought two baby presents: a plastic ray gun and a toy guitar with lights that flashed and buttons you pushed for different rock songs to come out. Together they cost fourteen dollars and ninety-five cents, not counting the tax. As he left the store he began to feel the financial weight of his new responsibility. He drove to Seaside Park. For more than an hour he stared despondently at the Sound. The surface, normally quite still, was full of whitecaps. Many times he heard himself sigh. The wind blew. The waves fell hard onto the shore. Joey switched the car heater to high. "A father," he said to himself. And he sat and he gazed and he sighed. And all the while he kept thinking: "Christ, fourteen ninety-five."

They were waiting for him in the room. He could tell Arlene had been crying. The doctor's colleague turned out to be a plastic surgeon. He had a Spanish-sounding name and he wore this real good suit and he used words Joey had never heard before, starting with "anomaly."


It was dark by the time Joey left the hospital. He drove straight to a cocktail lounge where he got stiff on five Old Fashioneds. He had slept very little and had eaten almost nothing apart from the Number 3 Breakfast Special at the diner. So those drinks at the bar, which he disposed of very quickly, one right after the other, went as quickly to his head and he got really pretty stiff. At one table sat a couple who were regulars at the video store and the bartender Zoli he knew since grade school but he did not speak to any of them except to ask Zoli for another Old Fashioned when his glass was empty. When Zoli, upon delivering the round, asked, "So how's it goin' anyhow?" Joey only answered with a curt "Good" and said nothing about anything and didn't even ask, "How's it goin' with you?" He just said "Good" very curtly, which prompted Zoli to murmur under his breath, "Well, fuck you then, *Junior Dirty*," and he went to stand at the other end of the bar.

He hadn't been able to say much to Arlene, either. Despite what the surgeon had said about the decision they needed to make, and the sooner the better, they had hardly talked at all. He had tried to hold her hand but she had snatched it away and kept it hidden under the sheet. The baby had been brought into the room, but she could not look at it, neither of them could. When it was time to feed it and she held it to her breast, she kept her face turned. Joey never got the opportunity to take out from the shopping bag the ray gun or the guitar with the buttons and lights.

Only vaguely did he remember the ride home. On one street he nearly sideswiped a car whose jerk of an owner had parked it way out from the curb where someone could run into it. Pulling into their driveway, he noticed the upstairs lights on but attached no meaning to it. "He'd just better not bug me," he muttered. He stumbled into the cellar, found the wine bottle in the refrigerator, poured a water glass full, and posted himself at the foot of the stairs. "You'd better not dare," he said up toward the door. "Out bragging to everyone. Old bastard. Who gave you the right?"

After waiting a minute for his father to appear, he observed the glass in his hand had become empty. He returned to the fridge and filled it. But now all his tiredness and despair caught up to him and he dropped heavily into an armchair. It wasn't right, he argued in his thoughts as he gulped his wine. It wasn't right that he had been mocked in school for nothing he had done; that his father without fail had given in to his mother each time she had sent him wimpering back to his lonely, night-filled room; that she, the competent, and not he, the feckless, had been the first to die; that by her death he had been compelled to marry a woman he never had loved. And now the worst of that which was not right: to have become the parent of a freak.

She hadn't even taken his hand. As if he and not her aging organs, not his father's cursed blood, had been to blame for whatever it was sprouted there between the child's legs. And whether they chose to make it one or the other, to whittle it down or try to enlarge it, meant surgeries and hormone treatments and more mockery and shame and goodbye to the money in the bank which was vanishing fast enough as it was.

Joey's throat began to ache. "Go ahead, that's it, blame me," he said hoarsely. His eyes stung. His breath surged sharply from his chest. Where was his father? Why didn't he come down? He must have heard him drive in. What was he waiting for? Wasn't he curious to hear about his *grandthing*?

He felt his forehead, his cheeks. He was burning. He just knew it: he was going to get really sick. With Arlene in bed and him down with a fever, who would look after the kid?—they'd probably make them bring it home soon. Sweat dripped down Joey's neck. He removed his coat and threw it aside. He felt into his trousers.

His underpants were all wet in the crotch. Once again he strode to the bottom of the stair. "I'm here!" he called up.

And in silence said Don't abandon me. Not now when I need you to say it, you used to say it *It's all right sonny don't be afraid it'll be morning before you know.*

He listened. Presently he heard a voice that did not sound like his father's. He grabbed the railing and went up. Lights burned throughout the house. On his mother's good sofa the throw pillows lay lopsided and scrunched. He went into the living room and turned off the TV. A half-empty glass sat making a ring on the bare wood of the coffee table. "Pop?" he said, full of fear. In the kitchen he found a plate with the scorched crust of a potpie. Again he called out his father's name. "Don't do this to me," he said.

He backed into the hallway. The thermostat on the wall had been pushed to seventy-five. At the far end the attic door was bolted. He was beginning to panic. "Where are you?" he yelled. Then he noticed the door across from his old room had been closed halfway. From it came the warm glow of a lamp. Joey lurched forward, bouncing in his drunkeness off the wall. "Daddy!" he cried.

What a showman! What timing! Mr. Piszkos lay propped on the master bed, his hands behind his head, his legs stretched luxuriously, his shoes all over the bedspread. To his son who stared incredulously, he gave his proudest Piszkos smile and just raised his chin and crooned his climax, the big crescendo verse of the Joey the Third Concerto:

"Sweet baby Joey our nights will be shared, side by side in our bedrooms so you'll never—"

These words, as it happened, were the next to the last ever to come out whole and comprehensibly from the lips of the composer.

The actual final word, uttered as Mr. Piszkos was lifted by his shirt front in such a swift and sudden flight that most all his breath was sucked from him, was: "Joey!" After that, it was quite impossible for him to utter anything, for his collision with the floor took what little wind remained. It was only after he had been dragged out into the hall and thrown into the atticway and the door slammed and bolted that he was able to gasp his son's name one last time, though Joey most likely didn't hear for his raging.

"There! Where you belong! Howl all you want!"

But there was no howl, only that one last gasping "Joey!" It wasn't till later that Joey heard the other sound that was to become his father's voice. He had pulled himself back up the stairs after downing two more wines and listened at the door. The noise frightened him. That was when he opened the door and saw his father and called the ambulance.

For the first couple of days Mr. Piszkos and Arlene and Joey the Third all lay in the same hospital, Arlene and the child in obstetrics and Mr. Piszkos at first in trauma, then in the general ward where he stayed until there was nothing more to be done but to ship him to Merritt Manor, the nursing home over by the parkway.

By that time husband and wife had settled into the upstairs of their pleasant home where they cooked in the kitchen, dined in the dining room, bathed in the bathroom, and bedded in the bedroom. As for the anomaly, it and its bassinet had been moved into the cellar temporarily, for the child often cried at night and kept them awake.

They were learning to refer to it as him. They had decided to let its little dangle see if it could grow. And so they called him Joey as planned. Grampy's eyes just filled with tears whenever they brought him to his bedside.

"He lived up there. We had a nice little in-law apartment for him. But the stairway was a tad steep. One of those attic-type stairways," Joey told the day nurse who looked after his father, which was also what he had told them in the emergency room, how he had heard a noise and found the old man lying on the stair, trying to rise, lifting his trunk an inch or two, then collapsing, his mouth voiceless save for the grunting which grew fainter as Joey waited for the ambulance.

"I used to tell him, 'Dad, you've got to be careful on those stairs.' But Dad is Dad. He must have fallen pretty much from the top," Joey speculated. "That could account for the broken rib and all that bruising."

The nurse and the whole Merritt Manor staff loved Mr. Piszkos. Such a kindly light shone in his eyes whenever they had to turn him or change his sheets. And they thought Joey and Arlene were just wonderful, coming like clockwork every other Sunday with their adorable baby. The younger Mr. Piszkos almost always brought his father one of the new releases from the video store.

How that man waited for those visits! Though he was somewhat twisted on one side and was unable to speak, he could move his head quite freely and his tear ducts remained in full function and after a time he was able to bring up some noises other than grunts from his throat. And with these, with the motion of his head and the flow of his tears and the wordless modulation of his voice, he spoke to his beautiful grandson. And once—the day nurse swore she heard it when the son lifted the child for the old man to kiss—he shaped a soft patter of sounds into its ear, a little one-two-three like the notes of a waltz.

*Richard Burgin*

# Cruise

"I'LL GO FIRST THEN CAPTAIN, THAT'S WHAT YOU WANT, ISN'T IT?"

Rider said yes, though he'd never said he'd wanted him to go first, hadn't even been asked the question and here was Anderson already seizing it from him. Wasn't that the way things always were, someone seizing something then pretending they weren't interested in what they'd just taken. All the more reason not to get too attached to things. That was why the second he saw the ad for the cruise in the newspaper he knew he'd take it, improbable though it was for him of all people to go. He simply saw an image of himself leaving everything behind him forever and fell in love with the image and its impeccable irony.

Anderson was barely audible above the competing sounds of the ship and sea and Rider asked him to speak louder. His story still seemed to be in the preamble stage as far as Rider could tell. It was odd how Anderson did things, even more odd that they were apparently going to go through with "the game" as Anderson called it, although they'd only known each other a few days.

They'd met because they were seated next to each other in the ship's dining room. There was no grand stroke of fate in that, Rider didn't think, especially since, as they each admitted later, there was no one else at the table even remotely interesting. Anderson struck him as a man who had suffered but still had a sense of humor and was still somewhat charming, which Rider found strangely touching. Later they met again by the shuffle board tournament and quietly mocked it together. That night after dinner they drank in the bar making fun of the whole cruise, which of course was steeped in absurdity, and then ridiculed themselves for taking it. It was in that spirit of self-mockery and margaritas that Anderson proposed the game. Already they'd fallen into the habit of talking quite openly with one another, or at least Anderson had.

"You can tell me anything and I wouldn't bat an eye," Anderson said, on their second night of drinking and Rider said the same thing. Good, Anderson had said, because he had a bad conscience over something he really wanted to tell him about. Feel free to, Rider had said, assuring him he was a good listener. That's essentially what the game was, talking and listening, its object simply being to tell each other the worst thing they'd ever done—a clean confessional at sea. They'd decided to play it on the lower deck at midnight. Not bad as a final gesture, Rider thought to himself, with a grim smile. Anderson said it would be cleansing for both of them and fun too if they kept their humor. Anderson didn't even seem like a man who had done a worst thing. He was overweight and laughed a lot with a beard that despite being mostly black (and despite his dark intensely focused eyes which almost matched Rider's own) still made him look more like Santa Claus than the Devil. Rider pictured evil men as generally being thin and sensitive, tortured men as also being on the thin side, as he was. Certainly evil men didn't laugh a lot as Anderson was doing now.

"You sure you're up for this, Captain?"

"Totally up, totally ready," Rider said, forcing a laugh himself, and forcing himself to pay attention though he was not at all confident that he could actually listen to Anderson's story. How could he be with what he was considering?

"Do you mind stories about women?"

"What else is there to talk about?" Rider said, and they both laughed. "I just lost my last lover so I'm sure I'll understand," Rider added, swallowing some of his drink. Anderson was clearly ahead of him alcohol-wise but in spite of everything, he was afraid to catch up.

"It's strange about women how once they're past forty-five they become more like us, while we get more like them. Or haven't you noticed? Maybe you're too young to notice, how old are you?"

"I'm twenty-seven," Rider said, lowering his age by five years.

"So you're even younger than I thought. I have the habit of thinking everyone else is older than they are and that I alone am younger than I really am. Anyway, what I mean is women get more aggressive sexually and more assertive in general while men become less so once we hit fifty. Instead we become more emotional and weepy. At a certain point I think the genders meet and form a kind of third sex. The point is, until I met Francine I believed I was following that pattern and was a new member of that third sex who had completely reversed his old ways."

"Which were?"

"I don't follow," Anderson said.

"What *were* your old ways?"

"To dominate, of course. To have as much power and control as possible in every situation, especially in bed. Wasn't that ever the way it was with you? Or maybe I'm way off base here. Sometimes I project stuff from my own life onto people simply because I think . . . well simply because I do.

". . . Anyway about my old ways with women all you need to know is that there was the usual amount of blindness and bungling—a wife, a divorce, some girlfriends, some one night stands and whatever you'd call the vast in between. Let's see, what else? There were a few stabs at having children though only one was born . . . who's quite a successful architect. If you ever asked him I think he'd say I was a good father or at least a nice man."

Rider made a noise to show he was impressed and Anderson smiled briefly before speaking again.

"Then one final torturous love affair that ended with my thinking that I'd had enough. That I didn't want another woman—ever. I began to get fatter then as the months went by—swollen looking like I am now. It was like all the hurts I'd been carrying around inside me had spread out on my body. But then, despite all that, eventually the old itch for them came back and I started answering singles ads again. After a few crummy ones I met Francine at a single's bar in Center City. Have you ever known someone who's both pretty and homely at the same time? I hadn't until I met Francine. She had natural platinum blond hair and pretty green eyes but her nose was too big, her lips too small. Swollen nose, shrunken lips I remember thinking in spite of myself and the new sensitive type man I thought I'd finally evolved into. It was the same with her body, that also had a swollen quality like . . . well, like mine."

Rider laughed, a little too loudly he thought, but Anderson continued, apparently without noticing.

"Homely or pretty, pretty or homely I remember thinking throughout our drinks. It was like a tug of war in my head. Later I realized that there would be moments when she would be pretty and moments when she wouldn't. That's what happens when women are ambiguously pretty."

"To say nothing of men."

"Yes, of course it applies to us too," Anderson said. "There were other paradoxes. She had a soft, tentative voice, the most vulnerable voice I've ever heard, touching and arousing but at the same time it was hard for her to talk and she often spoke or mumbled in an un-grammatical and confusing way. I'll need a hearing aid and a translator to understand this one, I thought. It was another tug of war, another stalemate. Finally my hand landed on her thigh, we started kissing and I was instantly erect, something that hadn't been happening a lot lately. Well I guess the tie is broken, I thought. She seemed to heat up right away too. After a few minutes she said, 'Let's go back to your place.' When we got there we continued making out before we even took our coats off.

"In bed, she was by far the noisiest woman I'd ever been with—as if she were making up for how quiet she was otherwise. It was like an air raid had gone off, and not just when she came but during the whole time. So noisy that she got me 'off message' at times, by making me worry that despite my thick walls my neighbors would think a homicide was being committed and call the police who would suddenly burst into my room shooting first and asking questions later. Then as soon as our orgasms were over she was quiet again. Disappointingly so."

"When you might have expected to collect your compliment," Rider said.

"Yes, despite my hints, it was always that way. Maybe it was her way of spiting me."

"Still, on balance it sounds like a *Playboy* fantasy to me," Rider said. *"Woman Who Has Nothing to Say Does All Her Talking in Bed."*

"Yes, there was an element of that. It might have been like that if I could have controlled myself."

"Oh? How so?"

"I mean that I was at least ten years older than her. I should have realized what I was dealing with, especially as the details about her life began to trickle in. Her sexual abuse as a child from her uncle, her physical abuse from her ex-husband, her brief stays in various psychi-atric wards. Part of me did realize it, of course, but I still couldn't seem to resist. It was like that part of me I'd thought had died out in my thirties was back stronger than ever. Already by the end of the first night she was addressing me as 'master.'"

So it's another slave story, Rider thought, as Anderson began to supply more details. It seemed men, particularly men he was interested in one way or another, were always telling him stories like that which he didn't want to hear yet he'd listen anyway, which made him a kind of slave too, didn't it? I should just die now to avoid hearing it, he thought, looking up for a moment at the rash of stars. Years ago he used to believe they had ultimate control over people's fate. Now they were all out but it meant nothing, of course, the stars being silent as they always were.

He had thought the cruise would be the ideal place to do it—to die among the people he could never live with—the straight world that had treated him as an alien all his life. The irony was airtight and Rider considered himself an irony connoisseur. But the idea that Anderson would be his last witness was disturbing on several levels. That this monologue by an aging, quasi-sadistic, egotist should be the last speech he'd ever hear was too depressing. Even now Anderson had more than a trace of a smile as he continued to describe Francine servicing him and waiting on him. He had expected more from Anderson too—but wasn't that the way things always were. It was like a law of human physics—in the process of observing people they disappointed you. He remembered some years before Neal, his last lover, had stabbed him in the back, going to the apartment of a man named Al who he'd met at a music lover's club in Boston, a man who was going to play the piano for him. He didn't know if anything sexual were going to happen but he knew they were friends and he admired and respected him and looked forward to his piano playing. When he got to his music room he saw photographs of Al's female conquests draped over his piano. Obviously Al wanted him to comment on how beautiful they were, and of course he didn't. Very disappointing. He'd had high hopes for him, at least as a friend, and now this Al syndrome was happening again with Anderson.

"In the first few weeks I used to occasionally go out to eat with her," Anderson was saying, (and Rider, in spite of himself, began to listen again) "and once even to a movie but increasingly I didn't want to be seen with her in public. Even now I'm not sure why. I thought it was simply because I'd finally decided she was homely. I'm ashamed to say that to you now, but we agreed the whole point was to be brutally, completely honest. Am I right?"

"Go on," said Rider.

"Other times I thought it was because of the guilt I felt about how I treated her. Anyway, we began meeting exclusively for sex. A few times she mentioned that she'd like to go to a movie or at least leave the apartment for some reason other than to bring me food but I reminded her, with a smile on my face, that it wasn't up to her to make decisions. Then she'd quickly say 'You're right' or 'I know, master' and the matter was dropped."

"This slave business," Rider said, lowering his voice as a young couple holding hands passed by, "I'm not sure I understand. How serious was it?"

Anderson looked away from him at the water. "It was something we joked about at times—though during sex we carried out our roles with complete seriousness. Don't get me wrong, I never hurt her physically. I never enjoyed that or condoned that in bed. Almost every time I'd ask her if certain things were hurting and she'd say one way or another and if it was hurting her I'd stop. Also I'd ask her, you know, if she enjoyed our roles and she'd say yes, simply and convincingly. 'Why,' I would sometimes ask. 'I like a strong man,' she would say or, 'I love pleasing you.'"

"This is not a very uplifting story," Rider said, "but on the other hand since she chose to act that way and told you she enjoyed it I don't really see where the sin is."

"Wait, I'll tell you," Anderson said. "You see, things changed. She began writing me long, romantic love letters. Though she was poor she also began buying me gifts. Plants and flowers and crystals with perfumed cards attached.

"'We could have did more last night,' she wrote in one of her letters. 'You could have held me a little afterwards . . . why don't you ever want to hold me or have me stay over. Where is this relationship going?'

"I never answered with a letter of my own but in bed that night I brought it up.

"'I read your letter,' I said. She looked away with an embarrassed smile. She was short, barely the height of a child and she looked at that moment just like a child caught stealing the proverbial cookie from the cookie jar. I told her the things she said in her letter were nice but I didn't understand her asking about what kind of relationship we had. Her face turned beat red then.

"'I thought I was clear about that,' I continued. 'We're having a sexual relationship, Francine, in which we each have our roles. I thought we both understood that.'

"'But you said you loved me,' she blurted, suddenly staring at me with pathetically sincere blue eyes. She was alluding to something I'd said during sex a month or two before, near the beginning of our relationship, something that I'd completely forgotten but which I now remembered vividly.

"'Yes, I did say that. And at the moment I said it I meant it.'

"Finally her eyes softened until something like a smile was back on her face. But somehow I couldn't leave it like that.

"'It was an expression of pleasure that I was feeling at the moment while we were having sex. . . .'

"The look of profound unhappiness replaced the hopeful smile like a shade drawn over her face. That wouldn't do either.

"'Francine, I do love you . . . in my own way.' I added.

"With that uneasy compromise we were able to drop it for awhile but I knew it wouldn't go away. Just a second . . ." Anderson said, as he stopped a waiter carrying a tray of complimentary piña coladas and took one for each of them.

"I knew I was in a mess," Anderson said as he swallowed his drink. "I was doing these rather extreme physical and psychological things with her for an hour or so and then after it ended I'd apologize, seeking reassurance that she really wanted it, really enjoyed it. And even though I always got that reassurance I never fully believed it especially after the love letters started coming.

"'Why do I do it?' I'd ask myself. 'I do it because I can do it,' I'd answer, 'and also because it's simply irrestible to do.' But I knew I had to do something to change things so I began answering other ads, going out on dates with other women, though I also continued meeting Francine for our sessions. For awhile things were in a holding pattern. I continued doing ever more bizarre things with Francine. Meanwhile she continued to do more things for me out of bed too. To shop and cook for me and meet me at the airport when I returned from business trips, though I still felt uncomfortable walking through the airport with her. By the way do you also travel a lot in your work?"

"Me?" Rider said, poking himself in his chest with his index finger. "I'm basically just a bookkeeper though I"ll answer to the word accountant. I picked a job where my emotions wouldn't be involved, where only a small part of my brain would be . . . taxed, you might say. Otherwise, there's too much stress and disappointment. And no, I don't travel for my job either."

Anderson laughed, finished his drink, then got them two more. "When my car broke down," he said, handing Rider his drink, "she drove me even more. She drove me for my root canal and then trips to a different suburb for my accountant. Too bad I didn't know you then, I'd have thrown my business your way. The love letters continued also, all about the power of unconditional love, and about our future. It was during this time that I found out about her uncle and her ex-husband who never sent her any money, although one of his teenage sons still lived with her."

Anderson paused while a big bosomed redhead in a clinging pink T-shirt walked by. He smiled at Rider and they each took a big swallow from their new drinks.

"You see," Anderson said, "it's not that I didn't care about her. I was even touched by her at times. Actually, I'd fallen into the habit during the apology segment of our sessions of trying to pump up her self-esteem so it was natural that I'd ask her about why hers was so low. When she told me about her uncle she said, 'I feel like the worst thing has already happened to me, that nothing else could ever be as bad.' I also found out that for the last five years she'd been on antidepressants which she got from some kind of doctor she'd been seeing.

"'Do you tell him about the things we do?' I asked in a worried tone.

"She shook her head no, back and forth like a pendulum. 'No, that's personal,' she said.

"'Good,' I said, 'let's keep it that way.'"

"How exactly did you try to pump up her self-esteem?" Rider asked, with a tinge of sarcasm.

"I told her she was a passionate, highly emotional woman who had a lot to give. I told her that if she acted important people would treat her that way. I urged her to get a lawyer too and to hound her ex-husband for money (some of which she finally got), and to demand more than the crummy wages they paid her at the floral shop where she worked. She was an incurable lover of plants and flowers."

"And did she get the raise?"

"She got the raise."

"So you did do some good for her life."

"Yes, in those limited areas, but I was meanwhile dating other women and finally started sleeping with one—in a very conventional way—that I was mildly attracted to. My point is I still didn't give up Francine when I should have."

Anderson put his glass down on the small table by their chairs. "'I do it because I can do it' became my mantra, my explanation for everything I did with her. It never occurred to me that I did it because she let me do it. That included my cheating on her. I didn't want to tell Francine about my other girlfriend but I didn't want to deceive her either. Of course what I really wanted was her permission to do what I was doing. One night in bed—"

"Where else?" Rider said.

"Yes, where else, I told her that she had to live by different rules than me. One of those rules was that she could never ask me about other women.

"'Is there somebody else?' she said with that comically sincere expression back in her eyes.

"'Stop right there. Don't you see you're already breaking the rule?' I said, and she mumbled that she was sorry.

"I might have left it at that."

"But you didn't."

"No, I didn't. Instead I brought it up the next two times we met and on the last time I finally told her I was sleeping with someone else.

"'I knew it anyway,' she said softly.

"Are you OK?' I asked.

"'I love you unconditionally,' she said, saying her favorite word again more loudly than usual. She was biting her lip a little but other than that looked all right.

"'Thank you for accepting me,' I said. After we had sex she fixed me a snack and I still didn't notice any difference in her. She spoke about the power of love again. I told her she could stay over, thinking it would make her happy, and she did. I remember that I did hold her that night, and that it felt strangely peaceful. I vaguely wondered why I hadn't done it more often. When she left the next morning I really didn't think anything was wrong. But, of course, something was wrong. Before she left my place she'd swallowed a lot of her new pills, began driving on the wrong side of the road and ultimately smashed up her car. Miraculously she wasn't badly hurt but she was arrested and taken to the hospital where her stomach was pumped. Then she was placed in a psychiatric ward where she eventually called me. 'I just couldn't see the point of going on,' she said.

"She called me a couple of other times from the hospital. After each call I wondered if she were still alive and hadn't really died in between calls. One night I dreamed that she *had* died and that it was her ghost talking to me on the phone. The next morning I managed to switch my vacation time and booked myself on this fabulous cruise."

"Just in the nick of time," Rider said, drawing a hard look from Anderson.

"Obviously you disapprove of that too, of my taking the cruise. But remember this is me at my absolute worst, which is what we promised to reveal to each other."

Rider stared back at him, catching Anderson's eye before looking away from him. He watched a man walk by and then a woman, noticed the different sounds their shoes made on the deck. The man was carrying a drink, the woman her purse. There was some nauseating pseudo Caribbean waltz whose name he couldn't remember being played by a few musicians on the deck above. Then he realized that the ocean wasn't roaring anymore and wondered if he had just gotten used to its sound.

"So I'm awaiting your verdict," Anderson said. "What do you think of all this? Should I walk the plank right now for what I did?"

"It's not a pretty story, is it?" Rider said finishing his drink.

Anderson shook his head. He looked like an old little boy.

"It's disappointing," Rider said. "But I often find myself disappointed with people, did I already say that to you? It's odd how we allow ourselves to be disappointed so many times. You'd think we'd learn."

"What was it that you expected?"

"I remember once I went to Cape Cod with a friend, a male friend named Jay. This was a long time ago; I was in my early twenties. My friend was young and smart and full of energy. He was even valedictorian of his graduating class or so he told me. But I believed him because he had a tremendous ability to convince people of things like you had with Francine, and so I believed him. We'd met at a record store where we were working in the summer. The kind of job recent college graduates did before grad school or setting out on a career. Soon we began pining for the beach and talking about it a lot at work. People in Boston, where I lived then, went to the Cape the way Philadelphians go to the shore . . ."

"Yes I know," Anderson said.

"And so we went to Hyannisport me and my friend Jay, who I had such high hopes for."

"What kind of hopes?"

"Just hopes for a friend you could trust. I hadn't known everything about him, of course, but I had hopes and belief in a general way that he wanted the same kind of thing from life and from—"

"You."

"Yes, from me. That he expected a certain code of behavior, of character, that didn't even need to be discussed because it was understood."

"You certainly thought about this friend a lot."

"I always take people seriously, probably to a fault."

"And so what happened?"

"And so we found a motel and went to the beach and had a magical time swimming and playing Frisbee and laughing – it seemed like we laughed all day. And then we went to a steak house and it just continued. I don't think I'd ever had as much fun as I did that day and to cap it off with some good steaks. . . ."

"Which we certainly haven't gotten here," Anderson said.

"No, hardly. But to have those kinds of steaks when you're so young and don't normally eat that way and then with our desert we had a glass of champagne which inspired us to buy a case of beer later that we took back and drank at the motel."

"You were young," Anderson said.

"Yes, I was young. And after this most perfect, this happiest day and night of my life I woke up in the morning and discovered that Jay, the valedictorian, had driven away in his car and taken all of my money."

"Really?"

"Yes, I found out at work two days later that he'd already given notice. He was leaving Boston for Oregon where he was going to live."

"So he left for Oregon with a few hundred extra dollars courtesy of your pants pocket."

"He left the day after he robbed me. I'm sure he planned the whole thing."

"That stinks. That's really dreadful. But it sounds like the worst thing someone ever did to you, not the worst thing you ever did. Aren't you still going to finish the game and tell me what that is?"

"It *was* the worst thing I ever did. It's like the worst things I do *are* the things I let others do to me."

"You've lost me."

"Because part of me knew he would rob me. I may have even heard it while it was going on but I let him do it anyway."

"I don't understand."

"No, you don't."

"You speak as if there was something between you two. I mean. . . ."

"You said I could tell you anything. Well, now I have."

"So . . . what I'm thinking is. . . ."

"That I'm gay and you're right. Think about it. I never told you I wasn't."

"That's true."

"As for my valedictorian, he. . . ."

"Wasn't."

"I don't know about that. I've thought about it a lot. Once someone lies to you, once someone misrepresents himself you can never really be sure of anything about him. I don't know how thoroughly he planned it. It could have been a spur of the moment thing when he woke up that morning and saw me asleep and my pants on the floor or before we ever stepped in his car to go to the Cape or at any point in between. I know that that night I gave myself to him totally, let him do and get whatever he wanted from me physically and emotionally and I was so happy surrendering to him (I would never surrender like that again to anyone), that it didn't bother me that he barely touched me or gave a thought to physically satisfying me."

"Possibly because he wasn't gay."

"Possibly . . . or else because he couldn't deal with it. But I'm sensing from your tone that this story is upsetting you, making you uncomfortable, or maybe it's just that I told you I'm gay."

"Not at all," Anderson said waving his hand dismissively.

"I mean you haven't looked me in the eye once since I told you."

"I rarely look people in the eye."

"And the expression on your face, your whole tone of voice."

"If anything, I'm feeling that you disapprove of me . . . profoundly. . . . That the story I told you understandably disgusted you and that you think of me as some kind of monster who you could never be friends with."

"I wouldn't say 'monster.'"

"What would you say?"

"I would say, I'd admit I thought you were different based on our earlier meetings. I'll admit that."

"So there you are disapproving of me while copping out on the game by telling me the worst thing that ever happened to you instead of the worst thing you ever did, like you were supposed to."

"But I also told you I'm gay. From your point of view isn't *that* the worst thing?"

Anderson sat up straight in his chair. "That's ridiculous. That's bullshit. You don't have any reason to say that to me, any more than if

I said what really disappointed you about my story is that I turned out to be straight."

"Is this the part where we get into a fight on the deck so someone can yell 'man overboard!'" Rider said.

Anderson didn't say anything but continued looking at him.

"You would probably win since as a faggot I'd surely turn out to be an hysterical and inept fighter. Still I'm probably a good twenty years younger than you."

"We haven't established your age. You've been too vain to really tell me."

"You're a fine one to talk about vanity. You tortured some pathetic creature just so you could feel good about yourself sexually one last time. And then telling me all this sex stuff full of such great remorse but really full of not so subtle bragging about how good you are in bed, and you want reassurance from me?"

Anderson's face reddened and Rider felt he should stop but for some reason couldn't. "You get on this cruise to do penance but what you really want is for the first person you meet to hear your story and forgive you. Then it will be on to new conquests, new lies, new—"

"So what is it *you* want? Why are you even on this boat? Aren't there any gay cruises on the ocean these days? This is a straight persons singles cruise and since you've spent most of your time with me what is it that you really want?"

"It isn't what you're suggesting, I can definitely assure you of that," Rider said, breathing hard. He could feel his heart beating. "Besides, it was you who were pursuing *me*, you who wanted to play the game and who did all the talking."

"Careful, fellah," Anderson said, pounding his fist on the table.

Rider's face whitened. "I'm leaving," he said, getting up from his chair and immediately feeling tremendously dizzy.

Anderson got up from his chair too. "Yes, it's better if we don't meet again," he said, but before he could continue Rider had turned his back and walked away.

Anderson swore to himself, felt himself turning an intense, insane red, brighter than he'd ever been, as if his face had been the subject of a child's fierce drawing. He felt he had to shield it from the other passengers as he walked mad and dizzy down the deck to his cabin.

Once in his room he punched his mattress twice then his pillow several times in a row. He should have hit that little pussy; he should never have let him say all those awful things about him. Incredible

how Rider, how people in general couldn't face the truth about themselves or other people, though in each case they thought they wanted to.

When he stopped hitting he lay down on his bed breathing hard
and feeling a strange kind of sadness. He looked at the round little
ship's clock on his bedside table, thought of the idiots he'd have to face
at lunch tomorrow and thought then that some of the things Rider
said were true. But how could he say them, how could he know? And
why did he tell Rider so much about himself in the first place? Part of
him must have wanted Rider to hate him, but why? Anderson felt old
then, older than he'd ever felt and closed his eyes trying to hear the
ocean. Instead he started thinking about his mother. He could still see
in his mind's eye her hugging him as a child so close to her heart, and
the thought of that made tears spill from his still shut eyes, that he allowed to trickle freely down his face.


Rider walked at a fast clip still holding his drink until he reached the
back deck. The water roared white and black beneath him. How absurd that even now when he'd thought it would be the end, he was still
reviewing and answering Anderson's questions just as throughout his
life he would do so after fights—even after his last lover, Neal, had left
him with nothing left to puzzle over.

Why did you go on this cruise, Anderson had wanted to know, and
he'd said nothing as if he were playing yet another game with Anderson and with himself. But perhaps he should have answered, he
thought, looking at the water. His ironic line came back to him "to die
among the people I could never live with." How absurd a thought, how
pathetically adolescent it sounded now. He always knew he wasn't
going to do anything along those lines so why pretend he might? Why
did he try to fool himself that way? Who exactly was he trying to impress? Himself? Anderson, on some level? He finished the drink he'd
been carrying, felt the high, and then thought of Santa Claus Anderson and the improbable way he'd told him off. At any moment Anderson could have punched him out and perhaps killed him by sitting on
him, but he stuck it to him anyway and the thought of that made him
laugh so hard it drowned out the ocean and was all he could hear in
his ears for a while. Everything was making him laugh now including
the fact that he was laughing so hard. Finally he turned away from the
water and began walking back to his room, thinking of Anderson's face
when he told him he was gay. He was still laughing at the image of it.

The old narcissist had kept him laughing a long time now. You couldn't really off yourself after meeting someone like Anderson, he thought, as he nearly bumped into a waiter. "So sorry," he said, bowing a little, "so sorry." Anderson made you too angry and then he made you laugh too hard.

Rider continued laughing down the hallway, passing people and not even covering his mouth until he reached his room and sat down on his bed. Well, he thought after he finally calmed down I am a twit but I've lived through my death. God, or whatever, is keeping me alive for some reason. I've lived through my death and no one could really say I'm old yet, not *old* old . . . and tomorrow we'll be in Jamaica, won't we?

*Stephen Dixon*

# Again—Part II

SHE WAS IN A WHEELCHAIR. HE DIDN'T KNOW SHE WAS IN ONE WHEN he first saw her at this party; thought she was in a regular armchair. he'd just come into the apartment, was holding his coat and didn't know where to put it, as the front closet was completely filled. There were even a couple of coats and mufflers on the floor of it, which he picked up and tried to find hangers for but there were none nor any room to put the coats on other coats, so he left them on a chair next to the closet, the mufflers on top. He looked around for the host; not only to say hello but to ask where to put his coat. He didn't want to leave it on the chair. He had a feeling it'd end up on the floor, get trampled on or put someplace where he'd have trouble finding it. That was when he saw her sitting across from a couch in the living room, talking to a few people. He was immediately struck by her: face, hair, smile, intelligent expression, wide forehead, simple attractive outfit she was wearing, no lipstick or any makeup it seemed, and what looked like a good body: nice-sized breasts and narrow waist and flat stomach—her legs were obscured by someone else's chair—and she was speaking animatedly and her voice had a lovely clear tone to it and sounded bright and pleasant. The host came into the room and they said hello and he said "Thanks for having me, seems like a nice crowd," and asked where to put his coat—the host said "On the bed or chair in the bedroom; I doubt there's room left in the coat closet, though you can always try." "By the way," he said, "that woman over there," bobbing his head toward the woman in what he thought was an armchair, and the host said "Which one, the dark-haired, Beth, or the stately blonde?" and he said "The stately," and she gave the woman's first name—"I believe that's it, or close. Came with Beth, and with so many people getting here at once, we were introduced too quickly. No, it has an 'a' at the end of it, so two syllables, and as for the last name— don't ask or you'll have me stumped. But you know Beth, right?" and he said no and she said "She's lovely and brilliant; a Russian scholar. I think her friend is too. You two would have so much to talk about— Russian literature, samizdat, emigrés; Beth's specialties and field. Here, let me introduce you, but first get rid of your coat," and he did and slipped into the bathroom right outside the bedroom to make sure his hair was combed back and collar was right and to check his nostrils, which he'd thought of doing, but forgot, before he left home for possi- ble hairs curling out of them; it'd been about a month since he looked. Saw two in one nostril and pulled them out with his fingers, then checked his ears. Five to ten hairs in each but not in a clump. He looked inside the medicine cabinet for any kind of scissors—hair, nail, cuticle, regular, even sewing, which he checked the drawers under- neath the sink for—but there were none, and grabbed hold of some hair in one ear and pulled hard, a few came out but made his eyes tear, so he thought just live with it and went back to where he last saw the host, but she wasn't around. So go over to Miss Stately without her, he thought; no, don't call her that, even to himself; it's stupid. So what was her name? Something with an "a" at the and of it, but the host said it too fast or he wasn't paying attention. But he doesn't need any- one to introduce him. Though maybe circulate first, don't show he's in such a rush to meet her, as she might have seen him come in and turn- ing his head to her a few times while he was standing there holding his coat, and get a drink. He got one—scotch on rocks with a little water, since it was a drink he could never drink fast and he didn't want to be even a little high when he spoke to her, flubbing over his words and so on and maybe seeming to her like a lush or schmuck, and walked around with it, said hi and hello to several people he passed but didn't know though nothing else to them, put the glass to his mouth but it was empty without him even realizing it—he didn't spill any, he hoped—and got another and some *crudités* off a side table—carrots and celery sticks, a cauliflower floret, no tiny radishes, which he liked, be- cause they'd make his breath stink—but skipped the dip that went with them because he didn't want to risk any of it dripping on him or the floor. Then he wiped his fingers that had held the vegetables so they wouldn't be wet if he shook hands with the two women, stuck the cocktail napkin into his pants pocket because he didn't see any other place to put it, and went over, smiled at them as he sat on the one available space on the couch across from them, said hello to the man and woman he sat between, who were looking around the room and nodded pleasantly at him, and leaned forward and said "Beth, you don't know me and might even be a bit startled—surprised, really's, the word—that I know your name. But our host gave it to me and said introduce myself to you and your friend, whose name, I'm afraid—she was in the midst of doing something—she didn't give . . . something about things in common and so on. I'm sorry that took me so long to get out," and gave his name, the friend gave hers and this time he concentrated on remembering it, and Beth said "We all already know mine. Maybe I should say 'Elizabeth,' my given name, to get equal recognition," and they laughed, the couple on the couch too, and he shook hands with the two women. "Nice to meet you. And very nice to meet you too, he said to the friend. That was when he saw—well, he saw it the moment he sat down; actually, as he was squatting over the couch, preparing to sit down while carefully holding his glass so it wouldn't spill—she was in a wheelchair. He didn't want to ask her why she was in one. Seen other people make that mistake. "Break a leg skiing this winter?" "I only wish it were that. No, I went into elective surgery for a relatively minor problem and the surgeon severed a nerve and I'm stuck with this for life." Or once: "My brother's in a wheelchair now too. Tripped over his mutt and sprained his ankle bad. Something like that with you?" "Not quite," it finally came out. "Bone cancer." Later, when he was getting them a plate of *crudités* with a little side dish of dip, he asked his host "Do you know what's wrong with her that she's in a wheelchair?" "No I don't," she said. "She's so healthy looking, I doubt it could be any serious." Later she stopped him when he was on his way to the bathroom and said "I think I was being much too sanguine about her condition," and told what she'd learned. The three of them started talking, but after awhile he was almost only talking to the friend. Beth of course noticed it, and maybe even wanted to encourage it, for she excused herself, saying there was something she had to do and when her friend asked what, she said "Personal, in the pantry," and she'd see her later, and left. "It wasn't anything I said or did, her leaving, was it?" and she said "Why would you think that?" and he said "Well, it couldn't be anything you said or did. And the suddenness of her move, the ellipticness . . . ellipticalness . . . damn, whatever the word is in regard to her personal pantry remark," and she said "She probably just got an urge to meet and mix and perhaps also wanted to give us a few minutes together. I don't mind, do you?" "No, why would I? But it was nice talking to her," and she said "Then I'll call her back," and he said "No, it's fine." So they continued to talk. How did she find him at first? "What a question," she said. After they'd been seeing each other a few weeks he asked it, "just for the record," and she said if he really wants to know, she found him that night kind of skittish—"Skittish?"—"Jumpy, nervous, hypersomething, overly self-conscious, awkward, compulsive and a bit more chatty and self-referential than I feel comfortable with. The truth is, you kept steering and domineering the conversation, less when Beth was there, possibly because you sensed she wouldn't sit through it." "You think that's why, that first time we all talked, she got up and left kind of abruptly?" and she said "Did she? That I don't remember. Anyway, I let you steer and domineer, when you and I were sitting there alone, since I'm not very talkative when I first meet someone. Although I was a lot more so with you than I usually am with a man I've just met and who seems reasonably interesting and whom I'm not unattracted to. But, to counterbalance all that, I also found you peppy, charming and legitimately funny." "Not intelligent?" "Somewhat, but it didn't stand out." "Charming? Me? You've got to be the first woman to say that, or to my face, anyway, or behind my back where I could overhear, and maybe the first to ever think it other than my mother, who almost always thinks everything highly of me—to build me up, you know. So she at least says it; I doubt if she really believes it. But what about how I first found you?" "You already said—some of it a half-hour after we met, once Beth left—and encouraging you to reprise it would only be dibbing for compliments, unless you changed your mind or weren't saying the truth." "I wasn't. It was all said to get you into bed and my hope was that night, but it didn't work. No, that's not true and was stupid. Forget I said it. That night I only had holy thoughts of you." He found her from the start very intelligent, in a way so much more than he that he thought she wouldn't be interested in him, and also composed, soft-spoken, beautiful, personable, desirable, everything like that, and again, so beautiful that he didn't see how she could ever get interested in him even for more than a thirty-minute chat. Articulate, deep. Every little and big body part. Nose, ears, eyes, forehead, breasts, et cetera. Mouth, teeth. Sexy, the rest. He could go on. Fingers, cheeks, hair, shoulders, neck. He couldn't see her rear because she was seated.

But judging by her flat stomach and small waist, and she wasn't in an outfit that was cinched there to make them appear small and flat, and that her buttocks didn't spread over most of the cushion she was on—he saw this when he got up to get them *crudités* and himself a drink—he guessed her bottom wasn't overlarge. Legs, he could tell, since they were covered to her ankles by her skirt, but the bulge her thighs made through the thin cloth indicated they were solid but not wide, and her ankles seemed normal if maybe a little swollen. But that, he thought, could be because she was sitting in the chair so long and something to do with circulation, for all he knew. None of which he told her. He remembered sniffing for smells, though, to see if she was sitting in her own piss, and not smelling anything but the food coming to the buffet table and already on a couple of people's plates. So he told her what? That he'd been thinking of her. . . but how'd he even get into talking of that? "I've got to tell you something. You might not like it—I swear it's not bad, or all depends how you look at it, I guess—but I'd still like to tell you unless you object before I say anything." "What is it?" "That means I'll have to tell you," and she said "All right, go ahead; I can't see any harm." They were still sitting wheelchair: couch. Beth hadn't come back. The piss thought came later, after he'd learned what she had. His hand was on her knee. The couple had left the couch at the same time, so they were probably together but he didn't see them speak once to each other, and no one else had sat down. He'd put his hand there without realizing it, and when she looked at it—it seemed unfavorably—he jerked it away. "Sorry. I'm always, you know, touching people's shoulders and waists when we're going through doors or I want to let them pass, and if I'm sitting across from someone and close enough, often the knee." She spread her hands out over her knees; that was when he first noticed her fingers: long piano-playing ones it seemed, without a ring. The buffet table at the time didn't have anything on it but silver, napkins and a tall stack of plates. "Don't you want something to eat?" a man said to her when people were helping themselves at the buffet table. "Not right now," she said. "Would you like me to fill up a plate for you? I'll tell you what they have and you can tell me what you like." "It's okay. I'll go myself when the line's shorter." "You don't want to miss out—neither of you. The good stuff's going fast, and I checked with the caterer and the very best specialties there's only one platter of." "I'm sure that whatever's left will be sufficient for me, but thank you very much," and looked at I. and he thought what, what? For she had this look she hadn't had before that suggested she wanted to stay here with him and he felt funny because he wanted to believe it but also didn't. That was about fifteen minutes after he said he'd been thinking of her . . . his actual words were he'd had his eye on her from the minute . . . what he actually said was he couldn't take his eyes off her from the moment he got to the party and was standing there with his coat over his arm and saw her sitting here . . . did she mind him saying this? He would if he were her, he said, but he wouldn't if she were saying this or something comparable to it to him. "Really," she said, "such a long prolog to what you started out to say. Maybe you better forget the rest of it. The food aromas are becoming so strong that I don't know how long I'll be able to concentrate seriously on anything but them." "That's not the reason, of course," he said. "Of course it isn't. Excuse me, but please don't pretend to be blank. We were doing quite well and at a comfortable pace till you ventured into your had-to-tell-me talk. Why don't we resume where we left off? Or anyplace not focused on me, since I forget what we were talking of. Unless you feel unduly chastised, and that it was especially uncalled for, coming from someone you just met, and would rather not have anything more to do with me." "No no, everything you said is right. I can be such an impulsive schmuck. So, what do you know: our first argument." "What are you talking about?" She looked angry. "You see?" he said. "Just what I said: impulsive, schmucky. But I was only doing it to prove it to you. No, that's a lie and I'm getting myself in deeper when I absolutely don't want to. Forgive me. But one more blunder or asininity like that and you should cut me off for good. Or maybe you already have. Listen, this doesn't—what I'm about to say, I'm saying, and don't wince, because it isn't at all focused on you—this doesn't mean anything but what it says, and that's that I have to go to the bathroom." He didn't have to but felt they needed a short break. Then when he came back in three to four minutes, if the bathroom wasn't occupied and he got right in and out of it; even if it was occupied, he wouldn't have to go in because he didn't have to pee— maybe the mess he just got himself into would have blown over. And he actually headed to the bathroom, through the crowd in the next room and was about to enter the hallway to the rear of the apartment when the host stopped him, grabbed his arm and said "Got a second?" and led him out of view of the woman and told him what she'd heard. He'd said to her just before he left "Now don't move. And I'm not being facetious and certainly not malicious or anything like that. I really do have to make in the pantry and I'll be right back. Of course, if you feel you have to go—away from here, I'm saying, and again, I wasn't making any joke or pun—the damn coincidences of language just seem to come at the wrong moments—then you should do what you want and maybe we could talk after." "Is that very serious?" he asked the host. "I mean, I've heard of it but don't know anything about it, not even how it's spelled, or know anyone who's ever had it. Because to me . . . well, she looks so healthy and strong . . . I thought maybe she had something like a sprained leg or fracture she was still healing from. At worst, a slipped disk, painful but not permanent. The host said "It can be serious and because she's in a wheelchair, it probably is, at least now," and told him some other things she knew about the disease. He said "I can only hope hers isn't serious—she's such a nice fine person, though of course for anyone in that situation. But now I really gotta get to the john," and went into the bathroom, peed because he'd probably have to in half an hour and the bathroom might be tied up then, and thought while he was inside—checked his watch and thought "Oh my God, I've been away five minutes already"—what is he getting himself into this time? He's already committed himself way more than just coming on too strong. He means by that? But suppose he really wants to go out with her? He does want to, at least once. So he goes out with her once, what's the problem with that? No problem. Though suppose she has a physical problem he finds difficult to deal with on that date? Oh come on, by now she must be so used to her illness and how to deal with it that she'd never put someone in a position like that. She'd take care of everything beforehand, be prepared for any eventuality and deal with it discreetly, see that nothing out of the ordinary, in other words, would happen while they were together. She wouldn't just . . . anyway, she wouldn't. And he'd push her in her chair if he had to, up and down curbs and such and in and out of a restaurant, if that's where they ended up going. On their first date, if she had trouble moving the chair herself—that is, if she was confined to a chair all the time, because tonight's confinement might be just a temporary setback—sure, why not? Get in back, push, find a curb cut, down that, up the next, and a restaurant—she must know the ones in her neighborhood, which they'd probably stick to for their first meeting, that are easy to get in and out of and move around in. So, one date, that's it, or all he should think about, because he can't back out now—wouldn't be right and it could end up hurting her: "Sure," she could think, "once he knew what I had, he changed his mind"—that is, if she wanted to see him even a single time. There was a good chance—maybe even a very good one—she didn't. He could go back and she might not be there. She might even have left the party by now. Got tired suddenly—her illness—or discomforted about something—her illness again—she felt she could take better care of at home, and asked her friend could they go? Or she left alone. She might be able to get around that independently. Called for a cab and was downstairs already or on her way down in the elevator and the cab would come and she'd be able to get in it on her own or her friend would most likely go down with her to help her into the cab and the cabby or her friend could fold up the chair and put it in the trunk. She was probably able to stand, just not for long. Walk, even, most times, on her own or with a cane. Just tonight might be a particularly bad night for her, but tomorrow or the day after or so she could be out of the chair and walking everywhere after that, with certain limits of course. Till the next relapse, or whatever the host called it, when she'd have to use the chair again a lot. But all that was something he felt he could deal with their first date. If she'll go for it, he thought. But now get out of here before she decides he's never coming back and he may even have left the party without a goodbye. That wouldn't make her feel too good. He washed his hands, made sure his hair was down again, for it had a habit of popping up on the sides, which with his balding front gave him a sort of clownish look, and left the bathroom, wanted to get another drink hut didn't want to spend the time getting it—the crowd around the bar was large again, people getting wine to go with their food probably—and anyway, he'd made enough mistakes with her already that he didn't want to chance getting even higher than the little he was, or sleepy, which is what wine often did to him, if he wanted to switch to a drink that looked more sociable and was less alcoholic. She was smiling at him as he approached. Good sign, he thought, for a nice sincere smile—glad to see him it seemed—though he bet all of hers were. The couch was taken by three people eating off plates on their laps. Same with the chairs around her. And all these people with glasses of wine or bottles or glasses of beer at their feet or on end tables. She had a plate but no glass, it seemed—the one she'd been drinking from must have been taken away—and was feeding herself with some difficulty and also having a tough time keeping the plate straight on her lap. "Good, you got food," he said. "Looks good too. Sushi, other Japanese stuff; great. But you sure the plate's safe there? I don't want to nose in, but it's not a bit unstable?" "I have no other place to put it." "I might be able to find you one of those fold-up trays or a small table, if there's one. Or I'll just hold the plate for you while you eat." "No, I wouldn't like that," she said, looking cross now. Oh damn, he thought, another careless remark. Well, he was only trying to help her, but he should use more sense when he does, and now how does he get out of it? "Thank you, I'll manage," she said, that smile again, so maybe she was trying to get him off the hook, "or I'll get food later when I'm at a real table. Why don't you have it?" offering him her plate. "I've barely touched it—in fact, just two sushis and a noodle—but you'll need fresh silver." "I wouldn't mind; I'm famished," taking her plate. "Forgot to eat break-fast, which is nothing unusual for me, and I don't mind using your fork. Though I'll look around for a chair so I don't have to eat stand-ing up." He thought: He could sit in her lap, how about that? But he won't say it because he doesn't know what that'll bring. "I think I have that solution too," she said. "This gentleman—Ronald is it?" and the man in the middle of the couch looked up from his plate and said "Ron, and excuse me, I forgot. I got too taken with the food." "Ron only wanted your seat till you got back. I told him I was saving it for you, though I thought you'd come back with food for yourself, you were away so long." "I had things to do," he said, and "No, sit, sit," to Ron; "really, I don't mind eating and standing," wanting her to think him gracious. "Deal's a deal, man," Ron said, getting his drink off the floor and standing. "And I'm done anyway, or with this round. Food's great," and left. He sat down and said "Wouldn't mind a little wine myself. Can I get you one too?" and she said "Please don't leave again. This time I doubt I'd do anything to save your place for you," and he said "Sure, and I don't need the wine, though food always tastes better with it. We can get a drink later, if you like." "Okay," she said, and he thought then it's sealed, or something is. That what he want? He al-ready said, at least for one date. They talked while he pushed the food around with his fork. Meat, which he didn't much eat—fishy sushi and that dish, what's its name again? with long cellophane noodles and a variety of vegetables and thin slices of marinated beef. But he didn't want to start anything about how he hadn't had any kind of meat but a bit of fish and half a chicken salad sandwich in months—saw a whole skinned animal torso, he thinks a calf, carried into his neighborhood supermarket on a pole by two men before the store opened and that did it for him—so had a couple pieces of each. Later he'd tell her, if they went out for dinner. But for all he knew she might feel the same way and was given a plate of food by someone like that man before who saw her just sitting there when almost everyone else was at the buffet table or eating, saw it was meat and didn't want to make an issue of it so ate a little, and that could be why she handed the plate over to him. About music, but how'd that subject come up? He was rapidly tapping his fingers on the bottom of his plate while deciding what to eat from it and she said "Do you play an instrument? Often, people who tap like that, do." "No," he said, stopping, "just, extemporaneously, the plate. But do you?" "Used to play piano and was taking lessons from a concert pianist up till three years ago. First my hands stopped cooperating, then the feet. Actually, the feet first, so till the hands became too enfeebled to play I only chose pieces where the feet weren't needed." Then she told him what she had. He didn't ask; she just came out with it. "I've got." "That so?" he said. "I've heard of it and figured you had something. How much can you get around by yourself?" and she said "You mean in the wheelchair?" and he did but thought oh no, not again; what do I say to get out of this one? Dumbhead, dumbhead, because her expression seemed to suggest it was a totally inappropriate question, and he said "No, just, you know, anyplace. Do you get around? I meant. Concerts, opera, museums, movies? Take advantage of the city like I almost never do except an occasional movie, which I invariably bitch about, so I'm not really a good one to go with, and a walk across the park to the Met when I need a break from my work," and she said "Not as much as I want, but I used to a great deal. Maybe I've just become too busy." Taught two humanities courses a year at Columbia and was on a postdoctoral fellowship she was surprised he'd never heard the name of. "No, that's not right of me—I apologize— because why should I think anybody would know of it other than someone planning to serve a life sentence in academia?" Also wrote poetry and he asked and she said yes, a few, though not in great places but the only ones that would take them." He ate another piece of meat, thinking when he put it in his mouth that it was a black mushroom, and had to admit to himself he liked it, just as he had the two other pieces he intentionally ate before, and finished the rest of it on his plate while she told him some of the magazines she'd been in— he'd asked before he stuck his fork into what he thought was a mushroom—and books she taught in this semester's humanities course and he thought he might even go back to eating meat again but on a semiregular basis, because why be a phony about it?—he liked it and especially this beef and a small amount of it each week can't be that bad for you—and that he also might go back to the buffet table for more. "Impressive magazines to me," he said, "and sounds like a great course.

I'd love to hear your ideas on those books, though a few I haven't read but would probably start to. Can I get you anything at the buffet table? Maybe something other than what was on this plate, since you hardly touched it," and she said she was taking a new experimental medicine every other day and had lost most of her appetite as well as some of her hair because of it and probably shouldn't have even had the few sips of wine she did. "Your hair? No, it looks too thick and rich; you couldn't have lost any." "Anyway, I can be a drag sometimes when it comes to eating and drinking. Unfortunately, the medicine must come first, but thanks." Just then Beth came over. He didn't know how he hadn't seen her since she left, but maybe that was an indication of how absorbed he was in the conversation. Or she came over about a minute after that medicine-comes-first remark—they'd started talking about Ovid's *Metamorphoses*, which she'd taught this semester and he'd just read for the first time ("I'm gradually making my way through all the classics")—and said to her "I'm afraid I have to steal you away, cookie," and pointed at her watch. "I know it's still early and you're having a good time, but it's already half an hour past the time we said we'd be there, and from what they said our presence is needed," "You have to go?" he said. "I'm sorry. And you haven't really eaten yet," and she said "There'll be plenty where we're going, not that I'll feel like having anything more there than here," and he said "Then we should get together some time. For talk, coffee—your books for your course and stuff," and she said "If you'd like," and gave her address and spelled her last name twice. "There's only one of me in the book—you can imagine, with such a complicated name—and two of the three with the same last name and who live on West 83rd are my parents." "And the fourth?" and she said "The fourth?" and he said "The other person in the directory with your last name," and she said "God, I can be slow, excuse me. It's been looked into. My father, who lost his entire family in Europe, is always on the alert for possible newly discovered relatives, no matter how distant. He called this fourth name the first year it appeared in the Manhattan directory and the man was in no way related to us and didn't even know what country his father's family had emigrated from and hadn't a clue what the name meant in German." She said goodbye and stuck out her hand to shake and he said "Let me see you to the door first," and got up and she said "That's very nice but there are some things I have to do before I go, besides other goodbyes to make." He shook her hand and said "Listen, when I call you . . . ah, nah, forget it," and she said "What?" and he said "No, another dopey attempt at a joke again, and I don't want to make myself look worse than I already have," and she said "What are you talking about? We'll speak," and looked at Beth who, already behind the chair, pushed her through the living room to the back hallway. He got himself a drink, wondered what she had to do—something personal probably, but that was her business—and sat on the couch, his back to the living room, since he didn't want to catch her eye again and do that ridiculous smile and wave and moving mouth routine. "Hello. Goodbye. I don't know what my wave means and I'm not really saying something and the smile's automatic." He do the right thing before? he thought, sipping his drink and staring at the floor. Good, sitting here could be used to think out some things. He actually going to see her? Didn't just say it and maybe even meant it at the time but won't call? He could do that? Got cold feet when he realized how sick and incapacitated she probably is? If he doesn't want to see her should he still call but say something like he's sort of involved with someone or he's too tied up now with his work and he'll call her soon as it's done? A deadline, he could say? No, those are ridiculous lies she'd either see through and get more hurt by than if he hadn't called at all or she could say "Why's that"—to either—"have to make a difference? Do what you wish, but I think anybody can find a little free time. We had a pleasant talk, we could continue it over a coffee, which is all I was thinking of anyway." He still attracted to her? What if he became more attracted to her—enamored, even—and she in some way to him? Why jump so far ahead? Jesus: one call, a single date, take it from there, because what's the big deal? And she's expecting him to call and he thinks he wants to see her again a lot. Does he? She was nice, she was bright, she was lots more that he likes, and that she's in a wheelchair and maybe can't walk and possibly other things wrong with her shouldn't change it that much. Love stuff, that's a different story. But again, why shoot so far ahead? There are other things though, right? He wouldn't feel a bit uncomfortable just walking on the street with her if she was in a wheelchair? Less so pushing her if she had to be pushed, because then he'd be behind rather than alongside and doing something useful. Alongside, two or so feet above her, leaning in lower and closer every so often while he walked so he could hear her and she him over the traffic noises, he might feel somewhat self-conscious or just, well, something like that. Oh come off it. You're with someone, she happens to be in a wheelchair, you make certain accommodations for her, so is it just a matter of what other people you don't even know think?

Passersby, or people you do know whom you might meet? Truth is, most would only be thinking good things about it, the few who thought anything at all except "Oh, what a pity this poor pretty young woman in a wheelchair if it's something permanent," but he wouldn't be doing it for that either, of course. And he did go through it with his dad. True, his father. Last two years of his life. He was the main one to push him, for by the time they got him to accept the fact that if he wanted to get out and around he had to be in a wheelchair, he didn't have the strength to push it himself or the coordination to operate a motorized one. As he said before: up, down, in, out, "See a curb cut coming up? . . . Watch your feet, lady. . . . Excuse me, please, coming through, coming through." If things go okay their first meeting they can continue seeing each other awhile, even if he started something with someone else. Though maybe not. But for now, once a month for coffee or dinner. Or every other week, or not so systematically pre-arranged as that, because then she might think he was only doing it out of some kind of duty. Or for a movie or play or museum or something to do with music: concert, opera, even a ballet. He in the seat next to the empty orchestra space set aside for her wheelchair. Or she in the aisle, he in the seat right beside her—that is, if it's difficult for her to get from her wheelchair into a regular seat. So it's done, yes? Don't even think anymore about it. Have another drink, or maybe just a glass of wine or beer. He'll call, they'll talk and see what they want to do, if she still wants to meet. If she leaves the eating arrangements up to him: dinner in a relatively inexpensive Indian or Japanese place, as he'll want to pick up the tab. If she insists beforehand on paying her share or dividing the bill in half, then maybe a better restaurant. If she picks the place he's sure, since he couldn't have looked well off to her by any stretch and she's only a little more than a grad student herself, it wouldn't be a very expensive one. And it's still possible she isn't always in a wheelchair, he thought. Tonight might be the anomaly, or for the last few days. Couple of days ago or so she suddenly wasn't feeling secure on her feet, he'll say. This, the host said—though she didn't claim to be an expert on the disease; just stuff she picked up from a friend who has it—could go on for weeks or just days. Then she's back on her feet with a cane or even without one, maybe a trifle worse off than before it started, or using a walker, even one of those with wheels. He'll just have to see. Of course what he hopes for, he thought, is that she recovers completely from this latest attack, as the host called it and if that's what it is, and walks on her own without any assistance, or close to it. He stayed at the party another half-hour, walked around, had a selection of desserts and a semisweet dessert wine, which was so good he had two more glasses of it, at the dessert wine table chatted briefly with a few people about nothing, really. The two or three women there he thought, by their looks and something they were giving off, he could get interested in seemed pretty much tied to their men, and said goodnight to the host and left. In bed at home, while reading, he decided he'll call her tomorrow morning, and because it'd be Sunday, no earlier than eleven. Afternoon would be better, he thought, putting his book down again—but only a few minutes after—since she might get to bed late tonight and also need to make up for a shortage of sleep the last week. For the next week he thought of calling her every day but something always stopped him mostly: maybe, because of her condition, it just wouldn't be a good idea. If he did want to get involved with her, he thought—if it reached that point, he's saying, for it has been almost two years since he saw a woman steadily for even a few weeks and he hasn't been to bed with one for months—what were the chances of anything really developing between them? For instance: for the last few years he's been wanting to get married (it's true he doesn't make much money, so in that respect isn't much of a catch) and have a child right away—he was forty-two and didn't want the age difference between him and the kid to be that great—and she might not want to conceive or carry one because it could send her illness into a steep decline. That's what something he read about it said. He'd checked a book on it out of his neighborhood library—had gone there to see what was on the new-release fiction shelves—and saw her disease in big yellow letters in the title of the book on the subject in the new-release nonfiction section next to the fiction one: A Guide for Patients and Their Families. He read through enough of the book to know that if she had the worst kind of case of it or that was where she was heading, and about twenty percent of those who have the disease are in that category, it would definitely be a major problem for him and probably scare him off. Visual and hearing loss could be a problem too for people with the disease. Constipation, incontinence, just getting on and off the toilet and dressing and eating and swallowing, though she seemed to see and hear all right and hold her fork okay and had no trouble getting her food down, little she ate that night. He once even had the phone receiver in his hand and was about to dial her number. She has to know something's wrong that he didn't call, he thought. If it did end up where they went out several times and kissed

and fondled each other one night and then wanted to go to bed together, how would they do it if she was, as so many people with the
disease are, the book said, partially paralyzed or unable to move or
maintain control over certain parts of her body? If she was in the
wheelchair, and he cant see himself kissing and fondling her while she
was in one—kissing her deeply, he means, but fondling her in any
way—could she just lift herself off it onto the bed or use some device
like a board to slide herself off and then back on? Or would he have to
lift her out of the chair onto the bed, undress her if she couldn't undress herself and eventually pry her legs apart if they were locked so he
could slip himself inside her? Does someone—an aide—help her get on
and off the toilet at home? She said she lived alone. So maybe someone comes in during the day, and also gets her ready for bed at night,
and is also there in the morning to help her get out of bed and onto
the toilet and washed and dressed. How does she teach, if all the rest
is so? Someone could push her to class, pick her up after and get her
home or to her office or the library or wherever she needs to go, and
shop and even cook for her. Her parents might help out a lot too; relatives, friends. "She might also have a motor cart or motorized wheelchair. Maybe the building she lives in is just for the handicapped, so
everything in it is much easier for her. Ramps everywhere, wider door-
ways, lower toilets and mirrors and sinks and stoves. But he's probably
carrying this too far again, he thought. It can't be as bad as he's making out, or it could be but he doesn't think it is. Something more about
it would have come out in her conversation with him, indicating how
bad it sometimes is for her. Or in the way she moved; some involuntary motion in her face or hands or legs, as the book said. Spasticity—
or contractions; he forgets what the difference is, if there is one—
which many people with the disease have, not just the worst cases, and
can be very painful. Maybe she took some powerful pills that reduced
all these symptoms for the night, so she could get through the party
without losing physical control over certain parts of her body. Pills, or
a drug in any form, which she can only take sparingly, like steroids.
She had no speech problem either, which hits a lot of people with the
disease, and no sudden fatigue, nodding off, things like that. It can af-
fect the brain—"intellectual deficits," was the way the book put it—
and memory. But she was one of the brightest women he'd ever spoken
to: sharp, witty, articulate, and. also funny and lively. She can't be in
that worst category, he thought, and he bets she's able to do most
things on her own like cooking and going to the toilet and showering

and dressing, et cetera. Just call, he told himself. One date—what the hell's that? And he wants to know more about her and also how she manages with the disease. But more than that, a lot more. Her brains, yes, and her looks, and he was definitely attracted to her in a sexual way too. If he doesn't want to see her again after that first time they get together (of course it can be the other way around too), he'll make it clear it has nothing to do with her illness. Not that she'll believe him—he can just imagine the things that go through her head, sitting in that chair. But maybe, if he acts convincingly enough—if he does a good job acting convincingly, he's saying—she will. So he called. She said she was happy to hear from him; he said "Same here, talking to you again, and I'm sorry I wasn't able to call sooner, but I won't bother you with all the reasons why I couldn't." They talked about a number of things for a long time. A play she'd seen. He'd heard mixed things about it, he said; what'd she think? and she gave a devastating review of it and also of the audience who for some reason thought it was participatory theater and he asked what she meant and she explained. "You ought to print that," he said. "The whole review, word for word in the act way—the *exact* way; I don't know where that came from—you said it. Of course: *act: theater.*" Then he said "Listen, we should meet, what do you say? It's what I originally called for," and she said she'd love to. What would he like to do? Coffee, lunch, movie, hour in a museum? "A movie," he said. "That way we wouldn't have to talk, for we obviously have nothing to say to each other." She laughed, said "Does seem that way." Oh, I'm glad she laughed, he thought. That was such a stupid remark. She's making me look good. But he better be more careful with what he says from now on. Think, you idiot. Don't just say the first thing that crosses your mind. "Actually . . ." she said, and he thought uh-oh, she's having second thoughts because of what he said, "does breakfast interest you? I love breakfast out on weekends, if it's not too early, and I know a good place around here." "Then let's do it this Saturday, whatever time you want," and she said "Sunday's a better day for me this weekend, do you mind? Or we could make it the next Saturday." "How could I mind? Come on. Sunday's fine." They set a time when they'd meet in her building's lobby. "You'll recognize me, right?" he said. "If not, I'll be wearing a rose tattoo in my lapel," and she said "I'll look for it," no laugh this time and he knew he'd made not so much a dumb remark but one that didn't make much sense if you didn't get the references. But that rose tattoo one: admit it; it really didn't make much sense. She must be wondering about him, he thought, and he wouldn't be surprised if she phoned him before Sunday—she took his number, "just in case," she said—calling it off. She was waiting for him when he went into the lobby. They said hello, smiled, shook hands. She looked so pretty, hair sort of shining from the light, flowing almost like water over her shoulders. "So, should we go?" he said. The doorman had to open the revolving door so she could wheel herself through. That the right verb for it? he thought. Or "move, push, propel"? Which word do you use when the person in the wheelchair wheels herself? Never thought of it before, and none of those seem right now, so he'll stick with the first word that came to him unless she uses a different one for it. He said outside "You don't have a motorized chair or anything like that? Because I'd think it'd be easier, if you're going some distance and aren't going to be taking a taxi." "I did; a motor cart. But it fell over with me in it a few times—deep ruts or unsuspected slopes in the sidewalk, mostly caused by burgeoning tree roots underneath—and one of those times I broke my shoulder and another time I cracked my skull." "Oh, I'm sorry, that's awful," he said, and thought: funny; he thinks of her shoulders and a minute later she tells him she broke one. And he's constantly reminded how brainy she is and she then says she cracked her skull, though that's less of a coincidence. "Can I push you then?" and she said "I'm doing fine on level ground, thank you. The curb cuts down here are fairly new and smooth, and it's needed exercise for my arms and hands. I could use, if you wouldn't mind, help getting up the hill on a Hundred-twelfth. Unless you want to continue on Riverside to a Hundred-tenth, which is a flat side street, and go to the restaurant from Broadway." "No, I'll push you up a Hundred-twelfth. Though the restaurant's between a Hundred-thirteenth and -twelfth, isn't it?—I thought I saw it from the bus. So why don't I push you up a Hundred-thirteenth?" and she said "That street's the steepest in the neighborhood; I doubt an unmotorized wheelchair's ascended it successfully in years." "Ah, it can't be that bad," he said. "And I pushed my father in these for I don't know how long, so I'm familiar with them. Anything to get him out. It improved his disposition—got him away from the house. You know, outside doings and fresh air, and ice cream cones, which he liked. Across the park, up the steepest hills there. Pilgrim Hill, from Fifth, if you know it, and Eagle hill inside, and not so light a guy in not as light a chair," and she said "If you want, you can give it a try." They reached a Hundred-thirteenth. It's going to be a bitch getting her up it, he saw, but he said he would, so just do it, though next time listen to her. He got about halfway to the top, could barely push the chair farther—he was already digging his feet into the ground—and said "I give up, you were right," and she said "I'm sorry," and he said "For what? My problem—thinks he knows better—not yours," and turned her around and going down the hill he had to grip the handles tight to keep the chair from rolling away from him. Oh boy, that would be something—awful, awful, and shut his eyes and shook his head to get rid of the thought. He looked at her as they went slowly down the hill. She had her eyes closed and was smiling as if enjoying the breeze or something: river smells, the air. "Not too cold for you?" and she said without turning around "I always overdress for the damp or cooler weather. I have to; otherwise I could freeze just sitting here." He shouldn't have said anything, he thought; just should have let her continue enjoying whatever it was. Maybe being with him has something to do with it also; who knows. At the bottom of the street he started pushing her to a Hundred-twelfth. He knew she could wheel herself, but he had his hands on the handles and didn't know what he could do or say to take them away. Let go and step to the side of the chair, he supposed, so she'd know he wasn't pushing anymore and she'd have to take over? Wouldn't seem right. And it was easy, pushing, and he felt good doing it and she didn't seem to mind. She stared ahead as they went, hands in her lap, smiling again, and when they got to a Hundred-twelfth she said "Hill doesn't look too much for you?" and he said "Nah, it's a cinch. But how could two streets so close together have such different declivities, or the opposite word of that—acclivities, I think, but that one seems so . . . I don't know; unnatural," and she said "It's not one I remember reading or hearing or looking up, but I bet you're right. The amazing thing is that the other side of the street has even less of a slope than this one," and he said "So I guess that's the one you usually take," and she said "Most of the time, if I'm heading downtown, though never if I'm pushing myself. But this one has more obstacles and cracks and in some places isn't as wide, so it's a toss-up." He pushed her up the street and didn't find it steep at all. She pointed out Bank Street College across the street and he said "Oh yeah, I recognize it now. Once had lunch in the cafeteria downstairs, but I forgot it was around here," and she said "The breakfasts aren't bad there either. Someone told me Dean and DeLuca were doing the food. But you have to pass through several heavy doors and take the elevator, and anyway, it's closed," and he said "No, I wasn't thinking of it for that. I'm sure the place we're going to is fine," and she said "I didn't mean it that way either." It was with a woman he was seeing who was getting a master's in museum curating; could that be right? School of education giving a curating degree? Her name? Barbara? Beatrice? Bernice? Come on, it was only three to four years ago. It'll come back to him, he thought, if he thinks of it again. Liked her, and she was smart and great in bed and pretty, but another one who dropped him flat—she knew he had no dough and little prospect of getting a good job, so marriage and having a baby, which they both said they wanted one day, and realize just continuing, with him for a long time were out of the question—a few days after she met another guy. Bitch, was what he yelled at her apartment door when she refused to let him in and probably was with her new guy inside, and the name he used whenever he'd normally refer to her after that. Ms. Bitch, to be exact. At the corner of Broadway she said "I can wheel myself from here on," and he said "Really, I don't mind," and she said "It doesn't trigger sad memories of your father?" and he said "I didn't mind pushing him either. I in fact liked it. It slowed my pace, for I tend to walk too fast and miss seeing interesting things on the street, and with my dad . . . well . . ." and felt his throat choking up but managed "Anyway . . . enough." "The truth is I'd prefer doing it on my own now, thanks," and he said "Of course," and took his hands off: and walked beside her. He held the restaurant door open for her and then the inside door while he kept the outside one open with an outstretched foot. "You want to sit in one of the chairs or stay in your own?" and she said "I'm fine as I am," and started moving a chair away from a table and he did it for her, didn't know where to put it because all the unoccupied tables seemed to have the right number of chairs at them and the place didn't have waiters and he didn't see any clean-up people and didn't want to bother anyone eating to ask if he could slip a chair into the empty space at their table, so he lifted it over his head and carried it—"hot chair, hot chair," he said and she laughed—to a wall on the other side of the room where there were three highchairs lined up and a couple of small tables, one face down on the other. "About your father," she said when he sat down across from her and looked at the huge blackboard above the food counter with today's date and specials, "I want you to know I didn't mean to assume, make sad or probe and I apologize if it might have come out that way," and he said "Believe me, it never entered my head. Now for a serious question: What do you think I should order?" He went to the counter, got their food, she had tea, he went back for several refills of coffee, they talked almost non-stop: art, movies, poetry, their families, ancestries, his work and her work and scholarship. About her illness—he didn't ask; it just came out—she said sometimes she's able to walk with assistance, mostly she's in this chair, it hits her hard and retracts for a short time like that and she's sorry to say she's always a little worse after. It's a big nuisance and a bit scary and she's tried and is trying everything there is to arrest it or slow it down—unfortunately there doesn't exist so far a treatment to reverse her condition. When she needs help she has friends or professionals or her parents to look after her or do some of the things for her she can't or does clumsily and sometimes hazardously, like making coffee and burning rice and toast. He took care of the check—"Please," he said when she protested, "it doesn't come to much and because it's self-service we don't have to leave a tip," and she said "I always like to leave something for whomever busses our table," and put down two dollars. "Anyway," he said, "if it did cost a lot I swear I wouldn't pretend to be such a sport. Though if you want you can even things up by treating me to dinner some night," and she said "All right," and he said "Only kidding; it wouldn't be fair. For dinner, we go Dutch, if that's okay," and was thinking why's he saying this? Does he mean it? and she said "We'll see," and her expression didn't give either possibility away. Outside, she said she had various chores to do on Broadway and that she hoped to see him again. He was about to say "But I already mentioned we'll have dinner out one of these days," but said "Good, same here; it was fun. But how will you get down the hill to your building, if you don't go by way of a Hundred-tenth, and then let the doorman know you're outside and he has to open the revolving door?" and she said "The way I always do." They shook hands—he stuck his out first, after he'd said "Good, you got things under control. So I'll see ya." He wanted to kiss her cheek— something be almost automatically did with women friends he says goodbye to—but didn't want to bend down to do it and possibly bungle it, kissing her ear or hair and end up discomposing them both, and she started pushing herself uptown and he headed for the bus stop on a Hundred-twelfth. Actually, the subway would be faster, he thought when he got to the corner and was waiting for a chance to cross, and he wouldn't mind getting home sooner and getting some work in, since weekends were when he did most of it. Then she was suddenly in his head again and he turned around to look at her and saw her moving slowly, hands on the wheels going back and forth and though the street had only a slight incline, the pushing seemed hard. Several people walking by glanced at her and one couple stopped to stare from behind. A leashed dog tugged to get up to her and she waved at it and its owner moved his head as if apologizing to her and pulled the dog back. It must be such a struggle for her in that chair, almost everything, he thought. Getting out, getting around and back, shopping, just carrying packages, what do you do outside when you have to take a crap or pee? Always being much lower down than anyone on the street but little kids, dogs like that big one before and some possibly lunging at her with teeth drawn or trying to lick her face, though she might like the friendly licking part of it, and all those pitying looks from people and she must have caught several times some of the ones who stop behind her and shake their heads and stare. He saw some of it when he walked with her but less so than when she's alone now. He felt lousy for her also, way her body was slouched to the side crookedly, as if she was in a seating position she couldn't straighten herself out of and which might be painful and what she needed was someone from behind to lift her under the arms to reposition her. She wheeled left to a drugstore. He hadn't helped her off or on with her jacket in the restaurant—didn't think she wanted him to; sensed she felt that anything fairly simple she could do herself, even if she didn't do it that well, was better than getting help from somebody—and the jacket collar wasn't folded down right, one side sticking up and the other was down. She reached for the door handle and tried pulling it open. Held the handle with what seemed like two or three fingers, but the door went back and she let go. Too far away to get a good grip on it, it seemed. She wheeled closer, grabbed the handle with her whole hand now—so the distance problem must have been it—and pulled, but only got it a few inches out. Either the door was too heavy or unwieldy for her or some part of the chair was keeping it from opening farther. Jesus, he thought, why would she go to that store if she knew the door was so tough to open? He looked around and saw another drugstore a block down on the other side of Broadway. But maybe that's the point. It's across this wide avenue, so more difficult to get to—the cars, trucks, curb cuts, good possibility of not making it across on a single light and being stranded on the traffic island, which has no curb cuts so she'd have to wait for the light to change there and not on the protected pedestrian space but in the street—and that store might have a narrower entrance and aisles than this one and a step up while this one—and he looked at it—didn't seem to have any. He bet most of her shopping was done on this side of Broadway and only on the other side when she had someone with her to get her up the curb of the traffic island and so forth. Should he go and help? As he thought before regarding her jacket: does he think she'd mind? She's independent—that came out in their conversation—and persistent, he can see, so he's sure she thinks the less. . . . Just then a woman pulling a shopping cart rushed over to her, said something, they both laughed, the woman opened the door for her, she wheeled herself inside and the woman went back to her cart on the sidewalk. He imagined her wheeling down a drugstore aisle looking for something and finding it but it was too high to reach so asking a customer or one of the store workers . . . but enough, drop it already, and he continued to the subway station, started down its steps but then thought ah, hell with getting to his work so soon, subways aren't good for thinking, busses aren't much better, or maybe one can get some good thoughts on them but for him his best mostly came on solitary city walks when he put his mind to it, so he'll walk the rest of the way home. He wanted to give himself time to think about her and what he was going to do next. Next, meaning, is he going to call her again? First of all, he thought, how does he feel about her? That should be the only reason he'd call or not. What's he talking about?—he has to call. And he has to see her again also—at least once—so he means the only reason to continue seeing her after the next time. Well, he thought, she's quite nice, very, maybe as nice as any woman he's known. And interesting, pretty, lovely everything, lovely in every way he can think of, unlovely in no way, really; a soft woman—soft is the word for her, just as anger, he supposes, could be the word for him. She's almost exactly what he thought she'd be when he called her the other day: sweet, deep, very smart, refined, and with a good sense of humor—she made him laugh several times with her quick wit and wordplay—so all those things and more and also someone who's interested and involved in many of the things he is and feels the same about many of them too, a lot of which he found out today. All that's important. Same religion, even, which never mattered before and which would be a change for him and might even be a good thing; who knows? It certainly can't hurt, since neither of them practices or observes it in any way and their interest in it—hers, from what she said about it today—is mainly for the poetry and wisdom and so forth and sort of *where they come from* and in some parts of it can't escape. So he was sitting there with her before and thinking yes, yes, yes and her voluptuous body and long he wants to say lambent reddish-blond hair, but she's also twelve years younger than he, which can be okay in different ways including the younger body and outlook and face. So they'll go out for dinner, he thought, just as he told her he would, and if she wants to go to one— he's usually interested, if something good's around—a movie after, if there's a way of getting her there, for the theater in her neighborhood has an awful picture playing, he saw on the way up, so it'll have to be one they can only get to by cab or bus. Subways, she said, are all but impossible for her to travel on, with only a few accessible stations in the city and once you've reached your destination you never know if the car doors won't slam shut on the chair and if the people rushing into the train won't prevent you from getting off and then if the elevator to the street will be working. True, if she were healthier and ambulatory and her life, as she cheerfully hinted, didn't look so grim, he wouldn't think twice about seeing her again and again. He would have thought when she showed some interest in him "Boy, am I lucky, meeting someone like her, but she's too beautiful and intelligent and elegant and everything else for her to really become interested in me," and that sort of thing. He would have made a date with her before he said goodbye just now. Maybe for tomorrow night: dinner, movie, something like that. Tried to move it along swiftly, get her into bed quickly. He'd probably really fall for her, he's saying, rather than be so reluctant or hesitant or whatever's the word in wanting to see her again. And do everything he could to make her—he means, help her—fall for him. Not show any anger, for one thing, or any disagreeable side to him, including the fakery he'd need to hide these things, till she was hooked. And that's the goddamn shame of it, he thought. He meets the ideal woman in almost every way—his dream girl, as they used to say—and she has this disease which could be incurable or many years away from there being any help for it, is what she said, and so will conceivably only get worse and where she possibly can't or won't have children because of it and who knows how it's affected her sex life. Though if she didn't have it guys would be beating down her door to go out with her, while now her condition and being stuck in that chair most of the time and all that they might imagine about it probably keeps them away, leaving the field pretty much to him, though he could be wrong on that. So, did he decide? To see her again, yes, though that decision he'd already made before he started thinking of her while he walked, but nothing about what to do beyond that. He'll see her once and then he'll see; not enough? He stopped at a bookstore along the way and browsed but didn't buy, though wanted to, because he was a bit short these days and also had plenty of books at home he'd bought and wanted to read, and at a market a few blocks from his he got some things to eat tonight: cheese, half-pound container of cole slaw, couple slices of smoked turkey, two tomatoes and a jar of French mustard on sale and a few loose carrots and a Bialy and roll, wished the liquor stores were open today so he could get a bottle of vodka—he only had a little left at home but nearly a whole bottle of rum—and an inexpensive wine. I bet I'm going to drink while I read and eat tonight till I get so drowsy or even soused that I fall asleep where I'm sitting and then have to drag myself to bed, he thought as he walked up his street. Unless a friend calls before he starts drinking or no more than a couple of drinks into it and suggests something like a local bar for a snack and a couple of beers or a movie. Then he'll probably just drink himself to sleep reading when he gets home. Anything to do with her? Sure, what does he think? even if half the nights of the last few months he's sat in his Morris chair and drank and read and ate, all the food cut into pieces he can eat with his fingers off the plate or paper towel on the side table, though he rarely drank so much where he fell asleep in the chair. But why? Because, of course, he was very much touched by her today. Not touched so much as depressed and upset by what he sees as the goddamn misery of her life. He feels miserable for her, is what he's saying, that she has to be stuck like this and then put on this great face at how she's dealing with it, which he thinks has to be fakery on her part so he or whoever she's with won't be turned off by her dejection and frustration and self-pity and envy and everything else she must be feeling. If only he could do something for her, but what a stupid thought. Why so? Because what could he do but continue to go out with her and marry her and try to have a baby with her and take care of her for the rest of her life no matter how bad off she gets? Then if there were some new kind of treatment or miracle drug that'd just about cure her or at least get her up walking, but why even bother thinking of it?—she's already said. He went into his building, checked his mailbox in case someone had left a note in it or one of the tenants had received a letter of his by mistake the past week and shoved it through his box while he was out, which has happened. It'd be interesting though, he thought as he unlocked the front door and started up the stairs to his floor, or not interesting or curious or anything like that but just something—what is it with him with words sometimes?—as to what he'll finally do about calling her in the next few days. For really, after all his thinking and deciding and deep concern and sadness for her and so forth, he's still not sure if seeing her again won't eventually make things worse for her than not calling. So we're on that again? he thought, unlocking his apartment door. But that'd be two dates since the party and she'd probably think he's getting interested in her. Well, he is interested in her, he thought, going to the kitchen, but there are all these other things. He doesn't need to make a final final decision immediately, right? So just put your stuff away and have a drink earlier than you usually do, while you finish today's newspaper. Then after maybe a second drink, take or give in to a nap, since he could never get any work in and drink at the same time, or nothing any good. And it's also Sunday and midafternoon and he has a lot of sleep to catch up on and probably won't have the time for it after today till next weekend. Maybe, he thought, opening the freezer for ice, when he wakes up from his nap and has something to eat and a cup or two of coffee, he'll be able to sit down and work. He called the next day. She said she was just on her way out and was very glad to hear from him but she only had a minute to talk. "A taxi service will be downstairs in five minutes." "Oh, you take those things?" he said and she said "When it's necessary, but I have to tell them it has to be a car with a lot of space in the trunk." "I've always wondered: are they expensive?" and she said "Once you get inside you have to arrange the price ahead of time, but it comes to the same—or on short trips, maybe a bit more—as a regular cab. I have a good service if you want their number." "Nah, I rarely use cabs, and hailing one in the street's okay with me. So, I'll be quick. Dinner tomorrow or the next free evening you got?" They had dinner in a neighborhood restaurant. He'd said in her apartment "We could go some other place further away if you want to take a livery cab," and she said "I'm feeling a little less able today to do things like transfer myself from chair to seat, so I'd like to play it safe and stay close to home." "I can assist you—I used to with my father for years," and she said "I'm sorry but I don't think you know enough yet about my condition for me to take the chance. I think I've told you: I've broken a few bones in falls, hence the gnarled nose." "No, I never noticed. And I won't say 'Let me see.'" He wheeled her to the restaurant, wheeled her back. Had a problem at one corner getting the chair up a high curb where there was no cut till she said "Turn the chair tippers upside down but don't forget to turn them right again or else I could fall backwards on my head." "My father's chair," he said, "wasn't so state-of-the-artish, and I remember those accidents." He went inside her building to tell the doorman she was outside and could he open the door. After she wheeled herself into the lobby, he said "So, I think you can make it up okay, and that was lots of fun again, thanks," and she said "Like to come up for a coffee or drink? My father brought back this wonderful cognac, he said, from Spain, and I wouldn't mind trying it myself." "I love cognac," he said, "but how can it be from Spain?" "Brandy, then? It has a name I keep forgetting. 'Find the door'? 'Fond of Law'? Spanish obviously isn't one of my languages." "Oh, there are others besides Polish, Russian and French?" She gave two more she was fluent in and said she actually knew enough Spanish to speak it but can't read it well, or not the more literary novels and poetry. "Me, strictly a *touché* of *francais*, from a half-year in France dix-cinq years ago, which is why I can roll *cognac* so easily off my lips. Yeah, I'd like to come up," when the elevator came, "in case I didn't say and the offer still holds." At her door she said "Would you do me a favor?" and gave him the key. "Turn it only once to the left and it opens, but please don't turn it hard because it's a ravenous lock and short of iron intake, I'm sure, and has already eaten three of these keys." "You ought to get the lock cylinder changed," and she said "The super says it's a perfectly good one and that I'm just not turning the key right. He may have a point, what with my hands the way they are sometimes on the harder tasks, which is why I asked you to open it now. One sudden involuntary manual jerk and the key's gone." "Maybe the lock needs a lubricating oil or something. I can bring some for you next time we meet and apply it," and she said "Any help like that to make my life easier would be very welcome." Inside, she told him where to find the brandy, a brandy snifter for him and a plastic mug for her, "since, as I nearly demonstrated in the restaurant, the stem kind have a way of slipping out of my hands." She excused herself to go to the bathroom. "This might take time, so have a drink or two." He got the brandy and glasses in the kitchen. When he came back he saw her in the little hall between the bedroom and living room, having trouble squeezing the chair through the bathroom door. "Can I help you?" and she said "No thanks; it's always a bit of a struggle but I always get through. Same in reverse." "Maybe you could get a different kind of door, like a sliding one, or not have any door at all, just a curtain," and she said "And when other people are here?" and he said "Then a sliding door built at the entrance to the hallway." "We'll talk about it later," and she tugged some more and was in and then seemed to have trouble shutting the door. He poured himself a brandy, sniffed it and drank. He heard the toilet flush about ten minutes later, and five minutes after that the water in the sink turned on. God, does she have problems, he thought; every fucking move. What did he get himself into, coming here, and if she suddenly gets romantic with him, what does he do? But she won't try anything like that, he thought, pouring another brandy. She doesn't at all seem the type to make the first move on the guy. When she was well and walking she might have been different. And she has to be aware of his trepidation and just the whole newness of it for him, and that if anything's going to happen it's got to take time to minimize the strangeness of it. So they'll drink, talk some more, and then he should go, maybe kiss her cheek on his way out and say he'll see her, even if he isn't sure he will. He got up to look at the titles of the books on some of the bookshelves and then at the river. Nice view, he thought, eight, or because she's on the eighth, seven floors up. Compared to his and the amount of space he has and decrepitude of his building, a great place, and good security. She said she's had it for years—long before she got ill—or first an apartment in the rear and be-cause of some deal she made with the landlord when she moved to the front, the rent's not so bad. No wonder she'd put up with narrow doors and most of the built-in stuff constructed for someone standing up and her having to summon the doorman every time she wants to get into the building. Rather than move, as she said she was eligible to, into a city-subsidized building with studio apartments especially designed for single people in wheelchairs and which might look out on a dreary street or wall. He heard her chair backing out of the bathroom a few minutes later. "Again, can I be of any help?" and she said "Thanks, but I have a system. It's slow but it works, and for some reason leaving's easier than entering." She kept moving the chair back and forth a few inches till she was out the door and able to swivel around to face the living room. "There," she said, "not such a big problem, just a long time in returning; I'm sorry. I hope you had a couple of brandies while I was missing in bathroom," and he said "Just a sniff or two. I poured but I was waiting for you." He poured some brandy into her mug and gave it to her. "So, where do we sit?" and she said "You sit anywhere you want. But please hold this?" giving him the mug, "so I can wheel the chair near you when you do choose a place." He said "The couch looks comfortable and if I sit on the left side of it I won't have to move the cocktail table for you. But is it really necessary to even have this table? Excuse me, and I probably don't know what I'm talking about, but if I were you I think I'd clear the room of everything but the essential furniture so I could move around freely." "That table serves several purposes for me, like where I put down things like my glasses, books and that mug, and I can also raise my feet on it, which I from time to time have to do. And I want the room to look like a normal one, though I can appreciate what you mean about moving around freely; the thought is delightful. As for the couch, either side is fine for me, and I can always push the table away myself. I work out, you know. Weights, pulleys, a stretch bar and this huge rig called a Murphy press. They're all in my unnormal-looking bedroom and a few of them are bolted to the floor or wall. My hands and legs might sometimes be a gummy or gelatinous mess, but I'm pretty strong otherwise from the waist up and I apparently, according to my physical therapist, have very strong upper arms. So don't try to fool with me, mister. Sorry, just lame-joking." "I was wondering how to take it. Let me feel your arm muscles," and she turned serious and said "If you don't mind, and I realize I was the one who first brought up the subject, but it just seems too stupid a thing to do, so I'd rather not." "Okay, okay, then I won't let you feel mine. Now that was dumb too, wasn't it," and she shrugged. They drank; she looked away: at her mug, a painting on the wall, and when he looked away, at him. He's losing her, he thought. And don't say anything either about a narrower wheelchair for the bathroom and such. She's sure to have thought of it and the chair she's in might be the narrowest made and she'll think he's too free with his unthought-out ideas or simply doesn't give her brains enough credit. "So, silent period over," he said after about a minute. "I can't stand it," and she said "I agree; it can be so self-generating and unrewarding. How about if we go back to the last good place we left off?" "And that was? . . . your drink," which he just noticed on the cocktail table. "So you were right about that, of course," and held it out to her. She reached for it, hand was shaking, so she cupped the mug with both hands as she took it from him. "I hate for you to see so many things wrong at once, but nothing I can do," and he said "Don't worry about it; I don't. And wait!" when she was about to drink, "we didn't do this yet, even if we already drank," and raised his glass—"You don't have to raise yours"—and was about to say something when she said "No toast; there's no call for it. Let's just swallow silently and continue our talk or meander at will," and they drank. "I have to put the mug down," she said, and held it out for him and he put it on the table. They talked some more. He hadn't quite known what his toast would be. Something where all the lines rhymed with "ight" had popped into his head just before he was going to make it. Something like "To the night, short of moonlight, river-filled window sight, may both our lives all our

lives go right, and my apologies for this toasty fright," and something
with "delight." In a way she saved him from embarrassing himself. And
while they talked he thought she looks so good, so pretty, lovely and
sweet, way her hair shines, those multicolored light eyes and soft smile
and perfect teeth. He was feeling good too from the wine at dinner,
three glasses to her one. And now—he poured himself another: "Is it
all right?" and she said "Please, you're my guest"—a third brandy and
thought "No more after this; brandy's strong stuff but awful in the
morning." And after he poured for himself he held the bottle up to her
and gave that expression and she said "My poor stomach, and there's
tomorrow and work and its preparation to think of. And one's plenty,
the way you poured, and see my mug?" and held it at an angle so he
could see inside: it still had some but was now spilling out. "Oh damn,"
she said, and he said "Why? It missed the rug," and wiped it up with
his handkerchief and she said "You can leave that with me to wash,"
and he said "Nah, I'll hold it to my nose on the ride home and think
of my wiping the brandy off the floor." And their knees were touching—he'd moved his closer to hers so they would and she didn't pull
back . . . and because of all of this he leaned forward to kiss her lips.
First, after he'd folded up his handkerchief so the dry part was out and
put it back into his pants pocket, he took her hand and held it while
they talked, both of them darting looks at his hand holding hers, and
smiling. Then he brought her hand to his face and kissed the knuckles
and she said "That felt nice but I bet doing it to the other side would
feel even better," and he kissed her palm and wrist and she closed her
eyes and made the sounds "um, um," and he said "You know, with your
eyes closed," and she opened them, "I probably could have stolen a real
kiss from you, but I thought instead I'd ask if you'd mind," and she said
"Go ahead, it's okay with me," and that was when he leaned forward
and she moved a little to him and they kissed. They kissed several
times, one after the other. Didn't speak much, looked at each other
briefly between kisses some of those times, smiled, but mostly kept
their eyes closed. He was able to get his arms around her back and pull
her to him and she kept her arms around his neck but without holding
on. She was a great kisser—soft lips, beautiful breath, just enough pressure, and her lips stayed on his for as long as he wanted. A couple of
times when their lips separated she said "Ooh, gosh, whew," without
opening her eyes, and once with her eyes open "You're making me
dizzy, that was so nice." "Ha," he said, and she said "It's true. If I were
standing and you weren't holding me like you're doing, I'm sure I'd fall

down." "Ha, again," he said, "and I think I better go. It's getting late. I have to also get to work tomorrow, though no preparation—I just go in and do and do." "Good idea, your going," she said. "This kissing was interfering with my breathing and the whole thing was clearly getting out of control." "That's not bad," he said. "I know, I know, they're good, but we both agree just not for right now." "I'll call," he said, standing up. He had a hard-on but didn't care and she didn't seem to notice although it was sticking straight out in his pants. She wheeled herself to the front closet, he got his jacket and muffler from it, looked down and his fly was now flat, and tried unlocking the door. "How do you do this?" and she said "I locked the top one—protective reflex— which I never do when I leave, since I like carrying only one house key. Judging by the position of the bottom lock, it needs to be turned to the right and the top one stays as is." He unlocked and opened the door and said "I mean it, I'll call." "I hope so." "I will, why wouldn't I? I want to. One more kiss?" and she said "Shut the door first?" He did and she put her arms out and he leaned over to kiss her. It didn't work as a big kiss. His body was too twisted, and something about the angle so their faces didn't quite meet. He got on one knee and brought her face down to his and they kissed. "That was better, no?" and she said "The you-stand-up me-sit-down kind is essentially good for thrill-less pecks, like quick out-of-the-house goodbyes. If I could switch subjects? Would you mind, if you didn't call in an indeterminate number of days, if I called you?" and he said "No, call me, anytime you want, but I'll still be calling you," and gave his phone number. "You'll remember it?" and she said it back to him, "and you're probably listed, though it's more probable I won't call if you don't. That's what's happened to me; I'd feel too pushy. Goodnight, and my advice is to go up a Hundred-sixteenth at this hour. It's wider and there's more light and greater car and pedestrian traffic, though another steep street." Problems? he thought on the way home. Really, none. Day to day, that's how to take it, and only at her pace. She says slow, then that's the way to go, and "No no, not the time yet" for whatever, et cetera, and however long, that's okay too. Doesn't work out, then it doesn't, but he tried. She called ten minutes after he got home. "Good, you got back okay. I just wanted to say I had a very good time tonight, which I don't think I told you. That's all," and he said "Oh, it showed, as I hope it did from me. And as long as we're on the phone—"and she said "That isn't why I called, you know," and he said "I know, but it saves me the trouble of trying to get hold of you tomorrow for tomorrow or the next free evening you got. . . . I seem to be repeating myself with that line," and she said she was free the night after; too much reading to do tomorrow. They went to a movie by bus. She said she could meet him there and he said he'd rather pick her up so they could have time to talk before they saw the movie and he also wanted to see how she managed getting on the bus. "It's quite impressive, technologically, though I irritate passengers sometimes when my entrance holds up the bus or my chair displaces their seats." "Hell with them," and she said "I can sympathize with them if they have to be somewhere on time—a job where the boss won't accept any excuses for coming in late—and are behind schedule, or the bus is. That's why I prefer the number 5 on Riverside Drive. Usually, when I get on, only a few people are on it, and it's a quick trip to Seventy-second Street because it has to stop so few times, so can make up for what it loses on me." Kissing? She offered her cheek when he came in—"Door's open," she yelled from the kitchen—and he thought fine, because he felt they were going too fast. The lift on the first bus didn't work, but the next one, after several attempts by the driver to lower the outside lip of it, or whatever it's called, did. "You have to wheel me in backwards," she said, "or I can do it myself. But it'll be faster if you do it, and because you're assisting me you won't have to drop in a fare," and he said "Great, money saved, I've nothing against that, and very *gallant* of the Transit Authority." "What I meant was that we don't have to pay it now but we're expected to mail it in the envelope the driver gives us," and he said "Sure, I can just imagine lots of New Yorkers doing that, but okay." "Maybe," he said after the driver had fastened the wheelchair in the bus and given him an enve-lope, "I can send enough money by check for the next ten fares of my riding this way. Then I can avoid licking and stamping nine envelopes—oh, I see it doesn't take a stamp—the next nine, or rather, four times, since I'll pay for you, and it's all on a good-faith basis anyway," and she said "You can do that if you want, though I don't see why I shouldn't pay for my own fares, but there's always the possibility you'll end up losing on the arrangement and with no way to get reimbursed," and he said "What can I say? If I lose, I lose, and I'm out a few dollars." The other passengers? They watched them through the windows getting on the bus, with no revealing expressions, and once she was settled inside and he was seated beside her a couple of people nodded and smiled at them. After they reached their stop and her chair was unfastened, he started to turn it around to wheel her onto the lift backwards and she said "No, the other way." "I don't get it," he said, and the bus driver said "It's so there's less chances you both don't fall off, and if you do, you don't land on the back of your heads." He couldn't find a seat next to one of the wheelchair spaces in the theater, so he sat few rows in front of her. He was hoping they could touch or hold hands awhile and do things like look at each other from time to time and maybe whisper or mouth or gesture something about the movie or he just looking at her while she faced forward. He did look back a few times but the theater was full and he couldn't see her. After, he said "A bite? Beer?" and she said "I'd rather go straight home. Sometimes it's inconvenient being away too long." "I was just thinking. When I first met you at the party and you went into the bathroom there—you did, didn't you?" and she said "I think so," and he said "Then I presume you had no trouble getting in it. The door was wide enough, I'm saying; you were lucky," and she said "Sometimes I am; most times I don't even try. But what an odd thing for you to think of." "I suppose it shows I'm starting to think of different less ordinary things regarding you; logistics; like that. Nothing wrong with it, I hope. I'd love, incidentally, to invite you to see my place. But it's all up, one long and two normal-sized flights, nothing but landings and steps." "I'm sure you could put me on your back but I doubt you could carry me upstairs, so for now it's out." On the street, after they'd talked briefly about the movie—"Why do I continue to see his films?" she said. "When is he going to shuck his adolescent fantasies and juvenile humor and grow up?" "I agree," he said—she said she'd like to take a cab home: "Just to give you the complete transportation picture. Though it might not be easy getting one. Typically, if I'm alone, and even if I push up my skirt and flash a leg, ten to fifteen available cabs will pass before an extremely congenial recent immigrant from Ethiopia or Afghanistan or Pakistan or India—very often Sikhs or someone who has a close relative who lost a limb in one of the recent wars there—will stop. And not only will he help me in and out of the cab but he'll wheel me to my building and notify the doorman I'm outside." The first cab he hailed stopped. "He's not from Asia, Africa or the Indian continent so it's probably that you're with me and he knows you'll do most of the work." He helped her slide from the wheelchair to the front seat and then, with her instructing him, disassembled and folded up the chair and stuck it in the trunk. The cabby stayed in his seat and read a magazine, was a recent Soviet emigré, she determined from his photo and name on the hack license, and spoke Russian with her most of the trip about the beauty of Leningrad and greatness of Brodsky and Blok and ineptitude and corruption and inevitable self-destruction of the Soviet government for good, and she said "Nyet, nye budet, uzhe slishkom dolgo," and he said "Nyet, budet, it will, vy nye pravay, not too long, but still, after, no go back I; it be mess." "Give him a generous tip please," she said when they reached her building. "Even if he didn't lift a finger to help us and is quite unpleasant, I want to encourage him to stop for other sitstills like me." In the apartment she offered him a drink. "I can't have anything—if you'll excuse me, too much fluid already—but help yourself and perhaps get something to eat from the fridge. There's plenty." He ate a piece of cheese on a rice cake and then thought "What am I doing? Cheese; bad breath," and had a carrot and celery stick, washed his mouth out in the kitchen sink, brought in a glass of wine and they talked, sat in the same places as last night, held hands, kissed, kissed several times, rubbed each other's backs. He put his hand under her shirt there and worked it around to the front. "If you want," she said after a minute of his hand touching her breast, "we can go to the bedroom," and he said "It'd be all right?" and she said "Yes, I have my landlord's permission; it's in my lease. Whatever do you mean?" "You know, nothing about that you'll have any difficulty getting on the bed, off it, and so on, if by 'bedroom' you meant bed," and she said "Ultimately, if you didn't mind the idea, that was my objective," and he said "Then you answered the question I was going to ask." "Not that there can't be difficulties beyond the inconvenience to you of my long pre-bed prep, which I'd do even if I were alone. This, like my liquid intake limit, so I don't have to get up during the night to go to the bathroom or, to be frank about it, risk wetting the bed. If there did turn out to be a problem—spasticity, for one—I'd try to let you know beforehand it was coming so you wouldn't be too alarmed. If at any point you felt the whole coupling thing wasn't worth it because my physical problems had become a bit too hard to take, don't worry, I'd understand." "Somehow I don't—" "Let me just finish please? If it were the other way around—you in the chair, I able to get to my feet—believe me I'd be somewhat anxious too, particularly after all I've just said and the rather programmatic way I put it." "I'm not anxious," he said, "and I like the way you didn't coat it. Or I'm a little anxious, but only a little more than normal for a first time. What I'm really thinking though is what problem can be so bad that can't eventually pass? Okay, maybe some, but let's forget it, hope that none emerge, and go to bed," and he stood up. "My bed prep," she said, and squeezed his hand, rubbed it against her cheek while he ran his other hand across the top of her head, and went into the bathroom and shut the door. He sat down, heard water running, toilet flushing, her getting off and then back on the wheelchair. He looked at the prints and paintings on the walls, furniture around the room, thought things like So, this is it; shouldn't be bad; he's sure she's got everything under control, done this a number of times before, shouldn't be any missteps or anything they can't get right back to from what they were doing. Relax, she's very affectionate, sensitive, she'd never bring him in to it if she thought there was more than a slight chance it could go wrong. About fifteen minutes after she went in he said by her door "Excuse me, everything all right?" and she said "Couldn't be better. I'm sorry it's been so long. Some things I have to do in here take their own time," and he said "I know, I'm not getting impatient; just asking. If you need anything, though I don't know what that could be, let me know." He got another glass of wine in the kitchen, looked out the window there at the river and lights of New Jersey and followed for a while what seemed like a big jet flying north, thought if he was ever going to work here, since she probably works in the bedroom, this is where it would be: small typewriter table over the radiator under the window, window sill for his coffee mug and paperclips and such and a chair pulled up for a thesaurus and writing paper and other supplies. In the living room he looked at the titles of books in a different tall bookcase than the one two nights ago. If these were his, he thought, few to throw out or give away. He thinks the ones from the other night were like that too. Five, ten in this bookcase at least he'd like to read, and maybe one day he will. He should borrow one he's been looking for in bookstores a long time, before he leaves. He knocked on the bathroom door a minute later and said "Excuse me, but do you think I should just get into bed?" and she said "Is it getting too cold out there? The bathroom, because the radiator's almost as large as the one in the bedroom, is a hot box, and because of some malfunction the super's always promising to fix, it can't be turned off." "No, it's comfortable here, very pleasant. I just thought . . . I don't know," and she said "Do what you want. But I won't be much longer and I'm coming out fully dressed. So maybe we should both start with our clothes on, something I'd like tonight, would that be all right?" and he said "Sure, anything." "Did that seem peculiar, my request?" and he said "No, I can understand it. And I should also wash up before I get into bed, so forget what I said." He heard her coming out a few minutes later. He'd just poured himself another wine, quickly drank it and rushed back to pull her chair the rest of the way out of the bathroom.

"Right or left?" he said in the hallway, and she said "Bedroom; left," and he pushed her into it and turned on the ceiling light. Double bed neatly made, nothing in the room, it seemed, out of place, and he was right: a long table with an electric typewriter, lamp, books and articles and a ream package of paper on it, another tall bookcase filled with books and stacks of manuscripts and piano music, some exercise equipment taking up a quarter of the room, "I should work too with things like this," he said. "A gym would be okay but they're so expensive and time-consuming to get to," and she said "A couple of these machines you could possibly use." "You mean I'm not in such great shape," and she said "No, you look fine, strong, big forearms, and the right weight. I meant 'put to use,' if you ever feel like it and I'm not working in here." "I wouldn't mind; thanks. And excuse me," and he went into the bathroom. Make it short here, he thought, and peed, saw a portable toilet seat standing up between the commode and bathtub, washed his face and hands and took out his penis again and wiped the head with an already-wet washrag, then thought Ah, come on, and wiped the shaft and dried the whole thing with a face towel and folded it the way he found it and put it back on the rack, rinsed his mouth, checked his nostrils and ears for hairs curling out—one or two in one of the ears, but don't worry about it—and went back to the bedroom. She was sitting on the bed, holding on to the wheelchair arms, Still in all her clothes including her sneakers. Ceiling light was off and night table lights on either side of the bed were on. There didn't seem room for her to get around to the other side in her chair—exercise equipment in the way—though maybe she could squeeze through or there was a switch somewhere for both night table lights. Now that he took a good look at the bed it seemed larger than a double—queen-sized, probably—and also specially made or just set up for her: mattress lower than normal and, from what he could make out, even with the wheelchair seat. "So you made it okay from the chair to the bed," and she said "For this transfer I use a sliding board," pointing to it leaning up against the night table beside her. "And in the bathroom—the board too?" and she said "Grab bars and toilet seat arms help me get aloft, which you may have noticed when you were in there," and he said "The special seat, yes, but not the bars. Where are they?" and she said "In the wall and on top of the tub rim." "They work okay then, bathtub isn't too far from the seat?" and she said "Sometimes, like with the sliding board, I forget to use them right or I just slip up, and then there's a problem." "What do you do if you're by yourself and this happens?" and she said "Didn't we talk about this before? Maybe it was with someone else. I work it out. If I can't, I phone someone for help. You might be lucky enough to join that list." "Okay with me. But from the bathroom? I didn't see a phone." "Then, if I'm on the floor or have hurt myself, it's a big problem. Thank God it hasn't happened often, and I've almost always got myself up somehow or out of the room." "Have you had to stay down or hurt in the bathroom for a long time?" "A few times." "You could get a phone extension there. Why don't you?" and she said "I've thought of it and I probably will. Please sit next to me?" He did. "And for the time being, don't ask anymore questions?" "I won't." They started undressing each other.

*Kathryn Watterson*

# He Did It for Morgan

EVERYTHING MATTHEW DID NOW, HE DID FOR HER.

He was setting out the two beautiful Japanese cups—blue and white they were, two tiny bowls—and singing a little song from "Oklahoma" that he'd made up for her.

> *"Oh, what a beautiful Morgan,*
> *Oh what a beautiful day,*
> *Oh what a beautiful Morgan,*
> *Everything's going our way!"*

Flames burst against the underside of the aluminum frying pan his aunt Frannie had given him, making the water boil. The bubbling water hid the bottom of the pan from view, but he knew it by heart, every dent and scratch. He'd spent the morning staring at those little bumps and crevices, running his finger over them, thinking that they looked the way Aunt Frannie's skin did now, with hills and valleys of flesh, pores opened like little craters ready for moon landings of miniature spacecraft.

A thrill ran through him as he looked at the beat-up frying pan. The newer things remained unpacked in his cardboard box—his extra towel, his three pairs of black socks and his new white jockey underwear, his extra shirt and the pair of pajamas Aunt Frannie had given him last Christmas. In the bathroom, he had his shaving cream and razor, his bar of soap and towel. In the cupboard over the sink, he kept a box of tea, some cookies, a white cup and saucer, his tin bowl, two plates, the Japanese cups, a sharp knife and two spoons. And in the refrigerator, he had food: eggs, a little cheese, a loaf of white bread, a jar of Skippy's, a bottle of ketchup.

He'd gone alone to the grocery store. The first time, he got the shakes, but he'd done it. He copied an old guy in front of him—got a cart and pushed it around, found the Velveeta and ketchup and other stuff. About every half-second, he wanted to run out the door. Pressure built in the top of his head and behind his eyes, but he kept his hands steady on the cart until he got to the checkout girl, and she took over from there. A mist formed around his eyes when he handed over his twenty, but she took it and gave him change—no problem. He was so shaken going out that he forgot his bag, but she called, "Mister!" The word struck the back of his head—"Mister"—and he missed a beat. She was talking to him! He turned and went back, picked up the bag and carried it home, feeling more triumphant with every step.

It was weird to think that the last time he'd been in a grocery store, he'd requested *their* money, not vice versa. Of course he'd asked for it with Baby in his hand, but he didn't shoot anybody. "I never killed nobody and I never would," he told the judge. "I only took Ba . . . , the gun, to convince them to give me the cash." Calling Baby "a gun" to the judge made him feel disloyal, the same as when he was 11 and tried to impress his older cousin by dismissing his Pooh as "a stuffed animal." It hurt too much to think about it. They'd taken Baby as evidence and he'd never see her again. He had to let her go. "Just release, release," Morgan was always telling them when they did their breathing exercises. "Breathe and let it go."

It was good to have food, to fix food he could eat. He also liked cleaning up the way he had this morning: showering with his Irish Spring soap, shaving, making his face smooth, seeing the strong lines of his jaw glisten in the steamy mirror.

When he first got out—had it been three weeks already?—he couldn't remember how to turn on a stove. He could turn the knob, but gas hissed out and smelled up the room, with no fire. He turned the knob off and on again several times. No luck. He sat down, panicked. He couldn't go knock on a neighbor's door and say, "How do you turn on a stove?" Fuck it. It made him want to break the thing in pieces or smash somebody. But just when he'd given up, just when he was beginning to think about food at the joint, about going through the line with his tray, about how easy it is to know the rules, even if you have to watch your back, he remembered what to do it. He stood, turned the knob, struck a match and whoosh Magic! A flame!

Since then, he'd become master chef—the Julia Child of North Broad Street. He couldn't even count all the eggs he'd cooked in that pan now, all the toast, the Velveeta cheese sandwiches, the cans of Campbell's chicken noodle soup. It had been more than four years since he'd cooked anything. "Forty-nine months," the hack said who walked him out; he'd spent forty-nine months and thirteen days inside those cold stone walls, inside that stone cold cell. That's how long he'd been there. How many thousand days? They were blank except for Morgan. And except for that hole in his mind he could step through. He didn't know how to go looking for it, that space where no one lived but him—the place he sometimes went on those nights when he shivered for hours under his one blanket, and when, even with his shoes on, his feet stayed cold. He would get to the end point, the point where he couldn't take any more. And then it would be there, that warm dark cave he'd first discovered when he was just a boy. It would open right in front of him, and surprisingly, just when he'd forgotten that it ever existed, he found it again and again. All he had to do was crawl through and he was there, safe and warm.

He tapped the handle of the pan to keep himself in the room, and tried to focus. He'd boiled more water in this pan than he could remember, probably enough water to drown in. It would fill the bathtub, fill the bathroom, climb up to the ceiling. If he poured all that water over Frannie, she would be a steamed pork dumpling.

This was his room, his studio apartment, his stove and refrigerator, and his card table, the one he carried home from the Vietnam Vets' store on Olden Avenue. Those were his cups—his and Morgan's—and together they were about to drink the tea he was making. From a distance, he saw his hand shake a little as he took the teabag out of the little yellow box it came in, held the square paper between the tips of his thumb and his forefinger and lowered the bag into the boiling sea of water. The water looked angry, accusing, but the tea bag calmed it. He turned off the burner, watched the teabag float—a boat connected by its rope to the edge of the land. Little waves of brown drifted out from the boat as it began to sink to the bottom. When the whole sea was brown, Matthew lifted the teabag out, squeezed it lightly in his palm and threw it against the wall with such force that it split and burst, its contents sticking to the wall and sliding to the floor.

Using the hem of his T-shirt as a hot pad, Matthew carefully picked up the pan by its broken handle and poured tea from its bent edge into each of the blue and white teacups on the table.

"There, my darling," he said. "For you."

He picked up the empty chair and slid it forward with a gallant flourish, helping his princess closer to the table. The muscles in his arms and chest rippled under his black T-shirt and he patted his flat stomach before sitting on a low stool opposite the chair.

"Oh, I forgot. Do you want a cookie?" he asked. "It's one of your favorites."

He stood up and opened the cupboard door, pulled out his package of chocolate chip cookies, and carefully placed two on his thick white saucer.

"I knew you'd like that," he said, his face breaking into a radiant smile as he sat down again.

He lifted his tea cup, and then he lifted hers. "Cheers," he said, touching the cups together. "Cheers."

He drank the tea, first from his cup, then hers.

He refilled their cups. Then he stood and approached the black telephone hanging on the wall. He had gotten it connected last week, and twice already Aunt Frannie had called, "just to say hello." Trying to make up, he thought, for her dead sister. Once it was his cousin, Alan, saying, "Hey man, how you hangin'? How long you been out?" But really only wanting money, hoping to sell him a piece for some quick cash. Now Matthew carefully picked up the receiver, held it to his ear, and dialed the number he had repeated to himself like a mantra every night before he went to sleep. When she answered, he couldn't breathe.

"Hello," she said. "Hello? Who is this?"

This wasn't how it was supposed to be. She should know.

"My Morgan," he said, "This is Matthew."

"Matthew Williams?" she asked.

"Yes." He breathed out a long exhale, trying to stop shaking.

"Well, hi." Her voice had little birds flying in it—little brown love birds that carried yellow ribbons in their beaks and waved the ribbons at him. "How are you? I didn't know you were out yet. When did you get out?"

His voice wasn't as steady as it was supposed to be. "Three weeks, close to four."

"I haven't been able to go in because of the lockdown," she said, "so we haven't had any drama workshops for almost a month."

He didn't want to hear about workshops. Dramas without drama. He didn't want to think about the other guys in there looking at her long smooth legs, her shiny black hair that smelled of lavender, her pale fingers that spread in the air and beat their wings to the tune of her words.

"Morgan," he said, bringing his courage to the moment, a boxer gathering his strength and center as he steps into the ring. "You are my woman."

The other end of the line was suddenly quiet, still as warm night air. "Matthew, I'm already in . . ."

"Don't say anything," he interrupted. "I'm not asking anything of you. I want you to know that I have two cups of tea here. One is for you, and one is for me. We are drinking tea together."

"Tea?" Her word sounded "swallowed," a term she always used when she told them to speak up and project their voices.

"I drink tea with you in the mornings, and in the afternoons, and in the evenings . . ."

"Matthew, I don't think . . ." her voice trailed off for a moment and came back with a slight squeak that lifted it around the edges, as if those big brown eyes were looking into the air around her head, her hand poised to pluck out the right words. "This kind of worries me. Do you have anyone you can. . . ."

"Please," he stopped her with the force of his voice. "Speak no more. I know. You have many demands on your time. I am not asking for a gift or a morsel—I am not a common bore." He paused. "But you are with me," he said. "I want you to know—what I do, I do for you."

The other end of the line was quiet—but he knew she was listening. She always listened with her whole body tensed, her eyes open wide. He could see how she looked at this very moment, her hair falling over her right eye—the way she pushed it aside and tucked it behind her ear and bit her bottom lip in concentration.

He took a deep breath and said with practiced, perfect enunciation: "Morgan, please know this: you are my gentle queen." He paused a beat and added, "I would never hurt you. I will be in touch."

Matthew didn't wait for a reply. He cautiously replaced the telephone on its cradle and backed away from it. Hands together, he made a slight bow, a Buddhist priest leaving the zendo.

He pushed the teacups together on the table. Their edges touching made his heart hurt with pure ecstasy. He bowed again toward the cups. Slowly turning, he walked—mindfully placing one foot in front of the other—to the front door, where his gray raincoat hung ready on its peg. He felt in the pockets, glad that it had pockets with no holes. In the joint—that pocket of poverty—there were no pockets except for pockets of the mind, pockets of the soul, pockets of the eyes, pockets of misery, pockets of hate and vengeance and depravity, all pockets with holes. But love wasn't found in pockets. It wasn't hidden and held. Love floated free.

Even loaded, Baby II, his new Berretta pistol, the piece his cousin Alan had sold, as light as an apple, an orange, a heavy banana.

Matthew put one arm into the sleeve of the raincoat and then the other, slipping it on. "Oh, my love, thank you," he whispered, as though Morgan was helping him dress, patting down his hair, straightening his collar. He squatted, brushed the tips of his brown leather shoes, tied the shoestrings tightly. He'd always been good at tying shoestrings—from the time he was tiny, he could do it himself. Such a good little boy, he thought; so much you can do yourself. Then he stood, straightened, and walked out the door. Fear made his hands quiver, but determination propelled him forward.

As he walked, he swung his arms and hummed, *"Oh what a beautiful Morgan, Oh, what a beautiful day!"*

The sun was shining, just as he had known it would, and if he listened carefully, he could hear the whooshing of tires turning on the streets, the whistle of transmissions through telephone wires, the pumping of blood through hearts all over the city.


When he walked into the swinging silver doors of the Broad Street bank, no one looked up. He kept humming softly. It was a beautiful day, perfection itself. He was going to visit Aunt Frannie, but first he was here. Being here surprised him. Even though he'd come several times today, it looked different. Everything was polished. The silver tables had an extra shine to them, the lights were brighter, the floor was glowing. He hadn't prepared for all this dazzle. Even the gold buttons on the blue suit of the guard were gleaming. Matthew stared at the buttons. Then he noticed the guard's eyes—bright brown buttons glaring straight at him—and the sounds of shrieking and crying. The guard's eyes traveled to Matthew's extended arm, his hand, the hand that was holding Baby II.

The sight of the Baby in his hand startled him, but he wasn't going to shoot anybody—he would never shoot anybody with Baby II—he was just going to buy some time. The phrase, "Time in a bucket," popped into his head, followed by, "Time, time, time. You got time, I got time, all God's children got time, time."

The guard's hand was on his holster, but he was standing perfectly still, saying, "Take it easy, buddy. Take it easy. Everybody calm down."

Then, resounding throughout the room, he heard his own voice, the voice Morgan had called "sonorous," which she told him meant "rich and grand." It was the voice he'd used during his presentations in the workshop, and the sound of it echoing in this vaulted theater made him stand tall. He was aware of his audience, but he kept his eyes on the guard. "Do not be afraid," he boomed. "I stand before you to stand behind you, to tell you something I know nothing about." That was a silly verse they had practiced, but no one here was laughing and he wasn't sure why he had even said it.

"Four score and seven years ago, before the time I was born," he said, conscious of his inflection, "the world was a kinder place, softer, perhaps a place apart. And now, here I am. Be not afraid. I will not harm you. I have just come to a place in the road where I have no path to follow, where the road is not clear before me, and where I must make choices. My fellow citizens, sometime, the flesh is weak or the will is weak. In my case, both. The inane, materialistic pace of city life makes me realize, as I stand before you, that it is time for me to retire, once again, to the country of my dreams." The faces of the people in this room were all riveted on him, and he waved Baby II at them. "Please do not move until after I exit, and no one will be hurt."

He had seen the slight movement of the teller with the dreadlocks. She probably was the one who had pressed the button to call the police. The piercing sounds of sirens were drawing close, getting louder.

"I hear the sounds of the proud defenders of the law approaching," he said. "So I bid you farewell." He bowed slightly and started to back out of the glass doors, but suddenly he stopped. The thought hit his brain that he did not want to be hurt or bloodied. He did not want a swollen and misshapen face when he saw Morgan again. Perhaps in front of witnesses, the cops would not claim that he had resisted arrest.

He took a deep breath. "I am without exit," he announced. "I lay down my burdens here, under the sun and before witnesses." Just beneath the sounds of the sirens, he squatted, smoothed his raincoat and lay down on his side on the marble floor, in front of the doors. Over his head, he cradled Baby II in the palm of his hand, his fingers nowhere near the trigger.

He would have to give her up, but he was forced to make a choice—and he chose Morgan. "Baby, don't feel bad," he whispered, patting the gun handle. "I love you, too."

Loud voices and bells sounded all around him, and closer, inside his head, he heard a tap, tap taping that he traced to his own teeth. Chattering. They were chattering because he was cold, cold, cold. He looked around, seeing only flashing feet moving on the shiny marble floor. He saw the black polished shoes of the guard standing near his head and the guard's voice saying, "Take it easy, everyone take it easy. This is under control." The guard's voice was close then. "Buddy, I'm going to take your gun out of your hand now. Let's just do it nice and slow here."

He felt Baby II leaving his grip—the cool touch of her leaving his palm, brushing beyond him to another realm—just before the doors burst open and there were whistles, shouts, and all kinds of polished shoes brushed by the fabric of blue pants. There were too many shoes, and loud voices—shrill, without resonance or timber—hollow voices, voices with no range, no pitch, no soul, no vision, voices that fell into a bottomless pit and drowned, voices lost in the wind, voices that would fly away with the slightest challenge, kites without strings. He saw it then, a voice sailing on waves of air, in its own boat of dreams. He was thinking about that boat when, suddenly, that old thing happened. That hole in the wall—that space—appeared. He always forgot it until it happened again, and then he remembered: *it's always there. It leads to that cave where I'm safe again.* All he had to do was to get through the opening. He began to move through the veil and slip inside, and a warm, dreamy feeling began to fill his body, making everything warm, everything perfect.

James Tate

# Of Whom Am I Afraid?

I was feeling a little at loose ends, so
I went to the Farmer's Supply store and just
strolled up and down the aisles, examining
the merchandise, none of which was of any use
to me, but the feedsacks and seeds had a calm-
ing effect on me. At some point there was an
old, grizzled farmer standing next to me holding
a rake, and I said to him, "Have you ever read
much Emily Dickinson?" "Sure," he said, "I
reckon I've read all of her poems at least a
dozen times. She's a real pistol. And I've
even gotten into several fights about them
with some of my neighbors. One guy said she
was too 'prissy' for him. And I said, 'Hell,
she's tougher than you'll ever be.' When I
finished with him, I made him sit down and read
The Complete Poems over again, all 1775 of them.
He finally said, "You're right, Clyde, she's
tougher than I'll ever be. And he was crying
like baby when he said that." Clyde slapped
my cheek and headed toward the counter with
his new rake. I bought some ice tongs, which
made me surprisingly happy, and for which I
had no earthly use.

# A Walk by the Lake

Patsy and I were walking around Blue Man Lake.
It was a sunny, spring day. I thought about pushing
her in. She said, "If you push me in, I'll kill you."
We walked on, admiring the lichen on trees and rocks.
"Lichen eventually turns rocks into soil," she said.
"Look," I said, "there's a moose on the far shore.
It's almost hidden by the brush, but I think it's
taking a drink. Can you see it?" "I see a heron,"
she said, "but I don't see a moose. I've never seen
a moose. Why should I see one now?" "Well," I said,
"I think it would give you pleasure, and because it's
there, now." "Beside the boulder, that's a mouse, I
mean a moose?" she said. "Yes, that's a six hundred
pound moose with and incredible rack on its head," I
said. "He's from another world," she said. "How
can he live in our world. There's not enough room
for him, with the cars and highways and shopping malls
and housing tracts. He doesn't fit. He's from
far away and long ago." We didn't speak another
word until he left ten minutes later. And then I
thought Patsy was going to cry, but she held it back,
and we both stared at our reflections in the still
water. "We look like aliens," she said. "Or lichen
spores blown by the wind. We'll find a place to
take root, you'll see. We'll be just fine, all
green and violet and gray."

# Reasons for Rod's Breakdown

Cybil said she wanted to talk to me about
Rod. When she arrived, after a few pleasant
exchanges, she said she was worried that he
might be close to having a nervous breakdown.
"Do people still have those?" I asked. "I
thought they might be a thing of the past."
She thought I was being facetious, but I wasn't.
"I'm serious, Leo, when he gets home from work
he's depressed and irritable, to boot. I can't
talk to him. I just want to know how he is
when he's around you," she said. "He's pretty
much the same old Rod," I said. "He's funny,
he's interested in what I'm doing at work. He
tells me great stories about his office mates.
We, of course, still run together, and he always
beats me when we race, just like he always beats
me at chess." Cybil was slowly inching her
skirt up her leg. She had beautiful legs, but
she was making me nervous. "Does he ever mention
our sex life?" she said. I couldn't believe she
was doing this to me. "We've never talked about
that kind of thing," I said. "I guess we think
of ourselves as gentlemen in that regard." Cybil
was giving me a come hither look that was impossible
to misinterpret. "I'm surprised," she said.
"Men should talk about sex more. Maybe they'd
learn something useful." I could see her panties
now, which were celestial blue. I was extremely
uncomfortable, not to mention riveted. "Do
you see anything you want?" she asked. "Yes,
of course, but there are other considerations,
not the least of which is Rod," I said. "What
if I told you that Rod was dead?" she said. She
was smiling and touching herself. "Get out of
here. Get out of here right now before I call
the police," I said. I stood there shaking,
trying to catch my breath. I had barely survived.
It is perilous to dawdle in the combat zone.

*Steven Monte*

# Just the thought

I would not have thought it so difficult
to speak from the heart, had I ever sought
to do so—rather, had I ever thought
the heart was not already made of words—

a letting go, or pulling out the bolt
and the rush of pure expression, unfraught
because un-looked for, as if the words were caught
up in the spirit of escape, like uncaged birds.

And really, not all things are difficult to say—
poets exaggerate—and yet, just the thought
that sometimes the urge to speak won't go away
even after speech, is hard for me to stand.

I would not have it thought so difficult.
But what we can't say, do we really understand?

# Lost causes

The un-inevitability of it all
stayed with him more than anything else. For he'd sense
what never happened mattered more than the events
that somehow did—at least the ones he could recall.
What happened was so distant now it almost seemed a lie
to think of it as something that existed and was gone.
The traffic at the corner light would stop, then hurry on.
The geese still headed south. A windshield caught a fly.
Through everything the thought that there was something not there
menacing his world with its absence gave him pause.
Out of this confusion he would find himself a cause
of things he never had for which he couldn't not care.


# No uncertain terms

And after all the heartache, after all
that has been thought and said and left unsaid,
the talk of talking, and the many small
gestures and underlying feelings read

into those gestures, moments they recall
(so unimportant) that turn out instead
to have been some turning-point after all
measuring how far away time has fled,

after the point of speaking, or the thought
of speech has long since passed or come to naught,
and not to speak isn't something one must
do or consider doing, it is just

the way things are (regardless of the pains
one takes, without one's choosing to affirm
or deny it's so)—after all, there still remains
an unsettled something, for which there is no term.

*Jason Sommer*

# The Man at the Art House

The art house, revival house, itself revived
three times, conceived first as a music hall,
shows foreign cinema, and resurrects
American films, new when it was first renewed.
The one on screen three comes from the forties.
A decade for which the man in the tenth row
barely arrived in time. In his forties now,
he is weeping at the movie in which a man
also in his forties, though playing younger,
has moved the necessary distance through
the plot's too rough, too neat, approximations
of what might occur to become the man returning.

The bus trip starts it: a small canvas satchel
held on his lap, the unsought conversation
with the nosey old fellow in the next seat,
the conversation he seeks with his old friend
who works at the garage near the bus stop
for news of someone in this town where he'd lived,
not his hometown, though he wants to come home
to it, to the woman he thought interim,
an accommodation, love as a low point's refuge
and no more, not more surely, until it happened
to him, he happened on it elsewhere, the knowledge
that true as she was then, demanding then
so little, she wanted so much—not gratitude,
she had had gratitude—but love from him,
all he had to give, and more than that,
she deserved by virtue of her constancy,
her love, that gift, if she still wanted it.

And to feel all this! To be that man returning,
to be able to return with a whole heart,
healed somehow and then suddenly, though
everyone knows what's coming, the moment comes.
They sit in a kitchen of the period,
calico pattern on the table cloth,
the pattern of their speech, period, too:
*Why come here now? Don't be such a mug.*
His hand offered, taken and released,
her movement away abrupt, getting up,
going to the window. His movement toward her—
the shot over his shoulder, over hers
as she turns at his hand's touch on her shoulder,
turning to him and into their embrace,
which signifies hearts given once again—
for it is a reprise of a sort for both of them—
but given once and for all. To see all this
from his seat in the dark, close to the center aisle,
and even if then and only then to imagine
there is such a man, revenant, returning whole,
but to know it's not him, never yet, never—
why, those are the tears of the man who watches the movie.

# An Origin of Prayer

*Help me* he would say,

and what voice within him
said it?
      Soft half groan
he hardly believed his

when he lay him down
escaping from a sigh,
          those words

every night during that
time of despair—
to calm himself he said them
in a sort of deadened
calm, but weeping, too,
over and over.

For months this went on,
the sound escaping
as words
          when he lay down,
eyes closed for just a moment,
as if something within him
needed to be roused
to address something outside
before he could sleep,
then looking
through the window
by the head of his bed
that sometimes had a piece
of moon in it.

And he found he'd gotten
into a kind of habit,
so years later
he would say it before he dropped off
to sleep, in that way,
hardly saying really,
          the words forming
themselves out of an exhalation
willy-nilly.

Even back in those bad days
in the daylight
when he felt a little better
before he really was better,
he had begun to think of it
as a clear line back
to some beginning,
the tribe's more than his own,

as much in this desperate
petitioning
as in the coinages of wonder, sky
gods thundering
and the like,

that awe which after all starts the bargaining:
o master of rain, of wind,
vouchsafe a measure
from your bounteous power
or forbear to visit
the full measure of the bounty
of your power
upon me, upon us
and if you . . . then I will . . . we will. . . .

He thinks he comes to understand
how it resembles the beginning of the rites,
this little outcry.
Yet he persists in it
before he goes to sleep,
sighed out, an inadvertence almost,
a remnant from a troubled time of his.

And once one warm, close September night,
the night he could have seen the meteor shower
had he stayed up late,
an amazing thing—
the fiery evaporations
of dust
          in the outermost air.

Instead he saw, or
thought he saw
                the little
exhalation he made
while summoning his strength,
confessing his weakness,
forming those words
so vaguely addressed

as a visible shimmer
three times out of his own mouth,
a vaporous dust
         fiery
in that weak light
in
       from the window
and was afraid.

*Susan Hubbard*

# Duluth

"Please, Kirsten," Melanie says. "Stay put. My arms are tired."
Kirsten, aged four, is trying to run away, but the red harness, snug
against her chest and straining away from her back, checks her mo-
mentum.

Melanie jiggles the baby in the crook of her left arm—Matthew,
seven months old, is awake, but placid as usual. A heavy knapsack
holding diapers, bottles, snacks, and juice-boxes, trailing a fuzzy yellow
blanket, hangs from her left shoulder, and with her right arm she firmly
holds the leash connected to Kirsten's harness.

The leash was Lark's idea. Lark is a native of Minnesota, but
Melanie thinks of him as coming from the Blue Ridge Mountains—re-
mote, independent, belonging to no one except himself. She watches
the back of her husband's head as he talks to the Northwest Airlines
representative. Lark's head has a characteristic tilt that seems confident and curious at the same time. Melanie knows he is smiling and
using his most charming voice, as he always does when he talks with
strange women.

Melanie's entire body is taut, aching from a week of hiking and
sleeping in a tent. Kirsten and Matthew had stayed with Lark's parents,
giving Lark and Melanie their first vacation alone since their honey-
moon.

It was also Melanie's first time camping. Lark hikes and camps reg-
ularly with a club he joined last year. They meet every Tuesday night

and hike most weekends in the Blue Ridge Mountains nearby. Lark said the camping around Lake Superior was tame by comparison.

Melanie's head throbs from the strain of watching the children and the baggage—backpacks and assorted dufflebags, one huge one holding the tent and Coleman stove—spread in a heap on the floor next to her. She wants to rub her temples and pull her hair more tightly into the barrette that holds it off her neck, but she lacks a free hand. She doesn't feel as if she's been on vacation. Hiking was hard work, and every day ended with setting up camp, cooking a meal, and cleaning up before going to bed. Every day began with collapsing the tent and making the campsite look as if no one had been there. These were the basic rules of camping, Lark told her, but they left her exhausted; every night she'd been ready for bed by 7 p.m., although Lark liked to stargaze, then read science fiction in his sleeping bag until 10. She dozed while he read, and after four or five hours of sleep she would wake to worry about the children and listen to his snoring. They'd made love only once the entire week—for the first time in over a month.

Kirsten makes a loud noise like a motor boat's. "That sounds like Granddad's boat," Lark had said when she made the same noise yesterday.

Granddad took Kirsten out on the lake several times while her parents were away. Melanie hadn't known this was happening, although Lark insists he'd told her. In any case, Kirsten has been badly sunburned, although both grandparents insisted they protected her with plenty of sunscreen.

Melanie looks at the part in her daughter's hair—reddish scalp against hair so blond it looks almost white. Her face is dark pink and her nose is red, with peeling white patches. *If I'd known they were going out on the boat, I'd have bought the sunscreen with SPF 50*, Melanie thinks. She makes a vow to cover Kirsten with aloe gel when they get home.

Kirsten is wearing a new outfit bought by her grandmother: a yellow dress with zoo animals embroidered along its hem, a lightweight green fleece jacket, pink tights, and green patent leather shoes. She's also wearing a new "Hello Kitty" backpack and new green barrettes in her hair, which Grandmom French-braided and pulled tight with a green scrunchie. Except for the sunburn, she looks well-tended. Melanie thinks, *Is Lark ever coming back?*

They've been standing in line for more than twenty minutes now, and the line hasn't moved much. Apparently some Northwest flights have been cancelled—at least that's what they gathered from murmurs along the line, and from the length of time customers are spending with the representatives. Finally Lark had stepped outside the black ropes and approached the one person at the counter who, instead of dealing with customers, was thumbing through a sheaf of papers.

*They've been talking for a good five minutes now*, Melanie thinks. *How long does it take to find out whether a flight's been cancelled?*

Lark looks over his shoulder, as if he hears her thought, and shakes his head three times. Then he turns back to the airline representative and spends another minute talking with her. *As if he were saying good-bye to someone he's known for years*, Melanie thinks. Kirsten suddenly surges forward, so hard and so fast that Melanie drops the leash. Kirsten screams even before she hits the floor.


"What happened?" Lark bends over Kirsten, who has turned onto her back, howling, but his question is aimed at Melanie.

Melanie squats next to them, balancing Matthew on her knees. "She pushed forward and I lost control of the leash," she says. She knows that all around them people are staring, making whispered comments.

Lark picks up Kirsten, whose howls subside into sobs as she holds onto her father's neck, sucking the thumb of her other hand. "Mommy hurt me!" Kirsten says. Her forehead is even redder than the rest of her face, and Melanie can tell that it will rise in a bruise.

Melanie thinks of the months just after Kirsten was born. She'd been a nervous mother, never sure if she was doing the right things. While the baby slept, she'd read every manual on child-rearing she could find, taking notes in a large book she kept by her bedside. She'd been a graduate student when she'd married Lark, and the old habits of reading and taking notes gave her some comfort. She also used the notebook to document Kirsten's development, recording dates for key events such as "first smile" and "first sleep through the night," as well as observations on feeding, crying, and bowel movements. She doesn't remember, now, when she stopped taking notes—she's kept none for Matthew—but she remembers finding them a few months ago and marveling at their precision. *As if I needed evidence that I was trying to do the right things*, she thinks now.

"Mommy didn't hurt you, Kirsten," Melanie says. "You pulled too hard and Mommy dropped the leash." But she hears uncertainty in her own voice, and she wonders if anyone believes her.

"Did—not—pull—hard." Kirsten's blue eyes flash with indignation.

Lark pats his daughter's back. "Calm down, Kirsten, and we'll go get some lunch." He turns to Melanie. "Our flight's been cancelled, along with a lot of other ones. A bunch of crew members didn't show up today—apparently one of them is getting married and there was a big party last night. Anyway, we're stuck here for the next four hours, but they're planning to schedule a new flight to Minneapolis around two. I've got to check back later about the connecting flight. But they gave us a voucher for a free meal. We may as well go sit down and eat something."

"Did—not—pull—hard." Kirsten chants the words as they gather the baggage, load it onto a cart, and take the elevator to the next level.

"Do you need to go to the bathroom?" Melanie asks Kirsten as they wait to be seated.

"I do *not*," Kirsten says. "I do *not* I do *not* I do *not*."


The Duluth Airport's coffee shop is called *The Afterburner*, and its logo is a fighter plane superimposed on a globe. Melanie sets Matthew in a booster seat next to her in the booth, and Lark sits next to Kirsten across the table. He removes Kirsten's harness and tucks it and the leash into his jacket pocket. Then he picks up the menu.

"They've got grilled cheese sandwiches," he says.

"Don't want grilled cheese!" Kirsten shouts.

"Not so loud, please," Melanie says. An old couple in the booth across from theirs is staring. "I have some rice cakes and juice in my bag."

"I *hate* rice cakes!" Kirsten shouts.

Normally they're her favorite food. Melanie wonders if Kirsten ate too many of the rice cakes she'd left with Lark's parents.

"I want a hot dog!" Kirsten says.

Melanie's eyes question Lark's, and he shakes his head. Their family is vegetarian, but Lark's parents are meat-eaters. "I don't think they serve tofu dogs here," Melanie says.

"Don't *want* a tofu dog. I want a *hot* dog!"

Lark says, "How about French fries?" Melanie knows this is a compromise and accepts it as such. They never have French fries at home.

"French fries!" Kirsten bobs her head and grins. The people in the next booth smile and tell each other how cute she is. "Ya, I want French fries, Daddy!"

As well as introducing her to meat, her grandparents apparently have taught her to say "ya" instead of "yes." Melanie wonders what else they taught her last week.

The coffee shop is crowded—they were lucky to get the last booth. A group of Outward Bound teenagers swarms the aisles, talking to each other, waiting for seats. Only one waitress is working, and she hasn't come back since she left the menus.

"What are you having?" Melanie asks Lark.

"I have to go to the bathroom," Kirsten says.

Lark says, "Okay, Kirsten."

"I have to go *now*."

Melanie stands up and steps into the aisle. Lark lifts Kirsten from her seat and sets her next to Melanie, who takes her hand. Lark slides into the booth next to Matthew.

Melanie leads Kirsten three steps before Kirsten lets go of her hand and breaks into a run. Melanie says, "Kirsten!" and chases after her, jostling two Outward Bounders. She catches up to Kirsten outside the restaurant, near a display of small stuffed animals. "I want a nanimal!" Kirsten shouts.

The sign by the display reads *WeeBeans by Princess Soft Toys*.

"Bathroom first," Melanie says firmly, and takes Kirsten's hand again. They trudge across the polished tile floor.

Kirsten says she wants to go all by herself, but Melanie knows better. Without speaking she ushers Kirsten into a stall, shuts the door, pulls down Kirsten's tights and panties, and sets her on the toilet seat. Then she remembers that she should have put toilet paper across the seat first. The restroom lacks paper seat-covers, but prominent over the toilet is a green and white tin box labeled "Sanibag. For Sanitary Napkin Disposal. Preferred by Discreet Women Everywhere. FOR PERSONAL HYGIENE AND CLEANLINESS." Next to the words is an image of a nurse—dark curly hair and white cap—that looks straight out of the 1950s. *Hasn't this place ever been remodeled?* Melanie thinks. *Do women who use sanitary pads really put them in bags?* She wonders if she could have used two or three of the bags to cover the toilet seat.

Outside the stall, women are talking. "In Phoenix our time never changes," someone says.

"I'm done!" Kirsten sings.

"But you didn't go," Melanie says.

"I AM DONE!" Kirsten bellows.

Melanie lifts her off the seat and pulls up her panties and tights. "You didn't wipe me, Mommy," Kirsten says.

"You didn't need wiping," Melanie says, and opens the stall door. Two middle-aged women are washing their hands at the sinks, and in the mirror both look at Kirsten, then at Melanie, disapproval in their reflected eyes.

Melanie dampens the end of a paper towel and blots Kirsten's forehead, where a bruise already is visible. Kirsten yelps and recoils, as if she's been branded.

"Mommy didn't wipe me!" Kirsten tells Lark and the couple in the next booth.

Melanie opens her mouth to explain and closes it without speaking. She stares through the window to the landing field, a broad flat expanse bordered by clutches of pine trees. Overhead, the deep blue sky is marked by three small clouds. Lark goes back to the other side of the booth with Kirsten and Melanie slides in next to Matthew. Matthew turns his round blue eyes toward her, opens his mouth, and emits a small cough—a polite "ahem," like a gentleman.

As if on cue, Kirsten responds with what Melanie thinks of as her tuberculosis cough—a deep, wracking bellow. She's been able to cough like that since she was one. Conversation in their part of the restaurant stops, and people turn toward them. Lark sighs. Melanie wants to say to the strangers, *I've taken her to three doctors, and no one could explain that cough.* The couple across the aisle are whispering, and someone says, "Poor child."

The waitress appears with a tray holding glasses of water, and Lark helps Kirsten take a long sip. "Such a little thing to have a great big cough like that," the waitress says. "That's an awful sunburn, too."

Melanie feels her face flush. "Do you have any specials?" she says, for lack of anything else to say.

The waitress says, "We serve what's on the menu. I'll be back to take your order in a minute."

Kirsten says, "Daddy! Lie down."

Lark collapses against the back of the booth, closes his eyes, feigns sleep. This is an old game of theirs.

"Daddy, wake up!" Lark pretends to wake up, opening his eyes slowly, yawning, stretching. Kirsten laughs loudly and Lark joins in.

His laughter is low-pitched, distinctive; it was one of the first things Melanie noticed about him when they met, five years ago.

They play the game again and again. Melanie remembers something June, Lark's mother, said: "Each of my children is good at one thing. I made sure of that."

Melanie thinks Lark is good at acting, although she's sure June had something else in mind.

June and her husband Bill, the doctor, are proud that all of their eight children are successfully employed. Chase teaches French at a small college. Baxter is manager of a bank. Among the rest are an investment counselor, a travel agent, a realtor, and a high school teacher. Lark (only his mother calls him by his christened name, Larkin) has a Ph.D. in medieval studies and makes lutes.

Melanie wonders who else in America makes lutes and how they manage to make a living. Lark has sold only two since she met him. They met at a medieval fair; Melanie sat on a bench watching Lark, encircled by a group of long-haired, rosy-cheeked, buxom women as he played a melody she later learned was the Aria Di Fiorenza. Since then, she's heard recordings of that aria and has come to think Lark doesn't play it very well.

The lutes are beautiful things—glossy, pear-shaped, made of thin strips of steamed pine and rosewood—but expensive to produce. And the glue Lark uses gives Melanie headaches.

Until Matthew came, Melanie worked full-time in the library of the private girls' college down the road from their house; for the past seven months she's worked part-time, and it's been increasingly hard to pay the bills. Rent is only $700 a month, but there's the medical insurance that the college won't contribute to, plus car insurance, gas and electric, and food; organic products always cost more. Lark believes in living frugally—he hates to buy anything new, and he wanted to drop the family's medical coverage until Melanie went back to full-time work, but Melanie refused to let the policy lapse. Even with careful budgeting, things are tight. She supposes Lark's parents volunteered to pay for their plane tickets out of sympathy—and, of course, their desire to see the grandchildren.

"Where's our waitress?" Melanie says.

"She's the only one working," Lark says. "We're in no rush."

"Are we going on the airplane?" Kirsten asks.

Before they can answer, she says, "I want to go on the boat!"

"Yes, we're going on an airplane," Melanie says.

"I want to go on the boat!" Kirsten yells.

"Airplanes are like boats," Lark says to her. "Airplanes float in the clouds and across the sky. Just like Granddad's boat on the lake, only airplanes cross sky instead of water."

Kirsten peels a patch of skin from her nose, then sticks the patch inside her left nostril. Lark pulls a handkerchief from his jacket pocket and, pulling her finger away, holds it to Kirsten's nose. "Blow," he says, and she blows her nose noisily. The people across the aisle watch them and smile.

Melanie feels herself tensing, bracing for Kirsten's next outburst. She looks across at her daughter's small, even features, and the phrase "fearful symmetry" comes to her from—where? A long-ago college poetry class? *Is she really* mine? Melanie wonders, not for the first time.

Lark puts the handkerchief back in his pocket. "I'd better check with the airline rep to see about our connecting flights. Find out what the soup of the day is," he tells Melanie.

Melanie and Kirsten watch him leave the restaurant. Through its glass walls they see him stride to the escalator and disappear.

"Where's Daddy going?" Kirsten says. She stands up on the seat.

"He's going to find out about our airplane," Melanie says. "Kirsten, sit down. Please."

Kirsten turns around and around in the seat. "I want a nanimal!" she says.

"Please sit down!" As Melanie begins to stand up, Kirsten slides back into her seat. "That's better," Melanie says, sitting down again. "Now we can talk about animals."


Kirsten is drawing giraffes and horses on a paper placemat with three crayons the waitress gave her. Melanie ordered French fries and two bowls of cream of mushroom soup, which the waitress said contains no beef or chicken stock. Matthew is asleep—his head has fallen to one side, his blue-veined eyelids twitch from time to time. Lark has yet to reappear.

In this rare moment of quiet, Melanie can hear the conversation of the couple across the aisle. They're in their sixties, she guesses, and both have white hair and bifocal glasses.

"Your shoulder hurts," the wife says.

"It will be a long time till we get home," the husband says.

"You can take a pill," she says.

"The waitress didn't bring us water," he says.

"I want to go on a boat!"

"We should both drink more water."

"I want to go on a boat! Mommy!"

Melanie opens her eyes. Kirsten is jumping up and down in the seat opposite hers. The respite has ended. Melanie says, "Airplanes are like boats."

A woman enters the restaurant. Her mouth has something dark oozing from its left corner. Melanie tries not to stare, but when the woman walks by their booth Melanie sees a long, dark birthmark just under the left side of her bottom lip. *Like permanent Halloween make-up,* Melanie thinks. She wonders how many stares this woman has suffered.

Melanie recalls last Halloween. Lark went camping with friends. When he came home three days later, Melanie looked through his backpack—for what, she can't recall now. For dirty laundry? For manicure scissors or a can opener? Instead, she'd found a long braid of brown hair, bound at each end with red rubber bands.

For several minutes Melanie sat on the bedroom floor, holding the braid. Then, when she heard a sound from outside, she went to the wood-burning stove that heats the house. She opened the stove door and threw the braid into the fire.

Neither she nor Lark ever mentioned the braid, or the smell of burnt hair that lingered in the house for days.

Kirsten tips over her water glass. She shouts, "Help! Mommy, help!"

Melanie pulls wads of paper napkins from the dispenser on their table. Water drips onto her jeans, but it at least it hasn't touched Matthew, who sleeps on. Next to the napkin dispenser is a stack of green postcards. As the napkins soak up the water, Melanie reads a card. "How was your Visit Today?" the card asks. There is a list of items, followed by boxes to be checked. The first item is "Atomosphere." Melanie hopes she'll remember to tell Lark about that. When they first were dating, they made a kind of game out of scrutinizing menus for typos and misplaced apostrophes. They called themselves the Menu Police.

"I need water!" Kirsten says.

The waitress arrives with a tray of food. When she sees the water-soaked napkins, she sighs and takes the food away. A few seconds later she returns with a soiled white towel and another glass of water.

"Had a little accident, did we?" The waitress removes the paper napkins and wipes the table.

Kirsten says, "Mommy made me spill."


The mushroom soup tastes strongly of beef stock. Melanie pushes her bowl away. Lark's soup already looks congealed.

Kirsten covers her French fries with catsup from a squeeze-bottle and eats two. Then she says she has to go to the bathroom.

Melanie is glad that the couple across the aisle has left. She tries to reason with Kirsten. "Let's wait a minute," she says. "Your brother is sleeping, and in a minute Daddy will be back to watch him. Then we can go to the bathroom."

"I have to go NOW," Kirsten says. The bump on her forehead has swollen into an egg-shaped bruise that reminds Melanie of photographs she's seen of children with encephalitis.

Melanie suddenly feels cold. "I'll take you to the bathroom," she says.

She looks outside and sees Lark stepping off the escalator. But he's not alone. He's talking to someone behind him—a young woman with long dark hair.

"Daddy's coming," Melanie says. "See?" She points at the restaurant window.

Kirsten stands up in her seat, staring. "Who's that lady?"

"I don't know, honey."

Lark has stopped near the escalator to continue the conversation. His head is bent toward the woman; his mouth is moving rapidly, and when it stops, he is smiling.

Kirsten bunches her skirt between her legs. "Mommy, I have to go *now*," she says.

Melanie nods. The woman is speaking now, and Lark is nodding, nodding. Then Kirsten screams, a full-fledged scream that makes Melanie's heart leap. The coffee shop falls completely silent. Every eye is on them.

Melanie snatches Matthew out of the booster seat and tucks him into the crook of her left arm. With her right hand she picks up her knapsack, slides it onto her shoulder, then beckons Kirsten out of the booth. She puts her hand on Kirsten's shoulder and propels her down the aisle. Matthew wakes up and begins to wail—a thin, high-pitched sound. The knapsack swings wildly from side to side as they make their way toward the door. As they leave the coffee shop Melanie realizes they haven't paid for their food. Didn't Lark have a voucher? She lumbers on toward Lark and the woman, who have stopped talking and are watching them approach.

Melanie wonders what she'll say when she reaches them.

Kirsten shrugs and pushes free. She heads for the display of stuffed animals, grabs the wire rack, tips it sideways. Small animals cascade over and around her: elephants, tigers, unicorns. Kirsten laughs. She bends and scoops animals into her arms.

Melanie walks ahead with Matthew, past Kirsten. She takes comfort from these thoughts only: no one knows them here, and in a few hours they will be away, on a plane bound for home. They will slip away unknown across the sky, back to their small house below the blue mountains, and this day will pass unremembered, and nothing whatsoever will have changed, for better or for worse.

Melanie stares straight ahead and, as she passes, hears the low music of Lark's laughter.

Cynthia Huntington

# Untitled

You will forget the shame of your youth,
and remember no more the reproach of your widowhood . . .
For the Lord has called you
      like a wife forsaken and grieved in spirit,
like a wife of youth when she is cast off . . .
For a brief moment I forsook you,
      but with great compassion I will bring you back.

Isaiah II, 54


You said to me, O Jerusalem I call to you:
the one forgotten, cast aside, shall again be cherished.
But you have brought the stink of her into our bed.
You have buried your face in her neck,
inhaled her sweat, licked clean her salt,
and I have no place to rest in this house
that cannot be made clean, that reeks of the foreign bride.
Your wife has no room in this house that is safe,
that is not stained by that woman's pride.

She has opened my cupboards, touching things that are mine.
Taken off her dress and stood naked before these walls.
She has fingered the chair arm, drunk tea
from a cup her hands cradled. How then should I come home?
With her fingers of wanting, her eyes of ambition,
with her hard, claiming steps on the floor.

With her shadow on these walls, her breath tarnishing
the air, that shade in the window
my certain death, and you, still holding
the outline of her face in your eyes.

*Larry Janowski*

# What Celibacy Is

> . . . And there be eunuchs which have made themselves
> eunuchs for the kingdom of heaven's sake. He that is able to
> receive it, let him receive it.
>
> Matthew 19,12

If this is what
it costs to hold
at heart a hollow
where no sparrow
lives (nothing alive
that needs light),

if this is what God
expects from Yes,
then it is too much
today, although
I pay it anyway.
Again. Some heroic

souls, though few,
I expect, accept
such terms without
complaint: those
who, full of You
to breaking, can

cut off every
other thing and
one, swallow
pain like wine,
smiling, drugged
on purest Spirit,

proof that You
exist, the mere dregs
of You enough
to feel or fill
another day. But
this hole in me

is not wholly
holy yet (if ever
it will be), is still
child-round and
lover shaped
by someone as like

yet utterly unlike
me as I am like
and utterly other
than You, who
haunt and echo-
ache in that space

You claim
to hallow, but
which feels
merely hollow.
I will now
meet You here.

Rachel Dilworth

# The Cloistering of Mary Norris

Are there stones of water on the moon?
Are there waters of gold?

Is it there that the drowned live?

—Pablo Neruda, "Planet"

I do not picture sheep anymore—
thirty, sixty, two hundred bounding
ceaselessly, magic-propertied
over wave on wave of stony wall.

For the birds, that. Rubbish.
My green mind forfeits no space to dreaming.
I am precious with it, fearful it become,
itself, a dream of what might have been.

I keep myself awake with words:
*razor, puncture, mitre, claw*.
Think of: the shards of bottles ripping atop
the convent wall—ramparts of glass

During the nineteenth and twentieth centuries, thousands of Irish women were institutionalized in "Magdalen laundries"—residential facilities, run largely by female orders of the Catholic Church, for the care and containment of "fallen" women. These women were detained behind locked doors, where they performed laundry labor that subsidized the asylums. "Magdalens" ranged from unmarried mothers to young girls merely suspected of sexual conduct, women with mild mental handicaps, prostitutes, victims of sexual assault, and others considered socially deviant or vulnerable.

fortifying the brittle castle.
>                Such a landing! for a sheep too great
>                with flesh, or weak, or young yet
>                for the strength to disregard the law

>                        of gravity, of physical properties . . .
>                        Who *would* I be to risk a lamb
>                        on that? (It's not a leap of faith
>                        unless there's something to believe.)

The dormitory orders even
the night, shadows of bed on bed
catalogued like books on a shelf.
They are so easily read: uniform

lines and matter, lack of substance—
the same old story. (I am too bright
for this, for the blackening of histories
to plots so dark they seem the same.

Normalization is slight of hand.)
Think: chicken white, fat vein,
soot plum, ocean, orange.
>                        I saw an eagle once. And a man

>                        with a gold front tooth. I knew six
>                        different dances. I lived on a farm.
So much just continuation
in these sleepy hours, each slowed breath

for someone else, for yet another
day weighed by labor, day fenced with silence.
>                Confiscate the right to claim.

>                                        But oh,
>                the machinery will not stop bleeding . . .

Breathe out, breathe in. This is no dream.
Breathe out, breathe in. Carbolic, bleach,

must from the rug. No hob, no sweaty rowan.
Breathe. Breathe. Something my own.

I soft-toe to the loo, bolt myself in.
There is a clear cold off the lino
and a milky film of cast-off
light from the moon in the window frame.

A plump, pale turnip, the moon
roots in the chunk of heaven
the wall hoists up. I name this
mine: night's growing season:

the smooth and girlish round
line of the moon and the porcelain:
the rise of the wall to the high window:
the box of glass making its own space:

my tears, the rain awaited all day:
moments

                                      entire.
I feel the shape of each one—like a coin
in a trouser pocket, summed by touch.

A brush of my hand confirms the loot
stuffing my nightdress pocket—news
from the papers villagewomen have used
to truss their clothes and tablelinens.

I try to find whole stories to save
from the bin in the sorting room. But
generally, the vital bit's gone missing—
the conspiracy theory or why of the riot,

the picture of the Race Week winner,
the mad price of beef in the crisis . . .
At least I know the half of it. At least
I know exactly what I'm missing.

I carry the news with me like this—
against my body in the dark—so as to hold
the world close, to dress myself with nearness
to the strange, great variations of the self-made.

　　　　The depth of these hours feels good,
　　　　as when your hand, plunged far
　　　　down in damp earth, has reached the place
　　　　at which it can cup a plant by the roots.

On the floor of the loo, I set out rows
of articles and bury myself in a field
of names, elections, brides, tractor pulls.
I steep there, a seed or skeleton, beneath

the soft-lit eye of the moon with its hinterlands—
its daily-changing shape a talisman—
until I can feel myself bulging against the room's
straight walls, shoved by their trellising

edges up, until I am something bent
and wandering, striking out and out
to the high light, filling what space I find,
urging, asserting, *I am this*

*big, this too is mine, I am this, and this*—

# Guarded

In care, she learned to guard against herself.
Against her saucy form, its dirty bits
pudging mutinously out: lips, bum, womb, tits.

And against her feebleness, her thick heart with its
baby hopes that love would sally in
the kip fishshop and like the look of her

despite the smell of mackerel on her dress
and the ghostly scales that always littered her
nail varnish like wet petals. They took that,

first thing: her Cherry Red. Then, her frock with
the pin-prick posies went for soapwater wool
and a starch-stern apron that tamed her shape.

The pong of fish for bleach. Her name for a saint's,
or rather, another go, since your one hadn't taken
to her. (Just as well with the loads of other Marys.)

Her head of corkscrew porter-colored curls
was humbled to a speckled lump—a seed
dandelion blown—in case of nits, and as first penance.

Confused, she watched the rest go: her rings,
her sense of time, the podge that had dogged her legs
since she was ten, her flair for song, her little one.

One night, even her father's face was gone
and she slipped in her bed without picturing his sheet-
white teeth or the raised mole under his breastbone.

Here, she was a new girl. She was in charge
of suitable things like mends, like blanching out stains.
No gutting of flesh. No semblance of a fishy past.

She found evident definition in walls, screened
safe from the huge blue night that bruised the world,
day in, day out—the awful con of the things beyond.

Grew to fear the bad job she'd always make of it
out there, the riot of life and its deceptions,
the rapaciousness of the homes and lanes

restrained by spikes and stranglings of wire.
Inside these grounds there was the surety of women
charged with caring for her—mothers and sisters

to school her into dreamless sleeps
and a correction in which it became possible
to forget she had, somewhere, a son,

and be, herself, a child again
with no sense of permanence: when a thing was gone
it did not exist. Perhaps had never been.

Like a memory unshared, she grew ever more removed
from her origins, from her first clear truths.
Year by year, she steamed, ironed, hemmed in-

to herself quiet days that let her give to God
the gift of clean sheets and silence: a good girl.
Only now, in her oldest age, is she jealous

of her few certainties: dislike of parsnip mash,
the wizardry of her cribbage game, and Tuesday morning
visits from pretty Bridget, the physical therapist

who comes armed with the scrapes of her gang: three lads,
one girl. There is some apology between them, a knowing
sense that things long gone aren't lost in the forgetting.

The young mum, on leaving, is always cagey
to the matron, gives up nothing more than *Sure,
Joan is keeping fine. Sharp for her age, that one.*

Aaron Fagan

# The Funeral Dinner

> "It is enough to tell of the books we've read
> and our biography is done."
>
> —Mandelstam

On the title page of Rose Hecht's copy
Of *A Child of the Century* you can see
She kissed her husband's name beneath
The inscription: *To Rose for whose heart*
*And out of whose spirit this book was written*
*By her grateful lover, Ben*

Rose, who after his death went through
Each book in his vast library, documenting
The mind of the man she loved in life,
Taping in extra pages where his opinions
Required more than simply highlighting
"Benny's favorite line" in *A Hero of Our Time*.

In a dog-eared copy of *The Brothers K*
She got to about page one hundred and
Stopped writing. You'd think reading too
Unless you turn to the last page, some
Five hundred later, where two words seem
To be enough to follow the closing passage:

*"Well, now we will finish talking*
*And go to his funeral dinner.*

*Don't be disturbed at our eating pancakes—*
*It's a very old custom and there is something*
*Nice in that!" laughed Alyosha. "Well,*
*Let us go! And now we go hand in hand."*

And it is as though she disappeared
Into what her hand guided her to say,
Right then, into the book itself,
And became the words: "me too."

Garnett Kilberg Cohen

# Afterlife

You're still dead. I was thinking it as I was driving home, listening to some sentimental pop tune from the seventies, a song you would have flipped off before most people had a chance to identify it. (I can still see the endearing twist of your lips that indicated disdain.) I was on my way home from the hairdresser—yes, I color it now, something I promised I would never do—who had just told me she was diagnosed with a terminal illness. She must have forgotten that she had told me the same thing (albeit, a different illness) four years ago when I had first started using her. (People should keep track of whom they tell they're dying and when.) I remember the exchange distinctly because I had wondered if I should continue with her or switch before I got too attached. Finally it had seemed too mean to abandon a dying woman without insurance, particularly since I'm such a terrific tipper.

So yesterday when she delivered this bad news with a quivering lower lip as if it was hard to reveal such a thing, I wanted to say, *but you're still alive four years after the diagnosis for an inoperable brain tumor.* (Of course I never say what I want to say.) And that, circuitous as it may seem, is how I came to the realization in my car. My hairdresser is still alive. And you're still dead.

Granted, it has been a much longer time for you. I have divorced and completed grad school. My daughter, Molly, about the age I was then, lives out on the west coast now. (You should see her. Beautiful. Tall and dark and lush. Like me, only she knows it and uses it in ways

I never could.) I have switched jobs so many times I'd have to write a list to remember them all. While all this has been happening, you have been dead. If you were trying to make a point, it was obviously a mistake. The point lasted a few weeks, months maybe, a year at best. Death much longer.

I think of you most often in the autumn—when the leaves turn and everything seems overgrown, beyond fecundity. But lately, thoughts of you have arrived unexpectedly, and, I must admit, with increasing intensity. The force of these remembrances make me want to talk to you, clarify what happened.

Did you wonder how I would learn the news? Did you think Yolunda would call and we would grieve together? Everything forgiven on her part? Well, I can tell you—it didn't happened that way. Carlos told me. (You know, the guy you used to buy your pot from. You wouldn't believe how rich he is now! Owns a string of video game rooms and a God-awful nouve riche house, closer into the city, with huge gargoyles perched over the double front doors. When we see each other, we pretend not to know one another. And we don't really. We were different people in the seventies.) Anyway, a couple of months after you and I broke up, I called him myself. Michael had already quit smoking dope. You were my only connection. *Too bad about your old man*, Carlos said in that stoned drawl that seemed so sexy back then. *Yeah, well, things end*, I had said, thinking he was referring to our break-up, though a little surprised that you would confide in Carlos. *Wow, you are one cold bitch, no wonder he blew his brains out*. I laughed, said *fuck you*, and hung up the phone without making arrangements to pick up the pot. I didn't believe him, thought it was just a crazy-dope-dealer thing to say. I learned the details of your suicide just a few hours later.

Your funeral was held in the forest preserve, in the dazzling autumn sunshine. You would have liked the sound of the leaves rustling in the trees, the way the bright light illuminated each individual leaf. And proud of Yolunda. She played her role—the brave widow—with more flare than I would have expected. Decked out in festive colors (LuLu, too), Yolunda told the crowd it was to be a celebration of your productive life, not a mourning of your one last desperate act. Everyone you would have wanted showed up. Even that guy, Landers, to whom you lost that last commission to compose a piece for the installation at the cultural center. They wanted you, I heard, but you refused to compromise. Even for five thousand—a lot of money at the time. (I always admired the way you stuck to your aesthetic principles.) About the only person who wasn't at your funeral was Michael. I talked him out of it. He had wanted to go, argued that it didn't matter that Yolunda and I had had a fight. After all, he reasoned, the four of us, you and Yolunda and Michael and me, had been friends so long. He stressed the fact that our kids, Molly and LuLu, were best buddies. (He also said that your mistake was marrying Yolunda, that you would have been better off with someone like me. I didn't tell him that you had been with me. Many times.) I stuck to my guns (pardon the expression) and refused to go, said no, I wouldn't risk upsetting Yolunda, making things harder for her than they already were. He never suspected that I feared what Yolunda might reveal to *him*. Why would he? Michael trusted me. But the second he headed down the street for the train to work, I called Edge and asked her to watch Molly.

I went by myself, wearing the only black I had, an itchy wool suit my mother had given me, without nylons—the weather was exceedingly hot for October. (I have since wondered if you would have done it in May when the daffodils were blooming? Not as many people off themselves these days. They have amazing drugs for depression now! It's a brave new world.) I stood in the back, like the "other woman" in a bad movie, and sweated and scratched and cried. The event was a retrospective of your work. Once they set up the speakers, the leaves stopped moving—or seemed to. Both of your two biggest commissions were played, a few soundtracks, and that sweet little chamber piece—I wonder what Yolunda would have done if she had known you wrote it for me? I cried a lot. As I was leaving, I spotted Carlos (standing on the periphery as I had been) and asked if he still had my pot. He said to meet him at his place, so I picked up Molly, swung by Carlos's, then went home and got stoned.

Molly is juggling two guys now, one on the east coast and one on the west. Her job forces her to coast hop a lot. I tell her the game she's playing isn't wise; the guys will be hurt; she'll be hurt; it will all end up badly. Michael knows about it too. He disapproves on moral grounds. We don't speak much. His second wife doesn't like it; besides, it's painful for both of us. When we do talk, we try not to get too personal. Yet in a recent, unguarded moment, he said it was my influence that made Molly so bold. Michael never knew about you; but I did tell him about the guy after you. So he *thinks* he knows the score. But he only knows what I let him know. Sure, I might have looked brazen (even to you, I bet), but that wasn't the case. If Molly does take after me, it isn't boldness—it's fear: fear of being left alone, fear of making the wrong decision, fear of not having enough, fear of disappointing someone. Though Michael has the cause of my actions wrong, I do wonder just how responsible I am for Molly's behavior? Remember those times I brought her to your studio when we thought she was too young to catch on, those times she saw us kiss, our thirsty mouths finding it so hard to separate. Maybe being exposed to all that had some kind of subliminal, postponed effect.

It was better when Molly wasn't there, when Edge would watch her so I could come alone. I loved that little building, encased in all those fiercely clinging vines, the way it was almost hidden at the back of your overgrown yard. Both our spouses at work. LuLu in day care. It seemed like we were the only people alive in a sea made of instruments and equipment and soundboards and music, floating on the musty mattress in the center of the room. We would smoke that pungent pot you got from Carlos. (Remember the tape you made of seeds popping over seeds popping over seeds popping, a symphony of grass, with the intention of getting a refund?) I loved to listen to you talk about music, how noise *made* an environment but most people didn't even recognize that what they were hearing contributed to how they felt. Then we would make love on that damp mattress (I still get excited from the smell of must), amidst all your sounds and scents. Our lovemaking had a long afterlife. Hours later, my fingertips and toes still tingled and my legs felt boneless. When I rode my bike home it seemed like music came from everything: the trees, the clouds, the smoke spurt, spurt, spurting from chimneys. We lost track of time so often that I'm surprised it took Yolunda so long to catch us. Though technically, I suppose, we were never really caught. She simply spotted me leaving the studio, wading knee-deep in the middle of your overgrown lawn.

"I thought you were my friend!" she screamed.

I wanted to say, *I am your friend. What does the fact that I love your husband have to do with our friendship? I love you both. You have always been so illogical, Yolunda.* But I understood she was responding on a purely emotional level. I wouldn't have expected anything else. So instead of saying what I believed to be the truth, I pleaded ignorance.

"Huh? What's the matter, Yolunda? I just stopped by to give Jake that herbal tea you both like so much."

It was what we planned to say if caught so our stories wouldn't contradict one another's. A plan concocted during lovemaking and laughter, for we didn't believe we would get caught. Yolunda was more likely to work overtime than come home early. But at that moment, looking into Yolunda's eyes the lie didn't sound right. My legs were jelly, my head humming, and your long overgrown weeds had begun talking to me, chattering wildly. Insects buzzed, as if they were as astonished as the weeds, as angry as Yolunda. I could picture the bees' furious little faces. The flies rubbing their miniscule mitts together. The noise seemed to paralyze me.

"Oh, right, Kay, do you really think I'm that stupid? Do you think I haven't noticed the way you two look at each other?"

And then, trapped in your tangled lawn, I realized she *had* been quieter lately. Somewhat curt even. I wanted to say, *Wow, Yolunda, you're so much smarter than we thought. You figured it out before Michael even, him with his fancy job and all.* I didn't want to gaslight her. She looked so pathetic in that silly uniform she had to wear to work so that you would be free to compose. Not that I wanted to betray you, but the weeds were talking even faster, reaching a low roar, then you came out, then there was all that yelling from Yolunda. You looked so calm and cool in your blue jeans and bare feet, me so innocent in the white, gauzy shirt from India. Was that the day you hosed me off in the yard with the green garden hose after our first storm of love making? Whatever happened before was blotted out by Yolunda screaming, screaming, screaming. A little like the piece you had created for your only New York commission. I must say, now, in retrospect: you were right; you were ahead of your time.

"Yo, knock off the hysterics, you're freaking LuLu out," you said.

I saw her then, LuLu, her curly little head peeking over the top of a clump of Queen Anne's Lace near your back porch. She was sitting on one of the bottom steps, her body camouflaged by the overgrown thicket. At the sight of her staring at me, everything fell silent.

I tried to call Yolunda a few times afterwards—did she tell you that? She always hung up on me, the second she recognized my voice. I can't really remember the sequence of events after that, how long it was before—well, you know. How many times you and I actually spoke to one another again. Since it was the last thing in your life, therefore more recent to you, you would probably know better than I. (That is, if you weren't dead, but if that were the case, it wouldn't be the last thing in your life, would it?) The exact course of events is fuzzy now.

I do know that I told Michael that Yolunda and I had had a fight over the girls. I said she was jealous that Molly was developing faster than LuLu. He didn't blink an eye, took it as one of those "chick" things. In fact he accepted it so easily that I considered upping the ante, telling him Yolunda was also jealous because she thought you were making eyes at me. I wanted to know if that would get his mind going, spark some type of epiphany. Yet I have never been completely reckless. I was already worried that he would run into Yolunda. I knew she couldn't tell him anything for certain; she had no proof. All she knew was the way I had looked frozen in the weeds, my sandals straps looped through my fingers, so that the sandals dangled from my right hand. If she later went into the studio, the sounds you had going and the smells—must and sweat—would support her instincts. But she could not document sounds and smells.

You and I never really saw each other after that, did we? Except that one time when you came by early in the morning, after Michael left for work. You walked right in the house, up the stairs into our room (no one locked doors back then, not where we lived) and waited for me to wake. I remember the sound of the birds outside my window. As I sat up, I pulled the sheet up with me to cover my naked breasts. You asked me to take off with you, head south. Head west. No, east. I pretended that I wanted to go, that Molly was my only obstacle. You cried. I cried. I don't know for sure what you were crying about—rejection, anger over being caught? I remember I was sobbing, *really sobbing,* for what I had lost, with you *and* with Yolunda. I think it was one of the first times I knew with certainty that all things had to end. The fact that I could have lost Michael, too, struck me for the first time when you were standing there in the bedroom I shared with him. I realized how Yolunda must have felt seeing me in her yard, a trespasser in her private world. It seemed like such a violation. (Didn't you even think about the fact that I was waking naked in the bed I shared with Michael?) When you begged me one last time to leave with you, I wanted to tell you that you had missed the point. The point was having *both* you and Michael. There was no point in leaving him for you. Besides, I didn't even trust your desperation, your claims of devotion. Your appearance in our bedroom occurred shortly after you had lost that big commission to Landers because of your final refusal to be coopted—Michael heard the whole story when he stayed in the city one night after work, went out with friends to listen to music. (By the way, Landers has made it pretty big. I see his name in credits sometimes. But I don't really hear his stuff, not the way I heard yours.) I thought maybe you were more upset about losing the commission. It is hard to lose two things at once. I told you that you had to leave. I guess it was-n't long after that that you blew your brains out on the mattress where we had made love so many times. (Where did you get a gun?)

Speculation was that you couldn't take being undiscovered. Prob-ably only Yolunda—and maybe Carlos—suspected there might be something more to it. They would never tell. Carlos, given his line of work, had learned never to speak out of school. And for the sake of her own sanity, Yolunda could not allow herself to believe I was that im-portant to you. I'm still pissed at you for letting her find your body. What were you thinking? I've tried to believe you were so distraught that you didn't know what you were doing to her. I have pictured you, alone in your studio, feeling like such a screw-up, such a failure. I know how painful it is to long for a person when you realize it is too late—I know because I longed for you in that same way for weeks after you killed yourself. And then, on top of all this, your music had let you down, again. You were just enough older than the rest of us to under-stand that big breaks didn't always come, regardless of how much tal-ent one possessed. And you were *so* stubborn. I'm sure Yolunda wasn't very sympathetic during that time. She did not have much of a sense of humor to begin with. I doubt my encounter with her in your back yard improved it any. Regardless of your feelings for me, I'm sure you hated to be such a disappointment to her. I try to imagine your despair, the taste of the metal barrel resting—for how long?—in the lap of you tongue, scraping the roof of your mouth. But, Jake, *really,* couldn't you come up with a better plan for having your body found?

You'll be happy to hear she never did remarry, though last I heard LuLu was a little messed up. The sort of act you took has tentacles that worm far into the crevices of the future. I was in therapy for a while. But no matter how much money I paid the lady with bright white hair and yellow teeth, a different paisley scarf knotted at her throat each session (her name escapes me now, after so many years), I couldn't get her to see my problem. She thought I needed to work through my guilt, get over the fact that I played a role in your suicide. She could not conceive of the fact that I didn't feel guilty—except, maybe, a lit-tle for lying—and didn't hold myself responsible for your actions. I wanted to explore the value of what I had lost. Understand it. The guy that I took up with later, the one I *could* confess to Michael, helped me get over lying. But you. You and Me. That was something else.

I remember the sound you made chewing my hair, the dry crunch. You wanted to record it. You told me never to cut it or dye it. I promised I wouldn't. You put gobs in your mouth and chewed. It seemed like the noise was entering my skull through the individual follicles, right to my brain, rather than through my ears. I guess it was the pot. My hair fell almost to my waist back then. We thought middle-aged ladies were crazy to wear bubble cuts and do touch-ups. Wouldn't long flowing white hair be cool on a fifty year old, you said? Well, I can tell you now that I'm almost there, that our bodies lose moisture with age. It isn't so easy to keep hair below one's shoulders without it becoming thin and wispy looking. And while white hair might be cool, steel gray isn't quite so striking. But who knows? Maybe I will let it grow out now. That's the only way I can avoid my colorist in the future. I don't want to use her anymore. There must be some huge hole in her life that she needs to cover by imagining her impending doom. Thinking about that hole makes me anxious. But I can't imagine confronting her or switching colorists.

When I got home from the hairdresser there was a message on the phone from Molly, a complicated plan asking me to pretend she would be visiting me this weekend in case Eric called. She was going to be with Drew in New York, his apartment, not a hotel so there was no other number she could leave Eric. Except her cell phone and she didn't want to have to answer Eric in front of Drew. In, fact, she was calling me on her cell on the way to the airport. (Cell phones, that's a whole other story.) Her message worried me. She was taking bigger risks and implicating me. I wanted her to face her situation, understand her actions. I wanted to tell her *NO*, I would have no part of her lies, but a second later the phone rang and it was Eric asking me if Molly had arrived yet. I told him she had just gone to the store to pick up some herbal tea. He said she didn't drink tea. *No?* I asked, *I guess it's only when she's home that she likes it. A mother/daughter ritual, sipping tea and talking.*

An odd thing is that your memory is clearer to me now than it was ten—or even fifteen—years ago. As if you have been lying in wait. I don't know what happened to so many of the people we knew back then. Those who have stayed around—like Carlos and Edge (she's a grandmother now!)—have transmuted so many times that the versions of them that remain are new people. No one wears tattered jeans (the sleeker and blacker, the better) and guys don't wear their hair long anymore (short and sharp as razors standing on edge). And, I suppose, in a way, everyone has "sold out"—at least by your standards. Those who did it young, don't have to anymore; and those who didn't, well, most of them are desperate for the chance. But it's not as bad as you might think. Even losing my looks is a bit of a relief. I still have whatever it is that attracts men, but not the thing that drew even the wrong ones to me and made me do the things I regretted.

I wonder if you—wherever you are now—can hear my thoughts? I'd like to know the *timbre* of my musings, their tone. The sounds of taste and touch. Is the cacophony of my contemplation richer than words spun from my lips? Are you in an environment made of noises we never knew existed? Do you hear things you never heard before? Strange pitches and exotic notes. Heavenly sounds. Do you miss me? Listen, while I brush my hair. Can you hear it crackle?

*Joan Connor*

# What It Is

THEY MET AT A CONFERENCE. IT DOESN'T MATTER WHAT SORT OF conference. It was a hardware conference, say, at a Holiday Inn. They mingled among the bins of nails, keyhole saws, socket wrenches. He liked the way she hefted her hammer. She liked the way he tested the haft of his chisel against his palm. They were professionals; they knew their tools, their monkey wrenches from their vise grips, their Philips heads from their screwdrivers. The nuts and bolts of life. They introduced themselves. He did exteriors; she did interiors. They lived far apart. As two professional lonely people, they liked that about each other. They could build a bridge to span their solitariness but keep their trestles separate. He thought she looked competent. She thought he looked cute. He liked the cut of her nail apron. She thought his T-bar was cute. They exchanged business cards and half-hearted promises to meet somewhere sometime. She thought his promise was cute. Before he headed home, he gave her a copy of his recent manual, *How To Build A Lean-To*.

She read it on the plane. The guy really knew his stuff. His plumb line dropped straight. His corners were true. She thought, hmm.

Courtship in the computer age. A reticulating web of options, electronic avenues: e-mail, voice mail, mail, airmail, answering machines, the overnight expressways to your heart.

She e-mailed a careful compliment: I liked your book, *How To Build A Lean-To*, especially the section on slanted roofs. Your paragraph on gradients and outwitting ice build-up was profound.

He e-mailed back: Thank you.

She e-mailed back: You're welcome. I just reread the section on ice jams and the life span of the twenty-year shingle. No one else has ever before explored this topic with such sensitivity yet thoroughness.

He e-mailed back: I'm a sensitive guy. And may I say with Excruciating Politeness that I could not help but notice that you are an architectural gem?

She e-mailed him back with the compliment that he seemed structurally sound himself.

He e-mailed: Thank you. Let's stay in touch.

She e-mailed him an expurgated autobiography of her life to date.

When he received it, he didn't have time to read it thoroughly because he was en route to see his girlfriend, Marla, the computer programmer who was telling him to get with the program or delete. He didn't like ultimata. While Marla sketched out her blueprint for his future, he found himself reflecting on slanted roofs, ice jams losing their grip and sheeting to the ground in glorious January sun. It *was* a good section, he realized. It was in fact profound.

She sent him a carefully selected card, an etched Escher print that played with the architecture of perspective. The woman pins laundry. The man stares above the terraced hill at the sky. They are as alien to each other in the building they cohabit as Hopper figures in separate paintings: Sunday Morning. Gas. The man contemplates; the woman pins clothes. Marine plant life blooms impossibly in a gallery garden.

He sent her a postcard, telling her that his new book, *Building a Snow-fence, Slat by Slat* was out.

She sent him a note thanking him, a carefully selected box of small chocolate hammers, two tins of cookies, and a hand-braided belt. She ordered a copy of his new manual.

He left a message on her answering machine, thanking her.

She left a message on his, inviting him to come visit.

He e-mailed her saying that he couldn't visit just now, because he was putting a greenhouse on his garage.

She e-mailed back that she was building a hope chest and she'd send him the plans. She sent him the plans.

He called to thank her answering machine.

"Hello," she said.

"Hello," he said. "This is Conroy Cardamom."

"Oh my," she said.

"Oh yes," he said.

They started talking long into the night. They started talking around their short-term plans. They told each other stories which featured themselves as heroes. They put on their best faces and forth their best feet. They sketched the blueprints.

Hmm, he thought.

Hmm, she thought.

This guy/gal really likes me.

Hmm, she thought.

Hmm, he thought

This gal/guy is really smart. This guy/gal has great taste in men/women.

She express-mailed him pickled doves' eggs, four leaf clovers, falling stars, mermaid songs in pale pink conch shells, and the completed hope chest.

He sent her a signed copy of, *Your Friend the Retractable Tape Measure*.

She sent him a hand carved tromp l'oeuil tablecloth of ormolu. She sent him fudge, butter cookies, ladies fingers. *Feed him, feed him, she thought.*

He wasn't home to receive the package because he was off with Marla, arguing about their future. But when he got home and found the box, he thought: This has gone on long enough. He called her, "I'm coming," he said.

"Finally," she said. "When?"

"Soon."

Soon. Soon is a word with promise, eventuality, rhymes with swoon, spoon, June moons to croon at with a wayward loon on a dune. But that was silly. Snap out of it, her Alpha female said to her Epsilon male. But.

She dreamed of him, alone walking somewhere across a treeless plain. She woke wondering why this man was ambling across her dreams. She woke, singing, *If I were a carpenter and you were a lady*, failing to notice the double conditional. She shored up her empty hours raising high the roof beam, building a bungalow built for two, putting out malt for the rat in the house that Jack built. In between, there was life, interior decoration.

He thought of her occasionally. How *not* to. Why is this woman being so good to me, he wondered. It occurred to him that she was crazy. But, hey, she liked the lean-to, the passage on the longevity of asphalt. She caught on to things. She fed him. Still it might be a pretty trap. Why was she being so nice to him? He got back to work. He bricked the floor of the greenhouse. On Tuesday Marla called and crashed the hard drive. He stared at his monitor, his own impersonal computer. You have mail, it said, and raised the red flag.

"Drive," she said. She sent him a road map, room keys, directions.

Maybe, he thought, possibly. We'll see. He failed to note the red flag. (That is a metaphor.)

As she cut cloth, scalloped it, contemplated window treatments, she sang, "The bear went over the mountain to see what he could see." (That is a song lyric.)

He called her. They exchanged histories, building tips, niceties, anecdotes, favorite movies. She laughed at his halting stories, sly asides. *Feed him*, she thought, *feed him*.

"I think structure is what is important," he said on the phone. "Integrity of building materials. Decor is cosmetics."

Integrity, she thought, we are talking. We are talking. Aretha wailed from the CD player, "But I ain't got Jack."

"Cosmetics?" she asked. They had so much in common. Uncommon much.

He explained his theory of cosmetics: pretty is as pretty does. They rang off.

He thought, she gets my jokes. She has a heart as big as the Ritz cracker. He ate all the care-package fudge in a sitting and sank into a sugar low. She erected skyscrapers of meringue and sang into a sugar high, "The handyman can cause he mixes it with love and makes the world taste good." (That is a song lyric and a metaphor.)

She mailed him a meringue of the Empire State Building with a note: I won't scream, King Kong.

He called her. "I don't even remember what you look like."

"Like myself," she, no Fay Wray, said.

"I'm having anxiety attacks of approach avoidance," he said.

"Relax," she said. "Just have fun."

"Fun," he said. "Okay fun. I think if I plan ahead I could find a few days clear."

"I'm afraid," she said. He was scheduling his fun.

"Of what?" he asked.

"Of this." It wasn't fun. "What is this?" she asked as women are wont to do after the fact.

"What is this?" He growled in a gritty blues voice, "Why, darling, what it IS."

She laughed. WHAT it is. She stocked the house with groceries, planted peppermint petunias, aired out the attic, propped his book jacket photo on her dresser, tucked a retractable measuring tape beneath her pillow, baked cakes with flying buttresses, broke the ground, cleared the site, raised a cathedral of hope. In her dreams he was still walking across a vast treeless expanse. (She wasn't receiving the omen.)

This is a bad idea, he told himself. Structurally flawed. Collapsing keystone. Bad foundation work. He jerry-rigged a Tom Swift rocket to the moon.

She e-mailed him: Despite all my kidding around, I really do like you. And I have no expectations.

We'll see: he e-mailed.

We'll see: she e-mailed.

They saw.

He drove, stoned, the tunes cranked, eating up the road, lost his way, recovered, the trip growing longer by the second, the road stretching endless, seven hours. Damn. Lost an hour. She'd be worried sick. Why did they do that, worry? Now what? Cruising, Joan Osborn crooning about God on a bus. Like one of us. Like one of us. The first six hours urgent, then fatigue settling in, numbing his shoulders, the highway elation wearing off. How far away did this damn woman live? Impossible distances to span. What had she said on the phone? Courtship by interstices. Overseas acquaintance by satellite. Make up for lost time. Rolled on the right through the intersection. Uh-oh. Blue light special. Easy now. Pot in the car. He rolled down the window. "Yes, officer?"

She took a bath. She put fresh water in the flower vases. She curled her hair. She changed her clothes. Three times. She wanted to look nice but not too nice. Lace shirt, too obvious: Come hither. Button-down too prim: Head for the hills. She trimmed the hedges, vacuumed the floors, then paced them. This wouldn't do. This simply would not do. They were both in their forties. This was silly. She took a deep breath. She stared into the mirror. Gadzooks. She looked like Yoda's grandmother. Six o'clock. Seven o'clock. She set out the cheese. Where was he? She rewrapped the cheese. Why didn't he call? They never called. He might be dead somewhere and how would she know. They never called. Anticipation become anxiety become anger become anxiety again. A woman's assonant declension. Then irony: Great, now she'd never get laid again before menopause.

An hour on the side of the road, an hour while the cop ran the registration. Fucking cops, man. Everyone was doing it, rolling through the intersection on the right. Okay, he broke the law, but everyone was breaking the law. Why should he be singled out for breaking the law. Give a guy a uniform, a big gun, and he's the biggest cock of the walk all right. Officer Dickhead. Gonna get myself a uniform, man. Officer Dickhead meet Officer Anarchy. Blow justice right back into the power-hungry Hitler's beady little eyes. Ka-poom. Ka-poom. "Thank you, Officer," he said, accepting back his license and registration. "Thanks very much."

Gonna cost a freaking fortune. All to see some chick who's a tool groupie. Got to find a phone. Ten o'clock. Cops. Give a guy a uniform and he thinks he pisses testosterone. Cops.

"Thank you officer." Where was the fucking JUSTICE?

He rolled up to a phone booth and dialed in the blue light.

"Hello," she said. "Hi. Thank God. I thought. Yes. How far? Poor thing." She unwrapped the cheese, put a bottle of wine on ice. What room should she be sitting in? Living room, a book, perhaps? No, no, the family room. His manual. Just a half hour now. Eleven o'clock.

When she paces in the hall, her reflection startles her. He's here. No, that's me. Where is he? She doesn't hear him arrive. She's in the bathroom, chobbling down antacids.

A knock. And then he was there in the full light of her hall. And she knew the instant that she hugged him that she had failed. He had built her from absence, raised a pre-mortem Taj Mahal from e-mail, letters, doves' eggs. She had failed. And the walls came a-tumbling down.

"Conroy," she tried on his name. Croy, it stuck in her throat. Offer him something, she reprimanded herself. *Feed him, feed him.*

Wo, he thought. This was not the Trojan Helen he'd erected in his imagination over one, two months, two and a half. No, this was what the horse rolled in. He looked the gift horse in the eye. "Hi."

She smiled, pretending not to see the flinch. "Hi. What can I get you? Something to drink? Wine?"

"Fine," he said. He didn't drink wine. No sandpaper would abrade those wrinkles away. No sir. No draw plane either. This girl looked every inch of her long days. Wrinkles, chicken neck. Be polite. The girl has chicken neck. Be polite. He followed her into the kitchen. Prefab mock oak. Lino tile. Trapped, he thought. Trapped like a rat in Kerouac's suburban nightmare of the dream house lit by TV light. Blue beams. Blue light. Thin blue line.

204

"You tired?" she asked. "You hungry?" Her questions pig-piled. "Wine?" She started heating something up on the stove before he answered. He hated that. Mother bullying.

"Cops," he said. "You should have seen this cop. Fucking police state, man." He looked around furtively for an escape but kept talking.

While he ranted, she stirred the soup. Let him run his course. It was a guy thing. Guys don't handle authority well. This wasn't the greeting she'd anticipated, hoped for. But still, he was here. Drove eleven hours. She'd feed him, rub his shoulders. They'd sip wine, talk, recover the easy banter from the phone.

He raved. She set the table. He waved his arms. She poured the wine. He thumped the counter. She served the dinner, smoothed his napkin.

"Here," she said. "Relax. Eat."

Ten minutes. He was here ten minutes and she was already telling him what to do. He smiled and sat down.

They thought, We'll just have to make the best of this.

"Do you want to smoke some pot?" he asked.

"Yes," she said. She didn't like pot.


They were high. She thought his eyes had gotten bluer since he'd eaten. He liked her crooked smile, he decided.

He impersonated the cop. "May I have your license and registration, urp, please. Would you, urp, while I urp this on the urp?"

She laughed. She fed him cookies, meringue. More soup? Wine? Yes, please, no, please, three bags full, please.

For a giddy moment, they became themselves. They thought that their laughter sounded genuine. They thought they were enjoying themselves, but, but.

She cleaned the kitchen. As she put things away, she was watching herself put things away. Butter in the butter cubby. Napkin in the basket. He was watching her. This was all too much. She was playing into his fear of her: That women always anticipated what men feared: Their domesticity. Which was what they wanted. *Feed me. Feed me.*

"Would you like to listen to this tape?" he asked.

"Yes," she lied. She wanted to run screaming blue murder into the blue moon of Kentucky. She wanted to slit her wrists and watch her blue blood trickle into a bottomless basin. Her nerves twanged like a bluegrass banjo. She was stoned. Neurally jangled. She wanted to talk.

He popped in the tape. Why did women always have such lousy stereos? He wanted another meringue. Maybe he could just stroll over and puff one nonchalantly into his mouth. He wanted to study her, but every time he tried a surreptitious peep, her green too wide eyes would catch him, appraising his disappointment, judging him for it. He hated that. It was going to be a long weekend. He sat in the easy chair. The arm was loose. Right arm. He listened to her laugh at the tape. She laughed in all the wrong places.

"I love Fireside Theater," she said.

"Firesign," he corrected.

It didn't register. "Remember that one—Don't Touch That Dwarf. Hand me the pliers."

He nodded and stared at her now downcast eyes. What was so interesting about her lap?

She stared at her suddenly old hands. It happened like this when she smoked. She turned twelve, but her hands turned old. Old leaves. Spatulate hands turned over an old leaf.

"Do you want to hear the other side of the tape?" he asked.

"Do you want to go for a walk?" she asked.

He wanted to be agreeable. He wasn't. "Sure."

They stumbled into the frosty air, clopped down the tarmac through the subdivision. He felt that he had squirted like a watermelon seed from his own pinched fingers. The pink pulp of Spielberg's suburbia, sweet watery nothing. Pretentious prefab structures loomed waiting for something ominous to happen, anything, wiggy skeletons to rise jigging from the ground, sentimental aliens to start guzzling Coke. Where was this woman leading him? What was she talking about?

"There's a field," she said, "at the end of the development. An old farm. Baled hay."

He squinted at the pond she indicated with her right hand, but he couldn't see a thing. She shuffled along a dirt road, the way becoming clearer as the development halogens' eerie orange vanished like Kerouac's vision. On the road, off the road, he chanted to himself as he kept pace with her.

"Here," she said. "Isn't this lovely?"

A thatchy field spread gray and rolling behind a ribby corncrib. The moon was a perfect quarter, a yellow rocker.

"Yes," he said.

And it was.

"I wanted you to see it." Then she said no more. She turned and walked back along the road. We are talking, she thought.

He followed her, slapped his forehead once. What? What am I doing?

"You must. You must be tired," she said.

"No," he contradicted, then, "actually."

The high was wearing off.

"I'll show you your room." He followed her up the stairs. Her ass was immense. Black leather. Maybe it was just the angle. "Here. Here's the guest room." She indicated the door. He set down his bag. They waited.

"You're welcome. I mean you can. If you want you can stay with me. I mean if you want. You don't have to."

He kicked his suitcase. "What do you think. I mean, I think maybe I should stay here."

"Okay, then. Let me get you some clean towels."

"Thanks." Why do I need towels to stay in the guest bedroom?

She flipped on a light. "Here's the guest bathroom."

He peeped in. "Fine, Thanks."

As she slipped into her nightgown, she heard water rushing, gurgling. She wasn't used to hearing water run. Only her own. It comforted her. The toilet seat flapped. The water shushed. Water, water everywhere. She cracked her door. He was there, Conroy. He was smiling. His face looked boyish, friendly.

He looked at her in her yellow nightgown, her face tilted up into the sifted hallway light. Her mouth looked like a forming question. She looked very small to him, her hair unpinned, her back bare. All those freckles. He could play Connect-the-Dots, maybe. He could constellate his own myths, find a quarter cradle of a moon to rock him.

He shuffled. "Thank you for dinner."

"You're welcome. A pleasure."

"You could come down to me. Later. If you want. It's okay." He walked back down the hallway.

"Be there in a jiffy," she called and laughed.

He stripped and crawled into bed, laughing, too. He pulled the bedspread to his neck, upsetting a tumble of pillows. "Doesn't this feel a little weird?" he called.

"Yeah," she called back. "I feel as if I'm in a pension."

He chuckled, letting the down nestle his head, wondering if she would come, nudge him, slip into bed, wondering if she would and if he wanted her there.

Down the hall, she stared out the window, fiercely insomniac. She pretended to read. *The Mystery of Edwin Drood*. I know what he's up to. He is making me decide. That way, he's off the hook. He can say, She started it. She wanted to whack him one with a hacksaw, tweak his button nose with a plumber's wrench. But did he really expect her to creep down the hall? He didn't want her there. He was being nice. But maybe. Still, why should she . . . And then she could picture herself not wanting to disturb the moment, the darkness, the surprise of it all, banging into the walls as she fumbled down the hall, stubbing her toe, hollering as she pitched headlong into his shins. Throbbing toe. A choked curse or two. Yeah, that'd be erotic. Nyuk, nyuk, nyuk. Curly does Dallas.

They fell asleep.

She woke first. Maybe it wasn't so bad. Maybe he didn't find her as loathsome as she thought. Maybe. The light spilled into the room, uncertain. Maybe. The morning was pink and yellow. She rose expectant. The sun shimmered between the pointed lace trimming her curtains. Maybe. As maybe as a butterfly's wings drying, as maybe as their iridescent color, their powdery charm.

So she went to him. The hall felt very long. She snuggled into bed behind his back.

"MMM, nice," he murmured.

But it wasn't. Something felt off. It was his stomach perhaps. She wasn't used to his girth.

He closed his eyes so he wouldn't see her chicken neck. He wanted her to be someone else, his old girlfriend Marla who was in her twenties. While he tried to recreate Marla with his hands, she slipped out of bed.

They were in the kitchen. He was complaining about the skim milk, only drinks two percent, he said. She said that she'd go out to get him some milk. He started eating Halloween candy from her freezer. "Please, don't do that," she said.

He glared at her and ate another peanut butter cup.

She wondered why he was doing that. He was overweight.

Chicken neck, he thought. They all want to be mothers.

She served him some popovers. He ate them.

"I usually have bacon and eggs," he said. She made them.

Why am I doing this, she asked herself. Why am I waiting on this boor? She hated herself. *Feed him. Feed him.*

They spent the day in book stores, CD stores. She knew what he was doing, avoiding her, avoiding talking. So many avenues for communication, but still men and women don't talk to each other. She was growing tired of waiting as he finicked over books and CDs.

When she asked him if he'd like to pick out a movie for that evening, he picked out three. Three. She knew what he was doing; he was finding more ways to avoid her, to keep from talking to her.

At the deli, she bought sandwiches for a picnic. He was throwing a hissy fit because he couldn't find ice. Milk, bacon and eggs, ice. She knew two year olds who were more adaptable than this. But she grinned. Her face felt tight.

They drove out to the park and sat by the lake. It was a beautiful day, late October Indian summer, drowsy sunshiny day. He wanted to climb a trail.

"Okay," she agreed and she followed. Men lead. Women follow. He got them lost, all the while pontificating about how to keep one's bearings in the woods. She pretended to joke along, but she'd had it. He'd apparently had it, too. She could feel his strain. She was getting on his nerves. They were lost in the woods, Hansel and Gretel, on a beautiful afternoon, and she felt like a witch. The path dwindled to nothing. He was playing scout, pretending to orient them. She was overdressed. Her sweater stuck to the small of her back.

Jack and Jill went up the hill. The quickest way out is down. "The lake is there," she pointed. "I'm going down." And she removed her shoes and skied down the steep hill of pine needles.

He followed, laughing, but he was pissed.

"Impulsive aren't you?" he asked.

"Maybe, but I ain't lost."

His eyes hated her. They were full of the dirty tricks he'd like to play on her, saw her chair leg three-quarters through, scatter nails on her garage floor. But she didn't care; she was skidding down the hill, holding her shoes to her chest and laughing. And Jill came tumbling after. Kit Carson, can go right to hell. I'm going back to the car. She put on her shoes at the base of the hill, found the lakeside trail and started walking.

He was brooding. It was in the hump of his shoulders. He was sulking. He was not having fun. His mood was her responsibility.

She offered to take him out to dinner. She hated herself for offering. She hated herself for opening herself to be humiliated, to give and give with no expectation of returning affection. But YES, he said, and she bought him dinner. The boy had an appetite. He ate his way through the menu. Afterwards, he said, "Thank you."

It was not, she realized, sufficient. She paid the bill.

They were lying on the living room floor. She was touching him. He was channel-surfing and trying to annoy her. He was successful. "Would you stop it?" she asked. "You're driving me crazy."

"No," he said. "You are driving yourself crazy."

"No, that is driving me crazy. Can't you find a program and stick with it."

He tuned in Tom Hanks in "Big." He snuck to the freezer and popped a few more peanut butter cups, unglued the roof of his mouth, said, "That's what all men really want. A room full of toys, a girl to screw. No responsibility. What a hoot."

He was using the movie to tell her that he didn't want her. He squirmed under her touch, got up, returned with his vest.

"Would you mend this for me?" he asked. "I popped a button."

And she knew then that she was damned. If she refused she was all the bad girlfriends he'd ever had. If she obliged, she was his mother. She obliged, cursing. She jabbed the needle in and out of the vest with angry little stabs. Damn him, damn him. He brought me his mending. This is over the top. This is the date from hell, but still she sewed. She bit the thread off. "Here," she said. He took the vest. She couldn't bear it. She poked him in his jelly belly and said, "Say thank you."

"Thank you," he said and poked her back.

She pushed him, thinking this is it, the nadir, the pits. Courtship as low comedy. Slapstick love. Pigtails in inkwells. Pinkies in the eye. Petty is as petty does. They looked at each other hatefully, embarrassed.

"I don't know why I act the way I do sometimes," he said.

She smiled insincerely and he stuck in a video tape, Bergman's *Howl of the Wolf*. They watched it, pretending that they were not watching themselves on the screen. Shadowy castles, death masks, hunched vanities, horrors of empty laughing and longing through naked corridors of wretched men and women shattering each other infinitely in cloudy mirrors. It was not a good date movie. At last, at long last, it ended.

"I'm tired," she said. There were two more tapes. "I'm going to bed."

He didn't shift. He stared at the television.

Okey doke. She went to bed. She woke up at one. The moon was sifting into the room, shifty light. The hall light was on. She felt the emptiness of the bed. He hadn't joined her. She rose in her pajamas to turn off the light. The satin made a shoosh sound as she walked. She hurt; her heart was full of ashes and orange rinds. She wanted to cup her hands and find them full. But she came up empty. In the sudden darkness she leaned against the wall.

Pain is pain. Despair is despair. These were not tautologies.

Then she heard her name, and she entered his room, sat down next to him on the bed, brushed the hair back from his forehead. She took a deep breath to steady herself, because she knew that she must say what he would not. "It's okay," she said. "I'm just not your type. I told you that I didn't have any expectations, and that's fine."

"I didn't know," he said. "I didn't know until I came up to bed tonight and I realized that I wanted to sleep alone."

"I knew," she said. "But sometimes it's better just to say it, to get it out there."

"I didn't want to hurt you."

"Sometimes there is less hurt in truth. Chalk it up to lack of chemistry. Too little contact. Too much anticipation. It's fine."

"I feel very close to you now," he said. "Would you hold me?"

She cradled him. Her hands and heart were full. The moon spilled into the room. Hansel and Gretel had lost their way. They were two scared children. There was a wolf in the woods and every way, they lost the path. They were hunted by their loneliness. Terror was everywhere. He. She. They, the motherless children.

She kissed his forehead. It was cool. "I'm tired now," she said. "I'm going to bed." She padded down the dark corridor to her room, slipped sleeplessly into her bed, and then he was there in her door frame.

"Are you going to sleep here?" he asked.

"That's the general idea."

"May I stay with you? I don't want to sleep alone."

Why, she wondered, why do they only come to us when we leave them. But, yes, she said, her heart was large, her bed, commodious. She suffered from a surfeit of affection for the world and all its sad and lost inhabitants. She was one of them. Come to bed then, child.

And together they lay hand in hand, staving off the night, the wolf beneath the bed, the squalor of loneliness, ulteriority of hope. He. She. We, two. Hansel and Gretel following a path of bird-pecked bread crumbs through the woods. We lose ourselves. We find ourselves again. We build cabins with small thatch. We raise homes in our hearts. We give each other places to abide. You're safe now, baby. You're home. For a while. This while.

What is this?

What it is, baby. What it is.

*David Williams*

# Bobby Angel

BOBBY ANGEL'S PLAYING, AND THE LUCKY PEOPLE HAVE GOT THEIR places in the front of the auditorium already, which is really an old movie theater which the new owner has changed into a nightclub after putting in some décor in front of the first seats: tables made from old copper wire spools and chairs brought in deluxe from the Salvation Army. It's a place where local-yokels play during the week but tonight it's gonna be the best-thing-in-life-you're-ever-gonna-see national act concert hall, even if whoever did the paint job on the walls forgot to make it all the way to the ceiling. The place is packed, the bar is hopping, and the drinks are flowing out of the waitress's hands like the fish and the loaves, miracles everywhere as everybody's getting ready for this grand earth-shattering event of a lifetime, for nobody can croon like Bobby Angel, who has also got a silver tongue way with words, who takes them straight from his heart and lifts them right into yours, so that you'd do anything for him, you'd get on your knees, you'd roll over, you'd even bark if you had to. And every woman knows this. Which is why we're here. Fleeing from exes and has-beens, kitchens full of dishes and kids screaming, and all the unpaid bills and alimony payments that haven't come, flat tires, cracks in the plumbing, and overflowing toilets. We've been waiting for this night forever it seems, when we can be taken someplace else, a place we'd been expected to go all along but never got to. My friend, Suzy, has on her best loopy earrings and a white dress cut so low that if I bend over to talk to her

I can see the dark area around one of her nipples. Sherry is dressed in black, Martha's in a red dress, that she couldn't have fit into in high school but can now, since she's on Weight Watchers, and I'm in my best: very tactful. It's a blue dress with small white flowers that puts me in mind of an open field where you can walk and walk and find the rainbow if you wanted it. That, and I have on my turquoise earrings that bring out the blue in my eyes.

We're all sitting at one of these tables, drinking various things: a Bloody Mary, a Rum and Coke, a Margarita, and a Vodka Sour, when I see one of the band members come onto the stage: this guy in black boots with hair down to this shoulders, but it's squeaky clean hair, and he has a perfect little black moustache above his lip that's so fine it looks like it was drawn on with a mascara pencil. He puts his guitar onto a stand of some sort, and the closer I look at him, I figure he's probably forty-five years old, about fifteen years older than I am, but his chest is still bigger than his stomach, which is something you can't say about many of the guys my age. Then another one of the band members comes out and sits down at the keyboard. He's not as good looking as the first guy, but he is younger, with about a dozen metal rings in his ears, but his hair is completely fantastic, naturally bright red that stands up straight, just like a bunch of carrots that are growing backwards out of his head. Then the drummer comes onto the stage and sits behind the drum set. This guy's totally bald, but really macho looking, wearing one of those T-shirts without sleeves and he has tattoos on both of his arms that look like dragons or snakes. Then finally the bass player comes strutting out, this tall drink of water who has a larger than average nose, and tremendous feet, and hands that look like they could fit around your waist they're so big, and then on top of it, he's got this jaw line that looks like Mt. Rushmore or something, I mean chiseled. And they're all tuning and looking at each other, and as they do a hush begins to build in the room, and the stage lights dim all the way then come back on again in a fireworks display of reds, greens, and blues, when all of a sudden he's here standing amongst them—Bobby Angel. His hair's disheveled. He's wearing black sunglasses, and it looks like he hasn't shaved for a day or two. But his face is so fine boned, his features so utterly perfect and slim. He's got tall black boots on and black leather pants, and he's wearing this plain white shirt made of muslin or something that's open halfway to his navel, so that we can see the hairs on his chest springing out. His mouth is this beautiful red ribbon that turns up at the edges, as he smiles at us and invites us in. Then he looks at the other guys in the band and as if by magic they go into the music all at once, and the place is hopping with sound as the bass jumps into the cavities of our chests and the electric guitar lashes us with these runs, while the piano's jumping, and the drums kick in, roaring, roaring, then just as suddenly, everything crashes to a purr, and Bobby—Bobby Angel puts his lips to the microphone and snarls. And out of his mouth and throat comes this tone that makes you sweat under your arms even if you've worn deodorant. It's a sound that oozes into you, that moves inside of you, till you find yourself wet in places you shouldn't be, but you are, and there's no distance between you and the stage, between you and him, and you know he's singing to you alone, behind those sunglasses. And my girlfriends want to tear our clothes off of him and jump into the limelight naked and dance. We want to feel that tongue of his against our skin, like sandpaper, shark-like, rubbing us in all the right spots making us into kindling, to ignite us, till we are nothing but ash. His words suck at us, his words of love, sweet love. Words that we've heard a zillion times before, but now they're like the first romantic words ever spoken, they're the first kiss, the first time a guy takes you into his car out on the back roads of your youth when you are so hungry for it, and god you want to be hungry for it again, as the car careens down the blacktop with Bobby Angel driving, a red convertible with the top down, before hitting gravel, which kicks out like a stampede from the chrome and rubber, flying in every direction with the dust, as the road narrows down to a single lane and the trees go whizzing by you so fast they become one, until the road itself disappears, and the car engine purrs softly at the edge of the forest, where he takes the key and turns it away from himself and the turbo engine mutters and falls till there is only the sound of crickets and the summer wind, which gets in your ear and makes you breathe so hot and heavy as his hands find their way inside you like music against your skin.

When the song is over we clap so hard that our palms begin to swell and sting, but we love it as the next song and the next, rocks us or lullabies us, takes us to heaven or hell, so that the things inside of us begin to move in ways we barely remember, and we sway in our chairs, feeling like the wood against us is the whole world in his hands.

Magnificent. Unbelievable. Nipples hard. Throats dry. We scream. Till the end of the night, when we stand, and everybody stands, raising their arms into the air and yelling, whistling, then applauding again and again, encore, encore, which he gives just once until the lights of the room go up and we are left amongst the throngs of others with the same unquenched desire.

"What's there to lose?" Suzy says. "We're never going to get any younger." So together, like a pack of foxes, we rush behind the curtain to the backroom, all four of us girls who are wearing our best and who've had our hair done and our nails, and we scratch at the back-door which opens for us, letting us in to the promised land where, thank God, we look good enough to enter, and where the band members sit smoking cigarettes and drinking beer and whiskey, carousing together, except for him. He's there in the corner with his sunglasses still on—Bobby Angel—smoking and drinking as well, but in a way different manner than the other guys, for Bobby has something unique and fills his own space himself.

Someone offers us beers, and we take them gladly, and everybody's laughing as we tell the band members how damned good they are, and why aren't they at Carnegie Hall for Christ's sake. But not a one of us dares speak to Bobby Angel, for he's off in his own cocoon, with some-thing different rattling through his head than the rest of them, as the guitar player strums something, and the girls ooh and ahh, as the bass player shakes his hips a little and invites everyone back to the hotel where they all want to be, but Bobby Angel he just takes another cig-arette out of his pack and lights it, his cherub red lips sucking the smoke in like this is all the matters in the world, like all the rest of it, the sidewalks downtown, the people streaming through the bars look-ing for each other, the busses and cars going, going, going nowhere, everywhere, are all nothing, nothing at all compared to this, to the moment he is in, this space he occupies, which is eternal, elemental, straight to the core, and I so much feel I know this, that I too am alone in that place, that I also inhabit that particular landscape, which is the secret reason I have come here after all.

So after the second beer I begin moving toward him, very, very slowly. I slide against the wall where he leans and move carefully into the perimeters of his space, which is wholly removed from the raunch of the rest of them who are now into the party mood, a mood that Bobby isn't, and then I'm there in that sacred circle of his, within dis-tance of a whisper to his ear, which is pierced with a small fleck of gold, a very delicate piece of metal, almost not even there, and I turn toward him and look at the stubble on his face, seeing the small black hairs poking out of his translucent skin, as my knees shake, and I light a cigarette for myself, feeling my hands shaking as well as the silver lighter rises to my face. Then as the flame shoots up I see him looking at me, knowing I'm there next to him.

One of hands, ringless, comes up and pulls his shades down slightly so that I can see the very color of his eyes, which are blue like mine, cold blue but with the greatest depths of the ocean, swimming with electric eels and rays, as his mouth opens slightly and behind it I can see his famous tongue ready to strike.

"You want me to fuck you, is that it?" he says so matter of fact that I'm startled and feel my legs begin to wobble on my heels.

"What?" I say, not believing this, and I don't even look back. I take a quick drag of my cigarette then toss it to the floor where my boot heel catches it and grounds it into the linoleum. When I do look back at him once, I feel I've turned to salt, like my skin has dried out and is flaking off in chunks, and already he's pulled the shades up again, over his eyes, so there's just the blackness of my own reflection looking back at me, my hair newly blonde, my lips radiantly red, but I feel this little quiver in my heart that shakes it, that gets it off beat, and I turn to the door at once and walk until I'm opening it. I step into the hallway which is as black as his sunglasses, blinding me with blackness, until my eyes adjust to that light and I see that I'm there behind the stage curtain where a half dozen empty beer bottles litter the floor and the ropes for the curtains hang thick and tangled, where the wires from the microphones all run together to a big black box that is plugged into the wall near the exit sign that has the "it" burned out of it, so only "ex" lights up in red, pointing the way.

When I open that door I can hear the sound of traffic, the roar and grind of engines, and I can smell the exhaust of diesel fumes from the trucks. The air is cold, and in the distance I hear a siren winding itself through traffic, worming its way into the chambers of my heart. It's a music of its own, that sound, a music that you taste many nights of your life, that sits there on your tongue, like the taste of metal, toxic, that has somehow leaked into your blood.

## Stuart Dybek

# Anti-Memoir

> If there is any substitute for love
> it's memory.
>
> —Joseph Brodsky

I

This is a street whose name and numbers
have been erased, although at dusk
smoke from its chimneys still hovers
as filmy as black lingerie.
This is a street to which love letters
addressed in the illegible smudge
of Ash Wednesday are delivered,
a street to which amnesiacs retire
to pen their memoirs, where autobiographies
are written in the third person,
and photographers erect their tripods
beneath black cloaks, then vanish
in a puff of light. This is a street
you can't step into twice,
it trails behind like footprints
in the snow or, on a summer night,
appears suddenly, a run in a nylon.

2

A street without trees, without seasons
(from where do the leaves come
tumbling in the wake of newspaper
raked by a cyclone fence?)  Autumn
of flying paper: moments torn
from diaries whirl through portals
left standing above plots of leveled bricks,
charred doorposts framing the icons
who wander from niche to niche,
tattered topcoats drafting down alleys,
drawn to the monument of fire
erected to those without a history.
In such a season it's easy to mistake
the watery reflections on shop windows
for a symptom of the body's gradual
dematerialization, when actually it's the soul
growing increasingly corporeal.
There's an audible friction of shadows
slithering walls, susurrations
as if in backlit rooms starched clothes
are being stripped from silhouettes.

3

On this street, nakedness is measured
in discarded documents—expired passports,
delinquent bills, unredeemed pawn tickets—
relics of identity from the lull
before that first, seemingly innocent
notation—long since blown away—a blue
ballpoint's unmistakeable scrawl
on a cocktail napkin from a seaside bar,
that read, *a freshly ironed blue sky,*
but meant instead to say, *the hot smell*
*of her in my car, black nylons*
*scorched against turquoise vinyl.*
A cinnamon-smeared bakery bag,
on which *a scarred skating rink ghosts*
*above a summer afternoon*—daylight moon
that, decoded, may still be waiting
for *a night that rearranged*
*the mnemonic structure of the heart,*
or later, penciled like music
along the staff of a foreign postmark,
a dated word: *betrayed* . . . what or whom,
others or oneself, left unsaid.

4

At this hour, grated pawnshops appear
to jail all the lovely instruments
condemned to exile by electric guitars.
Along this block of lyres for sale,
the singing head is junked
as if it were an antiquated radio.
Follow the streetsinger, mute and blind,
he won't look back a second time.
Here, virgins abandon their illegitimates,
and magdalenes, whose stiletto heels
on concrete mimic the obsolete, lonely
peck of a typewriter, hang bed sheets
to bleach back into a *tabula rasa*,
vast pages blank as shrouds scribbled
with the automatic writing of wind.

5

The walls are a journal kept by crowds
passing into a phantasmagoric mural,
graphite coats the tablets of tenements
with the scorched patina of angels
in Prague, manholes vent
the illusion of heat at the core
of every spiritual world.
In noirish fog lit by a sparking tram,
the slumlord of the Tower of Babel
absconds with the rent.
This is a street whose tentacles
ravel about you, drawing you in,
*la calle en su tinta,*
a street stewed in its own ink.
Late for a dinner date, the disciple
corners his reflection on the window
of a bar, and stops to tie his noose
into a Windsor knot.

6

Tonight, follow the mute street singer.
Unimpeded by sight, he leads
down passageways you thought deleted,
diction stripped like stolen cars,
barricades of syntax broken by emotion,
sighs of plaster dust, the haze
of white space between words. Don't pause
for punctuation, here, a comma
of indecision elides into a coma,
and, years later, one wakes
to the interminable typing of rain
in a hotel where transients waste
money good for alcohol's blue flame
on sleep. Outside, the homeless
congregate, while you continue to rent
all the rooms you've left behind,
addresses one must be lost to find
knee-deep in flooded storm drains
clogged with crushed revisions,
a shredded blizzard, a tickertape parade
gusting from the out-turned pockets
of the dead, enough litter
to trash the future, fuel without heat,
and yet, the past combustible enough
to be compressed into a fistful of soot.

## 7

Bell at an hour too late for the angelus,
abandoned shopfront with its flaking acronym:
MEAT, boarded shoe store where your foot size
is of interest to the Grand Inquisitor,
intersection where long ago desire
crossed into obsession. To proceed further—
step by step, word by word—requires
a map where *not* to go: avoid
the linearity of narrative, its illusion
of cause and effect, the chronology
of retrospect—a synonym for fate—
avoid the viaduct from which dice roll,
ghetto games of shells and shills,
the card sharks cheating at Tarot.
Avoid the past tense of the oracle,
the politics of mediums—reactionary
dictates from their silent majority,
the dead—the current plague of angels,
the collectivization of the unconscious,
the monopoly on memory controlled
by ancestors posing as Poor Souls
who promise as inheritance
the status of a victim.

8

A bell at an hour too late for evening vespers,
resonates through dark matter, flights
of lacunae limned in streetlight
migrate from the rookeries of a parish
that would vanish rather than undergo
an urban renewal of recollection.
From an open hydrant, the Lethe trickles
into gutters where neon fish
feed on the reflections of meteors
rising back to heaven. The past
defying its own gravity,
leaving the present with the cry
within a song—a *hey!* . . . *aye!* . . . *ole!*—
the *duende* of a single nighthawk
reciting an anti-memoir.
A testament that takes the fifth
amendment of sleep, nocturnal
history that renounces the past,
in which memory, more mysterious
and elusive than dream,
is conveyed in sign for fear
the future may overhear,
daybook of a somnambulist, prayer
that precedes recorded time, oral tradition
preserved on illiterate back streets
where street signs rhyme,
and the confessional of the last
payphone rings. Answer,
and a stranger's voice reveals secrets
you've mistaken for identity,
your uncompleted story told
in a prose for listing groceries—
the unremembered, unredeemed,
ordinary, neither true nor false,
and unaccountable as love.
Above a flickered corner bulb,
the symbol of the nighthawk flares
into silence impossible to write.

Alone, along a street that's suddenly
like any other, you're blessed
simply to continue
another night's walk home.

# CONTRIBUTORS

**Richard Burgin** is the author of nine books, including the novel *Ghost Quartet* (TriQuarterly Books, 1999) and the story collection *The Spirit Returns* (Johns Hopkins University Press, 2001). He is professor of Communication and English at St. Louis University, where he edits *Boulevard*. **Garnett Kilberg Cohen**'s fiction has appeared in *American Fiction, Chicago, Descant, Other Voices, West Branch, The Literary Review, Ontario Review,* and many others. She received a Special Mention from Pushcart 2000 for her story, "The Woman with the Longest Hair." **Joan Connor** is Assistant Professor in Fiction Writing at Ohio University and has published two collection of short stories, *We Who Live Apart* (2000) and *Here on Old Route 8* (1997), both from University of Missouri Press. Her recent work has appeared in or is forthcoming in *The Southern Review, The Kenyon Review,* and *Shenandoah,* among others. **Rachel Dilworth** is a recipient of a Fulbright Fellowship for her first collection of poetry, *The Wild Rose Asylum: Poems of the Magdelen Laundries.* Her poems have appeared in *Ekphrasis* and *Perihelion.* **Stephen Dixon** has published nine novels, 13 story collections, and 500 stories. "Again—Part Two" is the concluding section of an interconnected fiction, called *I.* Other parts of *I.* have appeared in *TriQuarterly.* **Stuart Dybek**'s novella "Blue Boy" appeared in a previous issue of *TriQuarterly.* The poem "Anti-Memoir" is from a recently completed manuscript.

He teaches at Western Michigan University and in the Prague Summer Seminar. **Aaron Fagan** is assistant editor for *Poetry.* His work has appeared in *Shenandoah.* **Alice B. Fogel**'s books of poetry include *I Love This Dark World* (Zoland, 1996). She lives in New Hampshire. **Carol Frost**'s recent work has appeared in the *Paris Review, Gettysburg Review,* and *Prairie Schooner,* among others. Her last three books are *Love and Scorn, New and Selected Poems* (2000), an American Book Club selection, *Venus and Don Juan* (1996) and *Pure* (1994), all from Northwestern University Press. **Ray Gonzalez**'s work has appeared in *Best American Poetry* 1999 and 2000. He is the author of seven books of poetry, including the forthcoming *The Hawk Temple at Tierra Grande* (BOA Editions, 2002). **Linda Gregerson**'s most recent collection of poems is *Waterborne* (Houghton Mifflin, 2001). Her poems have appeared or are scheduled to appear in the *Atlantic, Poetry,* and *Best American Poetry 2001.* **Susan Hubbard** is the author of *Blue Money* (University of Missouri Press, 1999), winner of the Janet Heidinger Kafka Prize, and *Walking on Ice,* winner of the Associated Writing Programs' Short Fiction Prize. **Cynthia Huntington**'s third book of poetry, *The Radiant,* won the 2001 Levis Poetry Prize and is forthcoming from Four Way Books in February 2003. **Larry Janowski** has won prizes in both fiction and poetry and has been the recipient of residency scholarships at the Blue Mountain Arts Center in New York and

St. Deiniol's Residential Library in Great Britain. **Willis Johnson**'s first published story, "A Prayer for the Dying," appeared in *TriQuarterly* in 1982 and won a Pushcart Prize and an O. Henry Award. It was later included in his first collection, *The Girl Who Would Be Russian* (Harcourt Brace and Jovanovich, 1986). **David Lynn**'s book of stories, *Fortune Telling*, was published by Carnegie Mellon Press in 1998. He is editor of *Kenyon Review*. **Doug Macomber** is an award-winning news videographer and landscape photographer. He lives in St. Louis and Cape Cod. **Stephen Monte** has published *Invisible Fences: Prose Poetry as a Genre in French and American Literature* (Nebraska, 2000) and *Victor Hugo: Selected Poetry* (Carcanet, 2001). **David Roderick**'s stories and poems have appeared in *Boulevard, Ontario Review* and *Quarterly West*. He is a Wallace Stegner Writing Fellow at Stanford University. **Donna Seaman** is an editor at *Booklist*, a regular contributor to the *Ruminator Review*, the *Chicago Tribune*, and elsewhere. She is editor of the anthology *In Our Nature: Stories of Wildness* (DK Publishing, 2000). **Jason Sommer** is the author of *Other People's Troubles* (University of Chicago Press, 1997). He received a Writing Foundation Writers' Award in 2001. **James Tate**'s latest book is *Memoir of the Hawk* (Ecco Press, 2001). **Kathryn Watterson** teaches writing at Princeton University. She is the author of several books, including *Not by the Sword* (Simon & Schuster, 1995), which won the 1996 Christopher Award, and *Women in Prison* (Northeastern University Press, 1996), which inspired an ABC documentary. She teaches writing at Princeton University. **David Williams** has published two books with Alfred A. Knopf (1997, 1993) and short stories in various literary magazines. He is a weekly cartoonist for the *Chronicle of Higher Education* and the *Rocky Mountain News*, and he runs the fiction writing program at Metropolitan State College of Denver.

**Subscriptions**

Three issues per year. **Individuals:** one
year $24; two years $44; life $600. **Insti-
tutions:** one year $36; two years $68.
**Overseas:** $5 per year additional. Price
of back issues varies. Sample copies $5.
Address correspondence and subscriptions
to *TriQuarterly*, Northwestern University,
2020 Ridge Ave., Evanston, IL 60208-
4302. Phone (847) 491-7614.

**Submissions**

The editors invite submissions of fiction,
poetry and literary essays, which must
be postmarked between October 1 and
March 31; manuscripts postmarked
between April 1 and September 30 will
not be read. No manuscripts will be returned unless accompanied by a stamped,
self-addressed envelope. All manuscripts
accepted for publication become the
property of *TriQuarterly*, unless otherwise indicated.

**Reprints**

Reprints of issues 1–15 of *TriQuarterly*
are available in full format from Kraus
Reprint Company, Route 100, Millwood,
NY 10546, and all issues in microfilm
from University Microfilms International,
300 North Zeeb Road, Ann Arbor, MI
48106.

**Indexing**

*TriQuarterly* is indexed in the Humanities
Index (H. W. Wilson Co.), the American
Humanities Index (Whitson Publishing
Co.), Historical Abstracts, MLA, EBSCO
Publishing (Peabody, MA) and Informa-
tion Access Co. (Foster City, CA).

**Distributors**

Our national distributors to retail trade
are Ingram Periodicals (La Vergne, TN);
B. DeBoer (Nutley, NJ); Ubiquity (Brook-
lyn, NY); Armadillo (Los Angeles, CA).

**Publication of *TriQuarterly* is made
possible in part by the donors of gifts
and grants to the magazine. For their
recent and continuing support, we are
very pleased to thank the Illinois Arts
Council, the Lannan Foundation, the
National Endowment for the Arts,
the Sara Lee Foundation, the Wendling
Foundation and individual donors.**

# MICHIGAN QUARTERLY REVIEW

## RECENT AND FORTHCOMING

**Essays**: Toni Morrison, "The Teaching of Values in the University" • An Interview (in 1961) with Clifford Odets • David Blake, "The Poetry of Celebrity" • Josip Novakovich, "Letter from Croatia" • An Interview with Comden and Green about *Singin' in the Rain* • David M. Halperin, "Homosexuality's Closet" • Emily Grosholz, "The Poetry of Anne Stevenson" • Juan Abreu, "A Memoir of Reinaldo Arenas" • Carolyn Steedman, "Going to Middlemarch: History and the Novel" • Ilan Stavans, "Borges and Faulkner" • Karen Miller, "Race, Politics, and Museums in Detroit" • Philip D. Beidler: "Solatium: A Memoir of Vietnam" • Marcel Marceau, "Working in the Resistance and on Stage" • Andrea Barrett, "Four Voyages" • Simon Gikandi, "Race and the Idea of the Aesthetic" • Mark Halliday, "Damned Good Poet: Kenneth Fearing" • Edmund White, The Hopwood Lecture for 2001

**Fiction**: Clark Blaise, Millicent Dillon, Lucy Ferriss, Greg Johnson, Jessica Francis Kane, Jody Lisberger, Joyce Carol Oates, Robert Wexelblatt, and stories from authors in Albania, Argentina, and Japan.

**Poetry**: Stephen Dunn, Daniel Mark Epstein, Susan Hahn, Mark Jarman, Carl Phillips, Lee Anne Roripaugh, Lynne Sharon Schwartz, Anne Stevenson, Charles Harper Webb, Stephen Yenser

**Reviews**: Geoff Eley, "What We Now Think About Nazism" • John Taylor, "The Poetry of Carolyn Kizer • Laurence Goldstein, "Nostalgia for the *Flyer*" • Paula Marantz Cohen, "Situating the Jew in American Culture" • Khaled Mattawa, "On Arab Detroit" • Jay Parini, "Anne Stevenson at the Top of Her Form" • Arlene Keizer, "Gayl Jones and the Postmodern Moment" • Roger Gilbert on the Laureates: Pinsky, Dove, and Kunitz • Gorman Beauchamp, "Cold War Intellectuals"

**Winter 2001**: A special issue, "REIMAGINING PLACE," guest-edited by Robert Grese and John R. Knott ($8)

**CALL FOR MANUSCRIPTS**: for a special issue, "JEWISH IN AMERICA," guest-edited by Sara Blair and Jonathan Freedman. Deadline April 20, 2002. See our website at: www.umich.edu/~mqr

Send a check for a one-year subscription ($25) or a two-year subscription ($45) to *Michigan Quarterly Review*, 3032 Rackham Building, 915 E. Washington, Ann Arbor, MI 48109-1070